Naming the Snakes

NEW WRITING SCOTLAND 44

Edited by
Chris Powici
and
Allan Radcliffe

Gaelic editor:
Anna C. Frater

Association for Scottish Literature

Association for Scottish Literature
Scottish Literature, 7 University Gardens
University of Glasgow, Glasgow G12 8QH
www.asls.org.uk

ASL is a registered charity no. SC054925

First published 2026

This is a work of human endeavour. No large-language models
or text-to-image generators ('generative AI') were used
in the creation or production of this book.

A CIP record for this book is available
from the British Library

ISBN 978-1-906841-68-3

Our authorised representative in the EU for product safety is
JGU Scotland HUB, Johannes Gutenberg Universität Mainz
Jakob-Welder-Weg 18, 55128 Mainz, Germany
scotland@uni-mainz.de

The Association for Scottish Literature
acknowledges the support of Creative Scotland
towards the publication of this book

Typeset in Minion Pro by ASL
Printed by Ashford Colour Ltd, Gosport

CONTENTS

INTRODUCTION

In 'Naming the Snakes', Lynn Davidson writes poignantly of the beautifully serpentine threads that bind a woman to her son and granddaughter. Kate Hendry's 'Sonnets for My Daughter' traces the joys and frustrations of motherhood, of what it takes to be a *good* parent, with a tender, down-to-earth honesty. As she puts it, 'My heart, as messy as her room, strains to stay hard.' The young sister and brother in Julia Cathcart's 'Condensation' reveal the cracks in family life when they turn the tables on their errant father simply by breathing (read the story to find out how).

These are but a few of the stories and poems in this edition of *New Writing Scotland* that focus on personal relationships, in particular how families come together, offer support and strength, and, sometimes, break. In their range and variety of tone, they give the lie to Tolstoy's famous claim in *Anna Karenina*: 'All happy families are alike; each unhappy family is unhappy in its own way.' There's a rich middle ground where happiness and unhappiness, heartbreak and healing, mistrust and, yes, love, intermingle. It's in this middle ground where most of us live. We know its terrain well.

Of course, writing about family life is no new thing, and we don't have to look to nineteenth-century Russia to find remarkable examples. Closer to home, Lewis Grassic Gibbon's *Sunset Song* and Janice Galloway's *This Is Not About Me* come to mind as evocative and searching portrayals of families. In fact, in the epigraph to her short story collection *Jellyfish*, Galloway uses a telling quote from David Lodge to signal her interest in exploring parent-child relationships: 'Literature is mostly about having sex and not much about having children; life's the other way round.'

There may be reasons particular to the current historical moment that have made so many writers turn to what happens in families to explore the nature of belonging. In a world driven by relentless and reckless change, and where the moral compass of the powerful swings crazily hither and thither, this is understandable. Where are our roots? How do we make ourselves at home? How does the stranger come to feel at home? Maybe we need to remind ourselves of what a family is, what it could be, and what it stands for, to begin to make sense of the wider world.

Indeed, while a significant number of the works included here explore family dynamics, they are not narrow in scope nor are they confined to the domestic sphere. 'The Ugly Sister's Story' by Nicola Fitzhenry is a delightfully playful reconsideration of the Cinderella myth, that gives agency to its title character, providing a fresh take on notions of 'villainous' women in fairy tales. Tony Garner's 'Three Men in Assynt' takes its title from a poem by Norman MacCaig ('A Man in Assynt'), creating a vivid travelogue-style account of a family excursion, warmly describing the bonds forged by a trio of men from different generations and cultural backgrounds. 'Koora' by Scott Ferguson, takes as its theme masculinity in Scotland, casting a nuanced look across what it means to be 'one of the lads'. The story is notable because it is narrated by a boy from a refugee family, who has his own experience of heroism and loss that goes beyond football and macho aggression. Wry and economical, it is a quiet reminder that the personal is political.

Still, some of the most powerful pieces in this collection depict quietly devastating moments in family life; the kinds of events with which most readers will be familiar. Among a smattering of works about ageing and elder care, 'The Toenail' by Simon Ewing stands out as a convincing portrait of a boy who is sent into his grandfather's hospital room as a proxy for his mother, who is struggling to cope. 'Weather Warning' by Áine King is a delicate insight into a mother-daughter relationship, with the day-to-day worries of the mother thrown into relief by her child's innocence. Meanwhile, Wendy MacIntyre's poem, 'Haircut al Fresco', is an evocative reminder of an experience many of us shared in recent years: the weird intimacy of having our locks chopped by a family member during the Covid lockdown.

In the Gaelic selections we have Màrtainn Mac an t-Saoir's poems highlighting the importance of connection, Niall O'Gallagher's 'Pangur Bán', a reworking of a famous Old Irish poem, and Meg Bateman's ability to show us the joy in the small things of life – running in the rain or tasting fruit straight from the tree. In addition, we have Donnchadh MacCàba's short but to-the-point poem about the loss of history and heritage, Eilidh Eglinton's reflections on a visit to New York, and Robbie MacLeòid taking us dancing, and back to the importance of connection to both people and culture.

In *Naming the Snakes: New Writing Scotland* 44, we find writing that looks at the nitty-gritty of life, as well as those dreams and memories that shine a poignant light on who we are to one another, and so illuminate that wider web of relationships that make up Scotland amid a turbulent, testing decade.

Anna C. Frater, Chris Powici and Allan Radcliffe

NEW WRITING SCOTLAND 45: SUBMISSION INSTRUCTIONS

The forty-fifth volume of *New Writing Scotland* will be published in summer 2027. Submissions are invited from writers resident in Scotland or Scots by birth, upbringing or inclination. All forms of writing are welcome: autobiography and memoirs; creative responses to events and experiences; drama; graphic artwork (monochrome only, of suitable size); poetry; political and cultural commentary and satire; short fiction; travel writing or any other creative prose may be submitted, but not full-length plays or novels, though self-contained extracts are acceptable. The work must be entirely your own and produced without the assistance of generative AI. It must not be previously published or accepted for publication elsewhere, and may be written in any of the languages of Scotland.

Submissions should be uploaded, for free, via Submittable:

nws.submittable.com/submit

Prose pieces should be double-spaced and carry an approximate word-count. Please do not put your name on your submission; instead, please provide your name and contact details, including email and postal addresses, on a covering letter. If you are sending more than one piece, please group everything into one document. **Please send no more than four poems, or one prose work.**

Authors retain all rights to their work(s) and are free to submit and/or publish the same work(s) elsewhere after they appear in *New Writing Scotland.* Successful contributors will be paid at a rate of £50 for the first published page and £25 for each subsequent published page.

Please be aware that we have limited space in each edition, and therefore shorter pieces are more suitable – although longer items of exceptional quality may still be included. Our maximum suggested word-count is 3,500 words, and the submission deadline is midnight on **31 October 2026**.

Donald Adamson
DÜRER'S HERMONY

***efter* The Great Piece of Turf/Das große Rasenstück**
by Albrecht Dürer

Renaissance-body that he wis
A've nae doot he wuid hae kent the nems
o aw the plants in his pentin,
fun oot whit they wis cawed
by kintrae fowk aroon Nuremberg,
whit cuid be chowed, whit the kye cuid eat
and the ailments they wis guid fur.

'Lat thaim gang thegither,' he'd hae thocht,
in yin daud o turf, a mindin tae him
o his ain bit, a celebration
o his ain kintraeside, his native sile,
an eemage tae tak wi him
in the ceeties – monie – he wuid travail tae
pursuin the refinements o his craft.

Merk, if ye wull, the caum thegitherness,
seein whit cam afore and whit cam efter
in his ceetie: the massacre o Jews,
the rallies o the Nazis, rairins, ravins
tae extirpate ilk pushionous 'alien growthe':
ein volk, ein reich . . . aye, but in this pentin
thir's peace, aw leevin things in hermony.

David M. Alper

ICARUS REWRITTEN

You were never the boy who fell. You were the boy who
jumped. Let them call it hubris – you call it hunger.

Your father warned you *Don't fly too high*, but he never
said why the sky was like liberty and the sea like a tomb
you'd already crawled out of.

You stitched your wings upon each other from the gap
between his commands. Your mother's pillowcase.
Candle wax drips which you were never meant to burn.
You did, however. You burned the house down
before ever departing it.

They say you fell. But you remember the sun as a kiss that
opened you up. You remember the air as a lover who held
you too tight. You remember the ocean as the first place
you were ever allowed to scream.

You are not the legend. You are the revision. The boy
who flew because he didn't want to crawl any more.
The boy who burned because he understood what cold was.

MANUAL FOR RESURRECTION

1. Begin with the lungs.   Open them like letters never mailed.
Allow breath to come back as betrayal – cold,   like a lover
who left and is thinking of knocking again.   Breathe in until
your ribs remember   they are not cells, but wings.

2. Purify the heart.   With salt. With psalms.   With the
names of the dead   spelled backwards in candlelight.
If it still refuses to beat,   sing to it.   Sing with your
mouth a wound   and the song the only thing   that is not
bleeding.

3. Rejoin the hands.   They will have to reach out to ghosts.
Let them.   Then teach them how to cradle fruit again.
Teach them to sign your name   without shaking.

4. The backbone is a prayer.   Torch it.   Break it if you
must.   But reconstruct it with gold   as the Japanese do
with bowls.   Let your scars be the reason   you're worth
keeping.

5. Don't trust mirrors.   They are liars.   They reflect the
body   before the tempest,   not the one that survived it.

6. When the night arrives –   and the night will arrive –
cover yourself with the shadows.

Like a second skin.

Name it armour.

Name it mother.

Name it something that cannot be broken.

Emily Arnold-Fernández
SCALE

I found the mystery, gleaming like a child's delight,
among the canned tomatillos and jars of dried beans
in the half-dugout shed that kept everything cool,
summer or winter. Tender at first under my tentative
fingers, it fought back when I squeezed, yielding only
until pressed. It smelled of saltwater and meat,
like a piece of brined cartilage sliced off a butcher's cut.
Two of its edges were slick, honed like a filleting knife.
The third was thicker, raw and bloody. Still fresh.
Maybe it was a delicacy somewhere, but all I felt
was a shivering revulsion, like swimming in a pond
full of rotting fish. Nonetheless it was too beautiful
or the rubbish bin, so I planted it wide-side down
in the garden between the mealy potatoes
and the blackberries that tasted okay
but were always mushy.

The next time I grabbed a handful of those
squishy clusters, sweet darkness staining my palm,
the mystery's edge sliced my passing wrist.
As the blood welled, I remembered that other
bloody body, washed up last year on the beach
outside my window where it stared up at me
as if it had never seen my like. I stared back,
remembering the tall tales told afterwards by the fishermen
down in the pub. I saw my own hair dark with blood,
my own chest smashed and chaotic, guts gaping,
bloody chunks of fat and skin staining the sand as if I
were the behemoth, as if I were large as a porpoise,
as oversized and unapologetic as the body on the beach,

the unpoised body with its untouched tail, pearled
and shimmering beside the wobbling gobs of rent
flesh, the fractured ribs and bits of lobe and lung
and on that tail not a mark, not a line,
just one rusty absence in the perfect pattern.

NO, I DON'T HAVE CHILDREN

I feel time in my ears like diving,
the alien sea a siren and a tomb.

I surface. Bitter salt slides away
like thirst slaked. A dog whines.

The circled moon wanes softly.

Above me, swallows make eager figures,
a baby's fingers grasping at my collarbones.

Floating, I make my own womb.
Today I do not struggle with freedom.

Matt Barnard
DARRAGH

Some say you should fish on a rising tide.
Some say you should avoid the sun.
No one knows for sure, no one knows where
the mackerel are, where the shoals roam.

All you know is that the darragh
has seven barbed hooks variously rusted,
each attached to an inch or so of silver plastic
and they shine like sprats in the water;

that sometimes you catch them when the sea's
rough, sometimes when the swell's
flattened to the pitch of a whale;
that you have to drop the line and let the lead

spin to the seabed and whip it back
and most days you'll have nothing to show for it.
But when you're in the fish, the line will go light,
you'll see them dazzling beneath the surface

and when you pick the darragh out with its string
of lithe, white-bellied fish twisting
and leaping in the unexpected air, you'll know
the bloody process has only just begun.

Meg Bateman

NIGHEAN NA RUITH

Chunnaic mi nad ruith thu,
d' aodann fliuch a' deàlradh mar dhaoimean,
d' fhigheachan a' sruthadh a-mach mar earball.
Dh'innis thu gur toil leat falbh a dh'àiteachan brèagha
gus ruith agus cànainean aosta ionnsachadh.
'Fiù 's san uisge?' dh'fhaighnich mi.
'Gu sònraichte san uisge', fhreagair thu,
is chaidh thu nad dhàn nam inntinn,
nad eilid thais ghràsmhor fhurachail.

Sa mhadainn an-diugh, air dhomh bhith crùbte
aig a' choimpiutair fad na seachdain,
thog mi fhìn rathad a' bhàigh orm,
nam throtan gu cachaileith a' bhaile,
dh'fhairich mi crodh is mìlse roid is seamraig,
chuala mi monmhar is plubadaich nan allt,
's ged a bha an nigheadaireachd a-muigh agam
b' fheàrr leam gun sileadh e
ach am faighinn blas na h-uile.

GIRL RUNNING

I saw you running in the rain,
your diamond face glistening wet,
your plait streaming behind like a tail.
You said you liked going to beautiful places
to learn old languages and run.
'Even in the rain?' I asked.
'Especially in the rain', you replied.
You became a poem in my mind,
alert and graceful and damp like a deer.

And this morning, after a week
hunching over the computer,
I set off myself at a trot on the road
round the bay to the township cattle grid,
smelled cows and clover and bog myrtle,
heard the murmur and splash of the burns,
and though I had washing on the line
I wished it would rain
the better for to taste it all.

DHAM DHALTA-SGRÌOBHAIDH

stèidhichte air 'Na Crotaich agus na Sìthichean'

Èistidh mi ri do ghuth
a' tighinn air an oiteig
mar anail flùir na aimsir,

Agus ma bhuaileas rudeigin orm,
mar *Diciadain*, tairgidh mi dhut e –
gabh no guait e,

Ach na leig leam
Diardaoin is *Dihaoine*
a thilgeil dhan ruidhle,

No sgiùrsar às a' chnoc mi
is croit air mo dhruim
airson do cheòl a chur tuathal.

TO MY WRITING MENTEE

Based on 'The Legend of Knockgrafton'

I'll listen for your voice
coming on the breeze
like the breath of a flower in its season,

And if something strikes me
like 'Wednesday',
I'll suggest it,

But don't let me throw
'Thursday' and 'Friday'
into the reel,

Or I'll be sent packing from the knoll
with a hump on my back
for putting your music wrong.

SEASGADAMH CO-LÀ-BREITH AN GÀRRADH LUIBH-EÒLAS PHALERMO

Shìn mi meas an loquat chun nam balach,
is le m' ìne, sgolt mi an rùsg, nam leth-mhàthair,
leth-ghocaid, is gu h-obann diùid, dh'fhàg mi
aca fhèin an fheòil a chladhach às.

Leum aon dhiubh gu gaisgeil air guailnean
an fhir eile gus meas eile a chosnadh dhomh
na chrochadh do-ruigsinneach air craobh sìol sìoda.
Bhrosnaich mi iad, ach rinn mo bhana-charaid

Trod 's tharraing i air falbh mi. Bha mi taingeil
gun robh na balaich a-mach à sealladh
nuair a nochd plaosgan an aon mheas nar slighe
is roileagan fuilt lèithe gan sèideadh romhainn.

SIXTIETH BIRTHDAY IN PALERMO BOTANICAL GARDENS

I proffered the lads a loquat, and with my nail
slit the flesh open – half-maternal, half-
flirt – then suddenly shy, left them
to gouge out the flesh themselves.

One climbed on the other's shoulders
and gallantly strived to win me a pod
dangling out of reach on the silk floss tree.
I cheered them on, but my friend

Scolded us and drew me away.
I was glad the lads were out of sight
when the husks of the same pod appeared in our path,
with rovings of grey hair blowing before us.

Martin Bowman
LICHT

Oan readin Ephesians in Scots

Muckle licht i' th' daurk,
Wee skelfs here an thair
An did ye see the wan that's burst?
Ah luik! A bricht wan ower thair!
An see thae farawa lamps ettlin awa
Fur traivlers no kennen whaur thur gaein.
Goad alane kens, as ma mither
Wha wis guid tae me,
Yaised tae say.

Pair sowel! that wumman doon the roadie
She's loast her bairn.
Whit dae ye say tae that? Somethin? Naethin?

At a freend's biddin ah went tae a scripture
But am feart ah've loast ma wey thair.
Ah couldnae git the threid o the tellin.

That baby bonnie as the yird but no broukit like it.
The luve ae her mither
and her bonnieness didnae sauf her, wee Gracie.

So whit wis Paul gaein oan aboot
In that letter tae the Ephesians?
An whaur's Ephesia onywey?
Is Ephesus its capital?
An is it a guid place tae dwal?
They cannae sauf thirsels if I git the drift
Ae whit ah wis readin.
An how dae ye thole that?
Ye cannae sauf yirsel?

Her mannie's in the farawa north wurkin in thae oil saunds.
She's alane in her loass, her grievin whummled by it.

An whit's a' this aboot the twa made wan?
An so wur a' wan!?
An whit's that aboot Paul bein prisoner?
As if ah'm in a woodie an ah canna fund ma wey oot ae it.
Are we a' fowk thit want howp?
But nae in the Inglis sense o desirin
But in the Scots o nae haein.

Nae haein Gracie
Nae haein howp
Nae haein luve
Ah no! haein far mair luve than she cud thole.

It's a braw inditin in Paul's letter
The luve o Christ
'in a' its breidth an lenth an heicht . . .'
– an dinnae forgit the guttural whan ye say that –
'. . . an deepth'.
So it's aw aboot th'apprehendin, is it?
Mair easy tae say than tae dae an mebbe ah'm no no wantin it
As in the Scots sense.
Twa thoosan year!
It's taken fell lang syne
fur us 'feckless bairns caa'd up an doun like cobles on a
jawin sea'.
An ah'm speakin ma ain truith, ye ken.
An am I speakin in a spirit o luve?

Is that Gracie's sacrifice?

Paul gaein oan aboot Christ
Giein himsel up a 'maumie-smellin offerin' fur us.

Whit's Gracie's deith-strak anent the big wan oan the cross?

Ar na we feart no o the wraith o God
But o the 'mirkie minds' o the haithens in oor midst
An at oor borders?
Are we a' no really Ephesians?

Thurs nae licht.
A fu' mune forby, greetin if it could
Fur the bogles stravaguin ower oor planetary hame,
A mune set tae birl awa intae space
Farawa fae whit cannae be tholed
Hurlin itsel oot awa fae its griefs
intae the starry pitch o the mitherless wurld
taibetless an wantin no the luve o Christ
But somethin that wis a stillborn dream.

Oh how ye grat an ye greet.
Luik!
Thurs nae licht
Or, mebbe a puckle
If ye rack yir wabbit een.

Note: Quotations fae William Lorimer's *The New Testament in Scots* (1983).

Julia Cathcart

CONDENSATION

There were plenty of spaces in the well-lit car park on the pub forecourt, but, as usual, Dad drove by them all and went round the side of the building instead. The narrow space there, between the pub and the hedge, was always empty, except for the bins, but Dad still expressed a gleeful triumph whenever he turned the corner and saw no other cars already parked there.

'Ha! We always get a space here!'

He'd parked there several times over the long summer just gone, when Mum had started going away for days at a time, and we would run out of things: potatoes, butter, toothpaste, forcing him to go shopping.

'Come on, you can't be left on your own!' He would bundle us into the back of the car and off we'd go to the corner shop, or, if it was late, to the all-night garage, where he'd send us, running, to find the things we needed on the shelves. On the way home, he'd almost always stop at the pub where we'd have to wait while he went inside – my brother Paul and me, forbidden to leave the car, bickering in the bright, sticky heat of that summer.

Now, however, it was November; it was icy cold and starting to get dark. Dad parked next to the hedge, facing the road at the front of the pub. 'Right,' he said, 'wind the windows down a crack.'

Paul groaned.

'Just an inch or two,' Dad said, 'that's all. Look, like this.' He demonstrated by winding the driver's window down an inch. 'That's all I want you to do!'

'But it's cold!' Paul whined.

'Listen, I'll only be a minute, all right? I'm just going to pop into the pub to see if your auntie needs a lift home. I'll be right back.'

We wound our windows down a fraction. Dad leaned over, grunting, and wound the front passenger window down an inch. The cold air felt its way into the car.

'There!' Dad sighed, satisfied, then launched with exaggerated patience into one of his 'What happens when?' monologues, which were his way of explaining the logic of something: by asking questions and answering them himself. 'Now, you remember what happens when you *don't* leave the car windows open in this weather, don't you? Hmm? They steam up, that's what! And when they steam up, what happens?' He paused for dramatic effect, 'I can't see out of them, that's what!' Another pause before the devastatingly simple truth: 'And I have to be able to see where I'm going, don't I?' When we said nothing to this, he half-turned towards us, eyes wide in question, 'Well? Do I or do I not need to be able to see where I'm going?'

'Yes,' we mumbled.

'Good!' said Dad, 'I won't be long.' He got out and made his way over to the pub, holding the lapels of his coat together under his chin. A patchy white frost covered the pitted tarmac, and he picked his way with surprising nimbleness for a big man. He turned the corner of the pub, and all that was left was his breath, trailing behind him. It hung for a moment, white and thin, before dissolving in the cold air.

The milk and bread, in the green polythene bag from the all-night garage, sat between Paul and me on the back seat of the car. 'You'll have to come with me to the garage,' Dad had told us earlier that night when we were eating tea – his signature dish of burgers and chips from the freezer. He was standing in front of the mirror, obscuring our view of the television while we ate, plates on our laps, sitting on the couch. He kept his eyes on his reflection, which made it look as if he was talking, sternly, to himself as he combed his hair carefully back and over his ear. 'Your mum's away and there's no milk and no bread. Do you want to get up tomorrow and find there's no milk for breakfast?' He passed the comb to his other hand and began combing the other side of his hair, up and over his other ear. 'No milk for your cornflakes?' he continued, eyeing his reflection appraisingly, 'No bread for your toast? How'd you like that, eh?' He turned from the mirror, 'Come on, let's go!' And we'd flung down our plates and forks and rushed after him, out of the house and into the car with no coats on.

As soon as Dad was out of sight, Paul wound his window up. It closed with a soft *thunk*. I was seized with panic. 'Dad said not to do that! It makes the window steam up!'

Paul shrugged. 'Who cares?' He leaned over and wound my window up. 'There, you can blame me. He'll be ages in there; he always is, and I'm not sitting here freezing the whole time.' He got out and opened the front doors of the car, one by one, and wound each of the front windows up. 'That's better!' he said when he got back in, 'Toastie now, eh?' He laughed sarcastically, blowing on his hands and rubbing them together. The windows were already beginning to steam up. I didn't smile back.

Paul sensed my discomfort, as he always could, and pounced on it. 'Wait! Are you scared?' he sneered gleefully, 'God, you're *such* a *baby*!' I bit my lip and turned to the fogged-up window.

Two years older and wiser, for the past year or so, Paul had enjoyed taunting me whenever he was bored and I was in his eyeline. Dad had started doing afternoon shifts at work, and Mum always seemed to be on one of her long phone calls at tea-time, so it was just Paul and me at the kitchen table. To the musical sound of Mum's telephone laughter through the closed living-room door, Paul would tease me about my appearance, my friends, the way I held my fork – anything and everything was fair game to him, but whatever the subject, his common theme was always that I was just a baby. He would only be smugly satisfied when I went from whiny protest to tearful exasperation, thus proving his point.

Now, in the cold car, I braced for the familiar, inevitable onslaught. But this time, Paul really surprised me. He was quiet for a minute, and when he spoke again, his tone had changed.

'Hey,' he said kindly, 'it's just breath!' He breathed out noisily, producing a cloud of vapour. 'See that? When it's outside, it just floats away, but in here it's got nowhere to go, so it sticks to the window. But look, you can easily wipe it off.' He pulled the cuff of his jumper over the heel of his hand and rubbed at his window to demonstrate. 'That's what Dad's got those old tea towels for.' Several of Mum's old tea towels were stuffed in the driver's door pocket. 'Listen, when he sees the windows are steamed up, he'll only be angry for a minute, that's all. Then he'll wipe them with a tea towel, and that'll be it! Gone! Don't worry!'

It was impossible, now, to see out of most of the windows; only Paul's was clear, where he'd rubbed it with his sleeve. He rubbed it again and peered out.

'Hey, come and look! You can see the road from here!'

I sidled over, shifting the bag of bread and milk out of the way. It was dark now where we were parked, but there were lights in the car park at the front of the pub and a streetlight on the pavement beyond it. From Paul's window, we watched people passing, all of them trailing their breath behind them. A man in a tracksuit jogged by, looking at his watch. A couple walked by. They had their arms around each other, but we could hear them arguing. There was a woman with a small black dog. She was wearing a long blue coat like Mum's. I wondered what would happen if Mum came back while we were out: did she have a key? Would she wait for us?

'She's not our auntie, you know,' Paul said, 'not really.'

I knew she wasn't, but I didn't answer. We returned to cold silence, and for a while, nothing much happened on the road.

Then the drunk man came reeling round the corner of the pub.

He was staggeringly drunk and heading straight for our car. He looked as if he would fall over at any moment, but, amazingly, he didn't. He swayed and he staggered, and he kept on coming. We both tensed and shrank back on the seat. I willed the man to slip and fall or change direction, but still he kept on coming, lumbering straight at us till he bounced off the car, and finally fell, cursing, to the ground. We could hear him scrambling and grunting and swearing before he managed to get back on his feet. He was right outside Paul's window, panting and peering in through the cleared spot, his hands on the car roof. His face was red, and his hair was black and straggly. We both froze. The man stared at Paul. Paul stared straight back. Then I saw there was no life in the man's eyes, not a flicker to show that he had registered the sight of us; he was just staring blankly, seemingly at nothing. Suddenly, he reeled away, pushing himself off the car and spinning round. He staggered over to the bins at the side of the pub, fumbled with his trousers, and peed against the wall, which made Paul snigger. We could hear his pee splashing on the ground. He threw his head back and sang loudly, but we didn't know what the song was. It just sounded like wailing. Steam rose from his pee and his breath. He zipped up his trousers and staggered out to the front of the pub and down the road out of sight. We let out our breath in a fit of nervous giggles.

After a while, our giggles dissolved, and it was quiet and cold again. I shifted back to my side of the car and sat on my icy fingers to try to heat them up. Paul blew clouds of breath on his cupped hands.

'You know the real reason Dad doesn't want the windows to steam up?' he asked.

'What?'

'Same reason he parks round here: so that no one will notice the car, or us inside it.'

I thought of the drunk man, his unseeing gaze. 'Must be working, then,' I said, and we both laughed again, but not like before. Still, I felt good that I had made Paul laugh. He threw his head back and imitated the noises the drunk man had made when he was singing. He did it to make me laugh, and that felt good, too.

When they eventually came round the corner of the pub, they were both laughing, too. She had one arm hooked in his, and she leaned against him as they both stepped carefully over the frosty surface. Her shiny black handbag, on its gold chain handle, dangled from her free arm, and a cigarette glowed red in her hand. When Dad opened the car door, his alcohol breath a sudden steam cloud, he shouted, 'I told youse not to close the windows! Look at them, they're all steamed up! Christ's sake!'

He grabbed a tea towel from the door pocket and impatiently rubbed at the driver's door window. 'Open those windows!' he growled, throwing himself into the driver's seat and swiping at the windscreen with the tea towel.

When she opened the passenger door, her voice was a big smile, 'Hi, kiddos, how are youse?' I couldn't believe how casual she was; she didn't seem to notice that Dad was angry. She got in, pulling her shoulders up into her neck and pretending to shiver under her faux fur jacket. 'Your dad's just going to give me a wee lift home, it's so nice of him. Saves me walking in this cold. Brrrrrr!'

She spoke to us in a baby voice, which I liked, though I'd never tell Paul that. She shut the car door and drew deeply on her cigarette. Suddenly, Dad stopped wiping the windscreen. 'Really?' he said. He shook his head at her 'Not in the car!' he said, very slowly, like someone who is tired of having to explain something very simple, over and over.

'Sorreeee!' she said, turning and making an 'oops' face at us. But then she took another long, slow drag of her cigarette. I held my breath, but Dad didn't say anything. She opened the car door, leaning out to blow out the smoke, and chucked her cigarette on the ground. I was sitting behind her, and it landed just outside my window, where it smoked and glowed red for a moment before it died on the frosty tarmac.

She clunked the door shut and reached for her seatbelt. 'Sorrreeee! Sorreee! So, so, sorreeeee!' she sang, as if she was making up a song.

I sniggered, clamping my hand across my mouth, and Paul snorted. The lingering cigarette smoke, her warm, sing-song voice and her perfume, even the alcohol smell from their breath, all made the air inside the car feel light and alive after the dead, cold air of before. It even felt a bit warmer. Dad threw a tea towel to her and two more over his shoulder to us. 'Here, wipe your windows. The back windscreen, too.' He even seemed less angry now.

I rubbed at my window, and Paul got up on his knees to wipe the back windscreen. She wiped her window very slowly, running the tea towel round the edges several times and then polishing it all over with small, careful circles, all the time looking sadly at her reflection. I watched her eyes in the dark window staring, trance-like, back at herself as she said, 'Is she still at her mother's?' She said this in a normal, flat voice, so I knew she didn't mean for Paul and me to hear. As if we could only understand her if she spoke in a baby voice.

'Yeah.' Dad sighed and put his seatbelt on.

We drove along with all the windows open a crack, the cold night air rushing in through the gaps. Just before we got to her street, she turned to Dad and said, in her normal voice, 'Just let me out here, I'll walk the last wee bit round the corner, save you trying to turn the car round in this weather.'

He had stopped the car before she'd finished speaking. She unclipped her seatbelt and, turning to us, said brightly, 'This street's a dead-end, kiddos, and if you drive down it, you might find you can't turn round to get back out because of people parking their cars on the turning point. And they park all down the street, as well – on both sides, and it's so narrow that everyone who drives down there has to reverse all the way back out. It's too dangerous in this weather.'

Dad turned to us, 'I'm just going to walk your auntie along home, and I'll be right back, okay? Now, remember, DO NOT close the windows, do you hear me? I mean it, now!' he said firmly, 'I need to be able to see where I'm going!'

They disappeared round the corner together into the dead-end street, her hanging on to his arm, their breath trailing and dissolving behind them, and then it was just her laughter, high and warm on the cold, clear air, and it made me feel sad, like I missed her. As soon as her laughter had faded, Paul looked at me, grinned and closed his window with a soft *thunk.* I grinned back and closed mine too. Then, without a word, we both got out, opened the car's front doors, and closed those windows, too.

Irene W. Collins

THE MASK THAT CROSSED THE SEA

The first thing Edinburgh gave me was rain. Not the heavy, slapping kind of Lagos storms, where water drums on zinc rooftops and the gutters swell with plastic bottles, but a fine, needling drizzle that soaked through my jacket and made the stones of the city glisten like wet bones. I pulled my suitcase over cobblestones slick as fish scales, the wheels rattling, my breath misting in the September air. Somewhere above me, a bell tolled the hour – slow, deliberate, like the city was reminding me that I was late for something I didn't yet understand.

I told myself I was here for knowledge, for the future, for the clean promise of a degree in a foreign land. But as I trudged past rows of grey tenements, I kept hearing something else beneath the wind: the muted throb of drums. Not the polite thump of club music, but the rolling cadence of the talking drum, familiar as a heartbeat. I laughed under my breath, embarrassed by my own homesickness. How could Lagos rhythms cross the sea and lodge themselves in this cold, northern air?

Then I saw them. Footprints. Muddy, wide, patterned as though made by raffia-fringed soles. They trailed me along the wet street, close enough that I could almost feel the heat of another body at my back. I froze, turned quickly. The street was empty, slick and shining, the drizzle whispering against my ears.

Yet the footprints remained, dissolving slowly in the rain, as if the city had opened its doors to a spirit that refused to be left behind.

Edinburgh never warmed, not even when the sun dared to show itself. The cold here was not sharp like harmattan, which stung your lips and left white chalk on your skin. This cold crept inside, slow and damp, until my bones felt steeped like over-brewed tea. In lectures, my fingers stiffened around the pen, and when I spoke, my vowels clashed with theirs, my words stuttering against their careful Scottish enunciation. 'Sorry, what?' was the phrase I heard most often. After a while, I grew afraid of my own tongue.

Back home, the world was noisy, overflowing. Suya smoke curling into the night. Bus conductors barking routes. Children drumming plastic buckets, daring you to dance. Here, silence lived like a tenant in every corridor. Even laughter felt disciplined, cut short before it spilled too far. I missed Lagos the way you miss a limb: constantly reaching for something that was no longer there.

It was Amara who found me on campus, her accent a softer braid of Scottish burr and Igbo cadences. A second-generation child, she explained, parents from Enugu but she herself was raised among these granite streets. She laughed when I told her about the footprints. 'Scotland has its own ghosts,' she said, eyes bright, voice half a warning. 'Sometimes they recognise ours. They like to talk.'

That night, in my narrow dorm room, I unwrapped the carved mask my grandfather pressed into my hands before I boarded the plane. Its wood was dark, ridged, worn smooth where generations had touched it. 'This will watch you,' he had said, voice low with seriousness. 'It will not let you forget.' I placed it on the shelf above my desk, telling myself it was protection, a reminder of home. But in the stillness of the room, when the radiator groaned like an old man's breath, I could swear the mask exhaled with it. The eyeholes shone darker than the wood, wet as if something behind them was waiting, patient.

I lay awake listening. Outside, rain combed the glass. Inside, the mask watched.

The ceilidh was supposed to be harmless, just a way for 'international students' to bond over reels and laughter. I told myself to be open, to let the fiddles pull me into a rhythm I didn't yet understand. The hall smelled of varnished wood and wet coats, rain steaming from bodies packed too close.

I tried to follow the caller's instructions, left foot crossing right, hand to stranger's hand. Everyone moved like they had rehearsed since childhood; I stumbled half a beat behind, my accent heavy in my throat even though I wasn't speaking.

That's when I saw him.

A figure in the far corner, standing utterly still. Tall, raffia spilling from shoulders like straw set aflame, a wooden mask gleaming with impossible light. The masquerade. My chest seized. He did not belong here, under these Scottish rafters, but there he was – the very spirit my grandfather once warned me never to turn my back on.

No one else noticed. Laughter swelled, skirts spun, feet hammered. The fiddler dragged his bow in a long high note, and beneath it . . . I swear I heard it . . . the roll of a talking drum, answering, mocking, threading Lagos into Edinburgh.

The masquerade's head tilted, mask-eyes fixed on me.

I dropped my partner's hand. My feet tangled, the floor tipped, the air thick with sweat and history. I bolted through the doors, into the drizzle, cobblestones slick beneath me.

Behind me, the music carried on. But threaded through the rain, I heard another sound: the sharp, laughing rhythm of footsteps not my own, keeping pace, chasing me into the dark.

When I was a boy, the air in my village used to vibrate with festival season. The whole earth seemed to tremble when the masquerades came out, swirling bodies clad in raffia, cowries flashing, wooden faces that were not faces but doors. Drums rolled like thunder across the red dust, and even the bravest children clung to their mothers' wrappers.

I remember one masquerade in particular, tall as a palm tree, its mask carved with lines that looked like tears. It stopped in front of me. The world seemed to hush, even the drums pulling back as if to listen.

'Never turn your back on a spirit,' one elder hissed into my ear. 'They don't like being left behind.'

That night, my grandfather pressed a smaller mask into my hand. The wood smelled of palm wine and old smoke. His eyes were milky but steady. 'One day,' he said, 'it will call you back. Do not pretend not to hear.'

I thought it was only a story, another way of chaining me to the soil I wanted so badly to escape.

Now, in Edinburgh, I wake with sweat chilling my spine. The rain lashes the window, but underneath it I hear drums, faint, steady, threading through the silence of my room. My suitcase sits by the wall where I left it, but on the floor, scattered like fallen hair – lie strands of raffia.

I tell myself it must have clung to my clothes on the flight, impossible though that is. Yet I can smell it, sharp and earthy, the same scent that once clung to the mask in my grandfather's hands.

The elders said spirits hate to be left behind.

What if one has followed me across the sea?

*

The library windows are too clean, too polished. When I lean close to read the spines of thick history books, I sometimes glimpse myself in the glass, only it isn't quite me. My reflection wears a mask, raffia trailing like a shredded crown, its hollow eyes fixed on mine. The first time it happened, I slammed the book shut so hard the librarian coughed. Now I pretend not to see, but the masked face waits, patient as stone.

In the lecture hall, footsteps come. Light at first, almost playful, padding between the rows. Then heavier, deliberate, a rhythm I know from childhood – festival drums made flesh. I glance back, heart hammering, but the seats are empty, my classmates bent over their notes. Only I hear the procession marching behind me.

It follows me into the library stacks, into the supermarket aisles, into dreams where raffia sways above my bed like curtains. One morning I open my course reader and a tassel of raffia slides out, brittle and damp with the smell of earth. I drop it, but the strands cling to my fingers, stubborn as cobweb.

I speak faster these days, words tumbling into Igbo before I can stop them. My classmates exchange glances, smile politely, but the gap widens. I become a spectacle, a stranger, the one whose tongue betrays him.

It is no longer just haunting. The spirit demands attention – no, allegiance. It crossed the sea not to chase me, but to remind me of a debt unpaid, a cord uncut. Each day the city grows colder, but the drums in my chest burn hotter, louder.

I cannot decide what terrifies me more, that the masquerade will not leave me, or that one day it will, and take everything I am with it.

The rain came hard that night, hammering the roofs and running in silver sheets down the closes. I should have stayed in my room, buried in books and deadlines, but the drums would not let me rest. They rose above the storm – low, insistent, a pulse that tugged me out of bed and into the soaked streets.

I walked without thinking, my trainers squelching, the city deserted except for shadows. Greyfriars Kirkyard waited ahead, its gates yawning like a mouth. The bells tolled once, then fell silent. Only the drums remained.

He was there.

The masquerade stood among the stones, taller than any man, raffia glistening wet, mask gleaming dark as riverwood. The storm whipped around us, but he did not move until I stepped closer. Then he circled, slow, deliberate, echoing my every shift of foot and breath.

I wanted to run. My chest screamed for it. But something older – something carried in the marrow of my bones, kept me still.

In that silence between drumbeats, I understood. He had not followed me to punish or kill. He had followed because I had left wrong. No farewell libations poured on earth. No words at the shrine. No hand on the old man's shoulder before I boarded the plane. I had carried a broken thread across the sea, and the spirit had come to tie it back.

The realisation broke me open. My throat burned with salt, my body shaking. I wept into the rain, relief and dread tangled like raffia strands. The masquerade did not reach for me, did not strike. He only danced, slow, circling, until the storm itself seemed to move in his rhythm.

I was not hunted. I was remembered.

I didn't want to face the masquerade alone. So I asked Amara to come. She arrived with jollof in a foil tray and music on her phone, the kind that shook loose laughter even from heavy air. We pushed the narrow dorm desk against the wall, spread food across its surface, and told stories until the room grew warmer than the radiators could manage.

At midnight, we poured palm wine into plastic cups. I spilled the first measure onto the floor, watching it soak into the cheap linoleum like red earth. My grandfather's voice whispered inside me: *Pour for those who came before, or else they'll pour their silence into you.*

We clapped our hands. We sang low, tuneless, but honest. I told a story about Lagos traffic that made Amara laugh until her eyes watered. She told one about her Scottish grandmother who swore the Highlands had their own spirits. Between our words, the room breathed.

The masquerade never showed itself, not in raffia or shadow. But I felt it – leaning in from a place the eye can't name. The air thickened, respectful, almost satisfied.

I understood then: it had never wanted to drag me back. It only wanted to be carried forward, stitched into my steps, even here, where cobblestones smelled of rain instead of dust.

I raised my cup. *To Lagos. To Edinburgh. To belonging without erasure.*

The wine burned sweet on my tongue, and for the first time since arriving, the silence in my chest loosened.

Weeks later, Harmattan has come back home, though I am still here in Edinburgh where the fog clings to stone like a second skin. My mother's voice crackles through the line – thin, stretched, but carrying the heat of Lagos even across the cold Atlantic.

She tells me she dreamed of my grandfather. Dancing. Smiling. Alive in the way only the dead know how to be. Her words stop me; they shake loose something buried beneath all this damp grey.

I press my forehead against the window. Outside, the fog thickens, rolls heavy through the closes and winds, not clean and cold but dry, dusty – almost like home. For a moment, I can taste grit on my teeth, hear the rattle of dry leaves in the gutter. The city exhales, and I breathe Lagos into it.

And then I see him – the masquerade. Not charging this time, not chasing me through foreign streets, but moving as though in step with me. Cloth alive with impossible colours even the fog cannot swallow. His body sways with a rhythm that crosses seas.

I do not run.

I lift my hand, and the figure mirrors me, a dance across the veil. I realise, suddenly, he has never been a threat – only a reminder. That no matter how far I go, the dust of home keeps its own passport, stamped into my lungs, my blood.

My mother is still talking, still describing her dream, but I am no longer only listening. I am inside it. Edinburgh fog and Harmattan dust folding into one breath, one dance, one inheritance.

And in that heartbeat, I belong to both.

Rachel Coventry
HAPPINESS

We are in love
and it is dusk

The Maghrib, echoing
from mosque to mosque

In *Fara*, which means
happiness,

you collect
the things we need

charcoal, wooden skewers,
bread, and sugar

from shop to little shop
on the dirty

narrow streets
remembering this and that

we will take it all to the beach
to cook and eat

I wait by the bike watching
a peaceful white chicken

pulled from its cage
screaming, slaughtered

I cover my ears with my hands.

MAGPIES

for Sara

After you died
I turned you into all living magpies.

What we, in the West, call consciousness can do this
and no other consciousness can offer anything against it.

Of course, someone well boxed might cut open a magpie,
point to its guts and ask triumphantly,
Where is your Sara?

Do not worry.
Insouciant as ever, I will reply,
Well where is your magpie?

Jemima Dalgliesh

LOWLAND KINGDOM

A mother drops a pair of tiny pants onto a pile at her side. Her child stands before her, belly prominent over a fresh pair of cotton underwear, still holding the toy that had so absorbed her when she wet herself minutes prior. The mother takes a pair of hand-me-down joggers from a stack of faded clothes and says to the child, 'foot up, no, the other one.' She guides the little left foot through the concertinaed cloth and through the cuff, then repeats with the right. All the while the child holds onto the mother's sleeves with both hands, pinching the flesh of her arms between her fingers as she tries to maintain her balance. The mother looks at the round white face, the beaky nose and big wide eyes, and remembers what someone had said about the child's looking like an owl.

Small and round and watchful. The child resumes her play and the mother says 'next time tell me when you need to do a peepee.'

The room is a tip. The aftermath of lunch remains on a table, a toddler tray caked with hummus, two fingers of milk in a plastic beaker, half a glass of water, a mug, a plate and some crumbs. A kitchen is fashioned from a discarded bedside table, the hob drawn on the top with black marker; play lemons and peppers, grapes and peaches, corn cobs and pears; plastic fish slices and cups, ice cream coupes and forks, cups and saucers; a notepad on which the mother had pretended to take Clean Cat's order; an upturned washing basket standing in for a table, two places set. There are books and wooden skittles, plastic figurines and dice, fragments of games scattered from corner to corner. The child is like a contract killer, methodically disassembling toys and stuffing their pieces into bags like body parts. There is the potty, pristine, resembling an upturned tooth.

The light outside is the light you get near the sea, thin and white, and it is fading. The mother thinks that they have barely been outdoors today. She looks at the stack of pissy pants and reflects that they have better days when they are outside and they are busy, when the child is occupied and content, bustling like a fishwife in supermarket joggers, carrying rocks in her little hands or clarting around with rainwater and sand.

The autumn humidity has triggered her mould allergy and the mother's eyelids are clammy when she blinks. She feels delicate and dehydrated thanks to the previous night's excesses. Her skin is speckled with rosacea and her teeth feel furry under her tongue. When she looks up, she sees the child squatting by a toy stroller, administering care to Clean Cat, adjusting his straps to ensure his safety and his comfort. A dark patch burgeons unmistakably across the ochre bottom. The mother takes another pair of joggers from the pile, a fresh pair of pants, and kneels beside her child. There is an amount of robust debate, agitation, and despair as the child – who if she had it her way, would pee her pants and carry on with her day – resists the ministrations.

A door opens and the mother's father, whose house this is, pokes his head around it like a thin bald bird. He is in search of company and conversation and seats himself on a chair at one of the tables in his disused bar. He and his wife, the mother's mother, had thought it would be fun to run the village pub, mutilated as it was, with its bowling green and portions of land excluded from the transaction. The child is receiving potty training in the remnants of a hospitality business, hence the surfeit of tables, chairs, and doors. As he sits himself down among the detritus of another day of tedium and incontinence, oblivious to the torrent of angry babble issuing from the child, he asks his daughter 'have you read much Salman Rushdie?'

The mother answers sparsely in the negative, repeats the pissy pants-clean pants process; the child tells her 'get back to the kitchen you naughty thing' and looks at her in fury, as though she had just eaten her child's children. When she, the mother, has gathered the urine-soaked clothes and sprayed the site with Dettol, she realises that her father is still talking at her about Salman Rushdie. She looks outside at the fading light, the scent of ammonia in her nostrils. There is a stack of nappies with tabs, four or five thick white slabs piled neatly one atop the other on a round table by a settle. She takes one and advances toward her daughter, pulls down her joggers, and affixes it over the cotton pants. Best practice would be to cajole the child onto the potty but her reserves are depleted.

The pram is parked out of sight by one of the many points of egress. The mother rolls it toward the centre of the room and unzips the footmuff. She cardigans her child and retrieves Clean Cat from his stroller, snaps her own charge into place with the efficiency of experience. As she leaves the room she hears the child tell her 'I don't nont to go for a walk'; when she returns she bears a slab of Hard Cheese, which pacifies the child. Her father, who is relating literal war stories, stands and says 'ah'll come with ye if yer goin for a walk' and she, the mother, replies 'I'll just go on my own, I'm going to listen to my book.' And she leaves him standing in his empty and untidy erstwhile bar, surprised, as she pushes the pram through two doors, and across the car park. The mother's mother works nights in a petrol station and is asleep in the upstairs flat, so the mother takes care to close both doors quietly, while her father stands open-mouthed, like a fish.

She is buffeted lightly by wind from the sea as she rolls the pram across first one road and then another. The child sucks contentedly on Hard Cheese, her muteness accepted as consent to the hood being lowered to protect her against the breeze. The mother hasn't changed her clothes in days, pants excepted. She wears only a heavy cardigan against the late autumn chill, and a long scarf wound round and round her neck.

Her back is to the setting sun as she rolls past a row of squat bungalows in varying states of repair. A few have small front gardens enclosed by low walls, behind which are strewn plastic toys and tricycles. Small bikes lean against some of the houses. She thinks about the streets where she lives, the solidity and elegance of the terraces, rows, and places, the private gardens quiet and greenly bright, and recalls her speculation as to the occupants and their occupations every time she glimpses portraits on the other side of lighted glass, or through front doors left ajar. She thinks little of these bungalows and their residents, whether they are turning the heating on, boiling the kettle, or watching television, their faces suffused by light in small rooms. She doesn't wonder if they work in solicitors' offices or motorway service stations, drive buses or put out fires, get home every day off the five o'clock bus or work shifts on chaotic rotas.

The houses sit between the village's arterial road and the train track which runs parallel and which is crossed at intervals by bridges. When she reaches the second bridge she turns left and pushes up the incline. She bends over the front of the pram and peeks beneath the hood where her child's eyes are shining, wide, and lovely, and adjusts the zips at either side of the footmuff. When she reaches the crest of the hill she slows her pace and looks out across the fields: to the northeast an estate of low houses loops and whorls; to the northwest the power station foregrounds, four clean grey blocks against the gradation of fields and hills and sky, gaps where the cooling towers once stood. A train shoots beneath her feet, is there and then is gone. It is dusk, and the grass to either side pools black in the shadow of the embankment. Crepuscular slaughter rustles in the grasses and the pram wheels whisper thinly over tarmac. She walks on, behind the backs of scattered houses, French doors throbbing black and amber with the changing of the light. When she looks again beneath the hood her child is asleep.

She sees a form at a kitchen window framed by pale curtains, a silver tap arching like a swan just slightly left of centre, and remembers a former classmate lives on this stretch of road. Almost everyone had called her 'Shovel', owing to the flatness of her face, a peculiarity which was only accentuated by her button nose, pert and round as a mushroom. The casual cruelty common to small towns and private girls' schools meant the mother had been able to slot right in when she arrived at Oxford, untouched, with her cheap shoes and immature notions of culture. She had lost the weight before going up, thank Christ, but can still remember being a heavy girl at school, and the stones whistling past her ears on her way home for lunch, and her sobbing and ashamed and in pain because one had hit the back of her skull, and her mother chirping like a harpy, determined to have the full story.

At the end of the road she turns right, discounting the westward dirt track which would take her to the cemetery where two of her grandparents are at rest. On her left, beyond fields of sheep, is the ambient thrum of the dual carriage way; to her right, pebble dash bungalows almost shine in the gloaming. The corrugated metal shed of the engineering business where she once temped looms large and cavernous ahead of her. Its car park is desolate, and she remembers that the men went home at four o'clock, boiler suited. She had a job in the office covering maternity leave, reconciling bank statements and booking cheap accommodation for the ones who worked away. During university summers, she waitressed in a hotel and served eggs to coach parties and wedding guests while her boyfriend, a milquetoast, faffed about in continental Europe and wrote about himself. During one long vac they went for weeks without speaking and though she thought this strange it had not troubled her unduly. She reflects that now there is one whose loss would break her irreparably, and she wonders not for the first time if she will only ever feel love negatively, and why love for her is at its strongest when it manifests as fear of the permanent absence of the loved, and if it has something to do with this place, this land of wood and hill and sea, of white skies and isolation and destructive boredom, this Lowland Kingdom.

She takes another right downhill, and manages the pram's descent past farmland. The bushes that line the roadside are out of control, the council has no money. She passes the black bars of farm gates and can barely perceive in the distance the sheep and horses that she knows are there; the sky in the east is purple to blue and the street lamps burn orange overhead. She adjusts her grip without thinking as she approaches the next bridge, flexing her palms and bending her elbows to push up and over.

Someone has planted evergreens to absorb the racket of the passing trains and now they stand tall and black over the roofs of houses and against the fading redness in the west. She passes another dirt lane and thinks of childhood gangs in summertime, an abandoned caravan, hide and seek, tennis balls batted against pebbledash, Findus crispy pancakes, DVD players and VCRs, Santa matryoshka, rollerblades, Pepsi, Asda and chips and gravy, the school bus, the utility room and the landline in the hall, headlice, social failure and academic excellence, as she crests the hill and glances westward. Her downhill grip is but a gentle pull to counter gravity. On the main road the headlights of cars thread yellow-white and the service bus passes by, lit up like a fishtank.

Once over the bridge she takes a left then crosses the road when it is safe to do so, avoiding potholes. She checks under the hood again: the child sleeps on. As she nears the village's outer boundary she passes a general store where she used to buy penny sweets, and remembers the ping-pong of the alarm, the hum of the fridge storing milk and clingfilmed baps, the scent of newspaper, a handwritten sign tacked to the door that read 'Only two school children in the shop at a time', the cool dark of the backroom and the sickly greenish light between the aisles of condensed milk and coffee granules, tinned Scotch broth, chocolate bars, and 10p crisps. Past the stone bus shelter that reeks of piss, where she exchanges short 'hallos' with an early evening dogwalker, the beast's claws clicking against the pavement and her pram wheels whistling, she takes another right and follows the curve of the town's perimeter.

She is now a Middle Class Fatty Who Likes to Run and chugs around the sweep of houses at least once per visit while her mother entertains or feeds her child. This loop of road contains the township like a net teeming with fish, and is lined with stuccoed semi-detached two-storeys and neat bungalows with hydrangeas spilling over pebbles. Many of the houses have names that are fixed in italicised metal lettering to the low walls enclosing the drives, or to one side of the front door. The rear gardens of those on her left incline toward the sea, which is sometimes mauve and sometimes grey but now is blue and still, and indistinguishable from land.

Across the firth are the hills and fells she began to offer as a reference point to those who asked where she received her earliest education, wholesome associations of daffodils and anthropomorphic rabbits, mint cake and cold air in the lungs. She supposes, as she steers the pram toward the declivity in the pavement and crosses a road that curls away to a cul-de-sac, that this began after the milquetoast's visit. He was a trust fund dandy who came to her ancestral home acutely conscious of the advantages of his classical education, with his reflexive disdain for mainstream taste and a small talent for writing the mystery of himself in furniture. His knees almost to his chin in the backseat of her mother's car, he had stared at the shabby high street of the neighbouring town, at the chip shop and the smiling children pushed in grubby strollers by their clinically obese mothers, thighs thick, hips and busts jutting like shelves, their poorly cut clothes faded and cheap. He said it was rundown and gave the impression of being displeased with everything and everyone around him while drinking their wine and eating their food. If she were to isolate a point in time, she thinks, as she enters the final stretch westward, the sun gone, it would be then that she became aware of how squat and poor and crude it all was, this Lowland Kingdom.

When she returns she finds her mother ursine in a fleece dressing gown, sitting by the fire. Motion arrested, the child snorts awake in the relative warmth of the former lounge, is unclipped and set loose. The grandmother encourages the child onto the potty, which has been fetched by the mother from the cold gloom of the bar, and the child squats blinkingly before releasing a warm stream of piss. The mother strokes the gusset of the child's pants with her knuckles: they are dry. Everyone claps and smiles.

Later, three generations of women eat around a small table. They share a meal of chicken, vegetables and potatoes. The meat has been cut into small white pieces for the child, who glugs milk from a plastic beaker and chews the chicken, condescends to have some peas spooned into her waiting mouth. There is ice cream and sauce in a small bowl afterwards, eaten with a teaspoon. The mother's father watches television in the flat upstairs and leaves his dinner to congeal in the kitchen on an oval plate; later he will tip it into the bin and make a sandwich with white bread and spam.

The child is bathed by the grandmother. They sing songs about fingers and thumbs and play tea party with the bathwater while the mother arranges pyjamas, vest, socks, and night nappy on the cot in the next room, switches on a nightlight and lowers the blinds. She fans the picture books in an arc and waits cross-legged on the floor, then remembers Clean Cat and fetches him from the lounge. Shortly following her return she receives the pinkly naked child into her arms and thinks of her birth, and of her crooked non-plussed gaze as she was held above the screen fashioned from a hospital gown.

Creams are applied, a nappy tugged up over small solid thighs. The child selects the books and the mother regales her with the humdrum exploits of suburban elephants. They argue over the quantity of books, reach an agreement with which, like the best negotiations, neither is fully satisfied. Then the mother lies on the floor alongside the cot and they hold hands until the child is still, her breathing rhythmic. She holds a hand under the sleeping child's nostrils until she feels the warm air.

When she leaves the bedroom it is briefly illuminated until she pulls the door behind her. It lacks a handle and cannot be fully closed. The grandmother has returned to bed for an hour's sleep before she must prepare to leave and commence her nightshift. The mother returns to the lounge bar where they had eaten earlier and reads news articles on her phone beside the fire. She drinks water that comes from the tap and is bright and cold and clean, and eats ice cream. She is tired and her reading is pointless and desultory. She decides she will go to bed early, to the room she shares with the child, and sleep.

The living room door is open and she stops on the landing. The father sleeps in his chair folded into himself, folded into a foetal position, folded to an egg. His head, also egg-like, is brown, like a smooth and shiny brown nut, or a seed. His legs, bent at the knee, are long and thin; they have the appearance of tense metal, jack-knifed in sleep. She watches him from the door, and knows that both of them are framed by the oblong of black glass that swallows up much of the opposite wall, but from where she stands she cannot see his reflection, nor hers. All she can see is him and his furniture, inside a room.

He had told her earlier that day that he had been hospitalised as a boy, had been operated on by a surgeon. His papa had brought his fat red dog to the hospital and stood outside the boy's window, stood with his fat red dog, which he had brought for the boy to see. The boy, her father, might have worn pyjamas with pale blue stripes and sat upright in his metal bed, with milky green blankets and stiff white institutional sheets. He might have walked to the window to wave to the fat red dog, and the boy might have smiled a smile that creased his eyes and sharpened his nose, which is the mother's nose, under a straight fringe of hair. The fat red dog would most certainly have barked, and it might have jumped. And her boy father would have smiled and waved again, and leaned forward into the glass, pressing his forehead against it, a soft peachy patch of flesh against the pane lit on one side with blue, on the other with white and milky green light.

Two rooms away, the child sleeps, face fat and flushed, scalp sweating under her curls. The child has an abundance of hair, it is plethoric. When she is put to bed in this cold Lowland Kingdom she is always overdressed, her mother forgetful of this inheritance of hair, and so the child sleeps and sweats, holds tight to Clean Cat, who is actually filthy and has lost his purr, and twists his label between her tiny fingers, while her mother's father puffs and snores in his recliner, jack-knifed to an egg, and the mother watches him from the doorway, framed like a portrait of a lady, then goes to bed.

Lynn Davidson

NAMING THE SNAKES

In the front yard of a suburban home in Meanjin/Brisbane, my son gently uncoils a python from the broad limb of a river red gum. Elliot is an ecologist, and part of his job is extricating snakes who have moved into domestic spaces. I watch from the footpath. Diamond eyes, half-diamond fork of tongue, diamonds on its back; the python suggests glitter, but doesn't glitter. Almost as thick as his arm and as long as he is tall, Elliot holds the python at eye level for a moment before easing it into a sack, tail first. The snake spirals in. Elliot puts the bag in the back of his ute and we drive to a piece of bushland where it is safe to release it. He gently lowers the sack onto dry, crisp ground, and opens its mouth. We watch the python slip out and away into country shaped by its Dreaming Ancestor, the Rainbow Serpent. That was Meanjin/Brisbane. That was then. I have shifted across hemispheres, from Aotearoa New Zealand, via Meanjin/Brisbane, to Scotland. I am missing my son.

In a quick, sudden wind, the gum tree shushes

I sit in an Edinburgh café called Wellington. Despite its below-street-level cool, its hip staff, the slightly too-loud music, and confident prices, my scone still crumbles in my hands when I try to butter it. Perhaps it is not the scone that crumbles, but me. I am sad that it is Wellington but not *Wellington*; another place holding someone I am missing: my younger kid, Tamara. The complexity of missing them and yet choosing to live far, far away is eloquently felt, but only clumsily expressed. It sits somewhere at the edge of language.

I live in Stockbridge, a ten-minute walk from Edinburgh's town centre. The Water of Leith curves through it. On my river walks I often stop at St Bernard's Well, whose mineral-rich spring water was believed to have healing properties. The well is crowned by a temple built in the eighteenth century in the Greco Roman style. Inside the columns of the temple is a graceful statue of Hygeia, the Greek goddess of good health. Hygeia was born into a divine lineage of healing: the daughter of Asclepius, the Greek god of medicine, and Epione, the goddess of soothing pain, and the granddaughter of Apollo, that god of many things including healing, light, music and poetry. Hygeia holds a bowl in one hand from which she will feed the snake that curves against her robes.

The medicinal snake represents the cyclical nature of healing, its ability to shed its skin demonstrating growth and transformation. The rod of Asclepius is a rod entwined with a snake; it is there on the building for the Royal College of Physicians of Edinburgh on Queen Street. I visit Hygeia to wish for my own good health, and the good health of others. I go there to pray for strength for the ongoing work of changing shape. These early spring days wild garlic scents the air and birds sing, and around the flowers, bees circle and hum.

The well is mentioned in Mary Wollstonecraft Shelley's *Frankenstein*, when Dr Victor Frankenstein describes 'The beauty and regularity of the new town of Edinburgh, its romantic castle and its environs, the most delightful in the world, Arthur's Seat, St Bernard's Well, and the Pentland Hills.' *Frankenstein* was written towards the end of the Enlightenment period, and Dr Frankenstein enjoys the order and beauty of the New Town, its uniform facades and generous town squares a shining manifestation of the Enlightenment. It was from this desire for order and control, and the new and fearless reason of science, that the very disordered Frankenstein's Monster emerged. It is no surprise that when the Monster plots its revenge on Dr Frankenstein for abandoning him, he invokes the snake, saying, 'I will watch with the wiliness of a snake, that I may sting with its venom.' No surprise that he calls on the snake, the skin-shucker, the measurer of change.

In Wellington, which isn't *Wellington*, I think of kākās with burnt orange flashes under moss green wings, their screeching calls at dusk. Aotearoa New Zealand does not have snakes. It has birds. Those otherworldly messengers. It has my old life, with its beauties and its disorders. I visit Hygeia at St Bernard's Well to remember the proximity of beauty to danger, love to loss. To remember the venom that that can also be medicine. In Wellington, more warm bodies gather at the counter to order what they order.

The coffee maker hisses

I leave the cafe and walk to the Modern Scottish Galleries where there is an exhibition by South Korean artist Do Ho Suh. The exhibition shows us how he has moved across the world, not just once, but several times. The exhibition is about the homes we find, the shelters; and the ancestry of those homes. He shows us how old homes live inside the new like ghosts, or babies, almost as though they might, one day, be born again, from ancestry back into this world. There is a drawing of Suh running along a street with thousands of threads sweeping up behind him, attaching him to a traditional Korean house, like the house where he was born. Life is circular, the drawing seems to say, no getting away from it. Haste ye back, is the Scottish saying.

By mistake, I start at the end of the exhibition, in the Ideas Room, where there is a display of books that inspired the artist. They include children's books, many of which are called, simply, *Home* – some with thick card pages, furry at the edges. Then I find James Bridle's *Ways of Being*; a book I gave to Elliot a year or two ago, about how we might make better homes for ourselves using our human skills to be part of, not separate from, the natural world. There is *Dark Ecology* by Timothy Morton. I sit down with *Dark Ecology*, a book which urges us, in the darkness of climate crisis and uncertainty, to find a new way of living in this world. Flicking through it, I notice that each section of the book finishes with a drawing of a snake in a perfect circle, with its tail in its mouth. An ouroboros, the ancient Egyptian symbol that means repetition and renewal, that eternal cycle of destruction and recreation.

Then I enter the exhibition itself, and walk through merged homes made of translucent fabric (everything is connected) and past the paper woven with thousands of strings of coloured thread (everything is connected) and the drawings that could be hundreds of little rocks one on top of the other, but are people crouched atop each other (everything is connected) and the drawings of karmic juggling (everything is connected). Finally, I am standing in front of the memorial he made to his long-time home, his apartment in New York. I have walked back to the beginning of the exhibition; to the beginning of Suh's story as an artist.

Before he left this apartment where, he says, he first became an artist, he took paper and stuck it to the walls, the whiteware, the cupboards, the meter box, the doorhandles, the evacuation directions, to the everything of his bare empty, beloved apartment. Then he rubbed the paper with something, perhaps crayon or pastel or chalk, to make the shape and the textures of whatever lay beneath it. He sees the gesture of rubbing as a very loving gesture, and the exhibition itself is called Rubbing/Loving. After rubbing/loving everything in his apartment, he carefully removed the paper, and he had an almost three-dimensional version of his home. To me, the shapes of the apartment hanging on the walls in Modern One looked like the shed skin of a snake, with all of its textures, its particulars, its more worn and less worn places. Its ghost. Its shape of *gone*. Its shape of *once lived in*. This is the sort of memorial Suh likes. Fragile, personal. I love that he memorialises the ordinary domestic. The shelter and safety of a home. A home where Suh could become an artist because the landlord was kind to him and let him make his art. *Do what you want*, the landlord said, knowing that Do Ho Suh would do no harm. Suh walked out of his New York flat, taking his shed skin with him. I want to touch it, the skin of the home that protected his dreaming.

The shed skin shivers

Then, I had a call from Elliot. He, his wife Ret, and their three-year-old daughter, Emily, had been on a farm-stay holiday, inland from Meanjin/Brisbane, with another couple and their children. On their last night, full of toasted marshmallows and the day's sunshine, they were outside playing charades; one person would make an animal shape, and the others would guess what animal it was. Then, right next to Emily, they saw a flicker. Elliot quickly identified a venomous small-eyed snake.

Inside, Elliot checked Emily for puncture wounds, and there were none that he could see, and she was, so far, fine. But it can take forty-eight hours for the venom to take effect, so to be sure, they drove to the nearest hospital. At the hospital the medical staff took them to the resuscitation room and put a canula in Emily's arm, taking bloods at regular intervals all through the night. At first, the doctors brushed off Elliot's claim that it was a small-eyed snake, until they connected him to someone they mutually knew who worked in ecology. Then they were sure that he knew what he knew about the small-eyed snake.

Before he started telling me the story, Elliot assured me that my granddaughter was safe, *Emily's okay, she's home in bed, but*. What does it look like, I said, as though that was important, but somehow, it was. It's got a rosy underbelly, he said. It looks a bit like a red-bellied snake, but smaller. Oh God, I said. It's quite pretty actually, he said. And I imagined it with its sunrise pink diamond-pressed underbelly. Flickering through the grass like a cold flame.

My breath rustles like a small snake parting grass

In ancient times Gaia created Python to protect her sacred temple at Delphi. The Oracle of Delphi was known as the Pythia. The original Pythia lived in a cave from which vapours arose from a fissure in the earth. When Pythia sat above that fissure and breathed in these vapours she went into a trance. Gaia entered her body, transmuting it into the form of a Python, and then spoke her prophecies through Pythia's mouth. Later, Apollo kills Python and steals Pythia who then must prophesise from the Temple of Apollo. The last prophecy of the Oracle of Delphi was given when the Roman Empire was supressing Pagan practices. Pythia prophesised that Apollo's temple was in ruins and that the prophetic spring had dried up, its waters were stilled.

Where did the Oracle of Delphi go when her job of prophecy ended? When she unstraddled the fissure and left the temple, did she also leave the cave? Did they go with her, these two sacred places, transparent as shed skins, one inside the other? Did she miss hearing from the earth? Did she miss speaking from her mother's mouth?

Apollo's granddaughter feeds the medicinal snake

A year ago, when Elliot, Ret, Tamara, Emily and I were visiting the Meanjin/Brisbane Museum, we stopped in front of a display unit holding around forty taxidermised snakes. Ret challenged Elliot to identify them. She did this by standing in front of the list of names and calling its attendant number. Elliot started naming the snakes by heart and people started gathering around, to listen to the saying of the names. As Elliot said the names, my granddaughter Emily and I stood together, her hand in mine. Me with my dozens of strings sweeping above me, connecting me to my many past homes, adequate and inadequate, each one ghosted by the other. Above Emily's wee self, a single string tethering a single home that is, to her, eternal.

Eilidh Eglinton

LORGAN ANN AN NEW YORK

Lorgan ann an New York
Casan calmain anns a' choncrait –
Sgròban itealain air seachran
->- ->- ->- ->- ->- ->-
->- ->- ->- ->- ->-
A' stiùireadh na slighe
Ach a' sgèith an taobh eile;
Bidh iad an sin gu sìorraidh.
Chan fhàg mo chasan làrach idir
An seo.

Lorgan ann an New York
An làrach far an do thachair e –
An dà thùr air an toirt gu talamh,
Air an slugadh dhan talamh;
'S ged tha 'n ainmean gràbhailte an umha
Chan fhàg *an* casan lorgan tuilleadh
Air thalamh.

FOOTPRINTS IN NEW YORK

Footprints in New York
Pigeon feet in the concrete
Sketch erratic plane-tracks
->- ->- ->- ->- ->- ->-
->- ->- ->- ->- ->-
Point one way but fly the other
They will be there forever.
My feet will leave no impression
Here.

Footprints in New York
The site where it happened
Two towers reduced to earth
Swallowed into the earth.
Though their names are etched in bronze
Their feet will no longer print
The earth.

Simon Ewing

THE TOENAIL

When we first moved Grandad into the care home, Mum and I would visit him together. She'd collect me from school, and as we covered the few blocks from here to there, I'd try to put on a brave face and answer her questions about my day as lightly and keenly as I could. But as we got closer, and especially when we rounded the street and the stern sandstone facade rose in front of us, I'd go quiet, my imagination running wild with the various terrible states we might find Grandad in. What if he'd soaked his pillow black with drool? Or used the toilet in bed? Or shifted in his sleep so his private parts had fallen loose from his pyjamas?

But each time we arrived, he'd be lying in the same position as the day before: thin arms at his side, pumpkin-like head propped up on his pillow. I'd take the chair at the head of the bed while Mum set out the folding wooden one at its foot. If he needed help, she always knew what to do: when to draw the curtain, when to give him water, when to simply lean across and stroke his forehead.

When I became upset, she would remind me of our holidays in Grandma and Grandad's caravan at Llannerch-y-medd, the night Grandad and I took his telescope onto the front lawn and he showed me the Dog Star, the time I made such a fuss about the seeds in the strawberry jam on my toast that he started to pick them out with tweezers.

'That's all we can do when the people around us get very sick,' Mum said. 'Remember the times that meant the most to us.'

I didn't want to hear it. 'If you got sick,' I told her, 'I'd make sure you got better.'

*

Every couple of weeks, she brought a small pair of scissors to trim his toenails. It reassured me that she was keeping him presentable, preparing him for the day we could bring him back home.

Once, he cried out, and she sprang away from his foot.

'Stupid girl!' he shouted, recoiling from her.

I looked from Grandad, whose eyes were wide as an animal's, to Mum, who had gone pale, to Grandad's foot, where blood beaded at the edge of the nail: she had cut too deep.

'Silly little girl,' he muttered, already drifting away again.

Over the next few weeks, I'd find Mum crying in her bed in the middle of the day or staring out the window at the top of the stairs. During our visits, Grandad was as docile as before his outburst, but she started to set her chair further from him, and when he needed something, she'd call for one of the staff rather than do it herself.

One morning, before I left the house for school, she explained she had a lot of work to get through that evening and didn't know if she'd make it to the home. Would I be a good boy and visit Grandad by myself?

I couldn't face the thought of sitting alone with him in that room, its wallpaper so drab you could hardly tell its colour.

When I didn't answer, her eyes fell. 'I shouldn't have asked,' she said. 'I'll visit him again as soon as things have quietened down at work.'

That evening, it didn't surprise me that she didn't seem to be working at all. She was quiet and distracted; when she spoke, it was with a brittleness I wasn't used to. At dinner, I knocked over my water glass. 'Can't you be more careful?' she snapped. 'Always spilling things.'

I lay awake deep into the night. I pictured Grandad in his bed, wincing with some new pain nobody knew about, asking his questions to an empty room. At the end of my night, my alarm would send me off to my school and friends, but his day would look just the same as his night had been. He'd lie there, hour after hour. That's all he did these days. He just lay there.

In the morning, I told Mum I'd visit him like she'd asked. She squeezed my hand.

'Just sit with him,' she said. 'That's all I need you to do.'

*

When I reached the home, I hurried past the front area and up the stairs. Voices boomed from the other side of the hallway, where a family was visiting another resident, hanging a birthday banner over her bed.

'Brought a bottle of the good stuff, Mum!' shouted a man with thin hair and a red face.

'And look, Linda – your favourite truffles!'

The old lady in the bed looked around like she'd never seen these people in her life.

I slipped into Grandad's room, relieved to find him sleeping. I took my usual seat (Mum's folding chair leaned against the wardrobe) and locked my eyes on the clock. Just one hour, Mum had promised – then she'd take me home.

As I watched the hands shift round, it struck me that they were the only things in the room that moved at all. When Grandad was awake, they must surely draw his attention to the time falling away, or creeping along, however he saw it.

I was determined to look anywhere apart from the bed. I focused on the chest of drawers – a black-and-white photograph showed Grandad in army uniform, his smile triumphant, almost taunting in its youthfulness – and then on the floor. The carpet's thickness highlighted a few flattened sections that showed how the furniture had been arranged – the bed against the far wall – back when another old person stayed here. Had the bed freed up and Grandad moved in the next day? Was some other old person out there just waiting for him to move out so they could take his place?

It didn't seem to matter where I looked. Everything seemed to chant: *dying, dying, dying.*

Someone opened the door without knocking: the man from across the hall. The lady's family started singing, *For she's a jolly good fellow . . .*

'Just you in here, son?' the man asked. He nodded at the folded chair. 'Mind if I take that? We're having a bit of a celebration.'

'That's my mum's,' I said. I didn't mean to sound so angry.

He backed away, hands up. 'Whoa, horsey,' he said, grinning. He danced back to the party: *And so say all of us.*

One of the carers stormed up the stairs. 'You must be quiet,' she hissed at the family. 'This isn't a function suite. And we've told you before. Only three of you at one time.'

I wondered if Grandad knew the lady next door had too many visitors while he had only me. All of a sudden, I felt that I was the only one keeping people from barging in and taking away his furniture, his photographs, his radio – from clearing the place out entirely.

I turned to him – and gasped.

His eyes were open, boring into mine with a focus I hadn't seen in all those weeks. I knew he wasn't all there, not yet, but still. Everyone else had written him off, but here I was, seeing him seeing me. My blood fizzed through me as sweet as cola.

I jabbered at Mum all the way home. 'And I said no, that's my mum's, and then he left, and Grandad was looking at me like he knew.' When she didn't say anything, I added, 'And he smiled at me!' I blushed at the lie. 'I can go back tomorrow. I can keep going as long as you need me to. Until we can go together again.'

'You're a good boy,' she said, smiling thinly through the windscreen.

*

She soon stopped making excuses for why she couldn't join me at the home. I started to bring a piece of schoolwork to pass the time. When she arrived at the end of each hour, she'd hover in the doorway, her eyes glimmering with tears. I'd grab my schoolbag and follow her out of the room as fast as I could, before she started to actually cry.

One month passed like that, then two. The lady across the hall never received the same rowdy group of visitors as that first time, but her son was there often. Bursts of his laughter and singing punctuated my hours by Grandad's bed.

During one visit, Grandad turned in his sleep, and his right foot dropped out from the duvet. The toenails, untrimmed for weeks, strained against the top of the sock. Queasy, I pulled the cover back in place.

On the rare occasion he drifted awake, he sometimes asked things I didn't understand, like, 'How long until the boat?' I knew he'd worked in the church and wondered if his job had prepared him for what was happening to him now. If that was the case, maybe he wasn't confused, and asking for the boat was just part of a process I didn't know.

Other times, he'd smack his lips: 'Pah, pah, pah.' Remembering how Mum had cared for him, I'd offer him water, but he wouldn't take it. I'd shift his pillow, but that only seemed to make him more uncomfortable. My hope of his recovery seeped out of me.

Once, he started coughing and didn't stop. I hurried downstairs and found the carer who had told off the family across the hall. Up in the room, she pulled him forward and rubbed his chest until his breathing steadied.

When she turned to go, she said, 'He's lucky to have you.'

'My mum's busy at work. But she'll be back soon.'

'Now, now.' She shook her head. 'Some of the people here, they never get any visitors. You'll be glad of the time you spent with him. You'll be glad to look back and see how well you looked after him.'

Blushing, I glanced away and saw with horror that during his coughing fit, Grandad's foot had fallen out of the duvet. The lady followed my gaze to where the nails gleamed through the thin fabric of his sock. She set out Mum's chair, took a pair of clippers from her pocket and removed the sock. The foot looked hard and dry as wood. I winced each time the clippers ticked shut, sure he'd cry out again, but he snored on. The nails were so long and heavy that they didn't dart away but simply fell onto the bed.

When she was done, she swept the clippings into the bin. My anger was the same as if she'd torn up his photographs or set his books on fire. As soon as she left, I shook his shoulder. 'You've got to wake up,' I said. 'You can't just sleep all the time.'

But he didn't stir. I looked at the ceiling and clenched my jaw, tensing myself against my shame. If he really was about to go, I knew I didn't have what I'd need to keep him together in my mind. My memories alone wouldn't manage it, and certainly not just the good ones. They simply weren't strong enough.

*

He died later that week. I was at his side, struggling through my biology homework, when all of a sudden he rose in bed and gripped the edge of the duvet. He was about to throw it off, launch to his feet, put on his coat and hat and take us both out of there.

Then he sank back into the bed with a terrible dragging breath. He lay still, his mouth open in disbelief, as though wherever he was now, someone had asked him to show some papers he had forgotten, and there was no way he could go back and get them.

At last, I could see just how bad he had gotten. His remaining hair was matted and ashen, while dark and wiry strands jutted from his nostrils. His skin had thinned to a discoloured film over his spindly bones.

I put a hand over his belly and watched it stay in place. His frown had already smoothed away; he'd slipped right out of his body. I thought of the last time he and I had cleaned our walking boots at the front door; the last time we made scones together; the last time he'd read to me from *The Once and Future King*. It felt cruel that nobody had told me those really had been the last times.

I stepped into the hall in a daze. I needed to tell someone. I stopped at the just-open doorway of the room on the far side. The man sat at his mother's bedside, taking photo after photo from a box and waving them in front of her.

'Remember when Jamie cut his fringe with the kitchen scissors?' he asked. 'We had a real laugh then, didn't we? Come on, Mum. You've got to remember that one.'

The lady was staring at me. The man shifted round. His eyes hung low and defeated. 'Hello, son.' He sniffed. 'You okay?' Surrounded by all those photographs, pleading with the woman to remember, remember, remember, he looked as ashamed as if I'd caught him stealing from her purse.

I ran back to Grandad's room, shutting the door behind me. I flung open his drawers and searched through his things: a comb, an antique cheese knife, ratty OS maps bound by a blue rubber band. I wasn't interested in any of that, the stuff of his life. I wanted something that would remind me of this last version of him, the confused and wasted version I knew I'd try to forget later.

At the foot of the bed, I crouched over the bin. It hadn't been changed from earlier in the week. I plucked out the largest of the toenails the carer had cut from him. It lay like a seed in my palm.

Someone knocked on the door. I was sure they'd take the nail from me if I didn't hide it somewhere, just like they'd take Grandad's body in the ambulance and box up his belongings.

'Everything all right in there?' asked the lady's son through the door.

I put the nail in my mouth. It was like a shard of plastic. My teachers said plastic lasted forever. I tried to bite it in two, but it was too hard to break. It tasted mostly of nothing but a little of mushrooms. Gritty particles came off it, like soil from the ceramic pieces I dug up in our garden. It was foul, but its foulness made me happy – so happy that when the man pushed into the room and I swallowed the nail, I couldn't help it: try as I might, I couldn't keep the smile from my face.

Gabriel Featherstone

GOD HAS A PLAN

Some people say that God has a plan for all of us. When he was five years old, my cousin Benjamin had a plan for his Sea Monkeys. That plan was to flush them down the toilet so the goldfish he'd already flushed down there wouldn't get lonely. Sometimes, I worry that God is a massive Cousin Benjamin, with a toilet beyond our comprehension.

It is sometime before the birth of time and Eurynome, the ancient Pelasgian Goddess of Creation, is incredibly bored. She floats in total isolation above an infinite lifeless sea and beneath an infinite empty sky. Eventually, the boredom becomes intolerable, and she decides to create a second form of life. Seizing control of the wind, she sculpts it into a creature named Ophion the Serpent. The Serpent is grumpy, ill-tempered, and a terrible conversationalist, but, by virtue of being the only candidate for the position, quickly becomes Eurynome's lover. This is how sex was invented. This is how the universe was conceived.

It is sometime later (or whatever passed for time before time was born) and Eurynome, while in the form of a beautiful dove, has laid an enormous egg. This is the universal egg. Everything around us will hatch from this egg. Ophion the Serpent coils himself around it for unimaginable aeons to keep it warm and safe.

Eventually, the egg explodes with a Big Bang and the universe begins to expand and evolve from within. Eurynome and Ophion watch in amazement as their child develops stars and planets and water and life. Shortly after the advent of mankind, Eurynome says 'Look, Ophion! Look at our beautiful child, the universe! Look at its infinite possibilities and miracles! Its radiant galaxies and oceans of consciousness! Look at the light and the mountains and the majesty of time! What an amazing thing we've made together.

I can't wait to spend the rest of my life watching it grow and change with you.'

Ophion, drunk on his own ego, snorts derisively and says: 'What the fuck are you talking about? I made this all on my own, you fucking bitch! Fuck off and leave me alone!'

Eurynome doesn't appreciate this. She kicks out his teeth and hurls him into the universe to fend for himself.

*

It is 2001 AD. I am five years old and listening to my grandma telling the story of Isaac and Abraham. Henry, her orange tomcat, is purring contentedly on her lap. Grandad has been banished from the living room for calling Henry a protestant. He likes to tease Grandma, but also fears her greatly, because she makes all of his food and has memorised his long list of severe allergies. Once, when they were arguing, Grandma wished that a bee would come along and sting Grandad on his arse. Immediately, a bee came out of nowhere and stung him on the arm.

Presumably, the bee had either misheard my grandma's instructions, or had a very poor grasp of human anatomy. Grandma is nearing the end of the story. God has just explained to Abraham that he actually doesn't want him to murder his only son after all. 'I know how it ends!' I yell with cat-disturbing excitement. 'It's a test! God's trying to teach Abraham that doing bad things just because someone told you to is wrong!'

Grandma and Henry both look at me with concern.

'No, Gabe,' explains Grandma. 'That's not how it ends at all.'

*

It is around 9000 BC. Ophion the Serpent, in a variety of different disguises, has convinced the inhabitants of planet Earth that he invented the universe on his own. He told some of them that he created everything in seven days and expelled their ancestors from paradise for eating a magic apple. It amuses Ophion to put his true self on display in the story of Eden. The primitives have no idea that God and the Serpent are one and the same! He tells many other stories, in many different languages, all over the world. The earthlings will come to know him by many different names, including Zeus, Ra, Odin, Brahma, Jupiter, Shangdi and Yahweh. The people of Earth, hypnotised and overwhelmed, give him love and affection, devotion and fear, and, in return, he takes credit for everything good in their lives. His lies inspire civilisations, atrocities, generosity and extreme pettiness.

Humanity is shaped, for the better and for the worse, by the serpent from beyond time hissing threats and promises into its ears. Outside the universe, Eurynome watches everything unfold with endless fascination. She no longer remembers what boredom felt like.

*

It is 2023 AD, and I've been stopped in Edinburgh by two pleasant young men who wish to talk to me about Jesus. One of them tells me he used to be trapped in a life of debauchery before Jesus saved him from himself. He also tells me that a demon used to pin him to his bed every night and whisper deranged threats into his ears. Now that he's accepted God into his heart, the demon never visits him anymore. The demon is too afraid of God to bother one of his servants.

I ask: 'Why didn't God stop the demon before you became a Christian? Are you sure they're not in cahoots? This sounds like it might be some kind of protection racket.'

He says that God has a plan for all of us, and we would all do well to let him into our hearts.

I say: 'The plan might not be good though! What if he's farming us all in some kind of soul factory? Maybe our entire universe is a battery farm, and our souls are the main ingredient in some kind of delicious chicken nugget thing that gods love to eat when they're drunk! He wouldn't tell us if that's what he was up to!'

The men tell me to stop being silly.

*

It is 67,000,000,000 AD. Humanity has been extinct for substantially longer than it ever existed. The Earth, the Milky Way and several of its surrounding galaxies are now ruled over by a highly sophisticated race of octopus-descended geniuses. Ophion the Serpent, detained by a dazzling metaconceptual containment field, is on trial for crimes against reality. The language of the octopuses is non-verbal and comprised entirely of changes in skin colour and tentacle placement, but Ophion understands it perfectly.

'Mr Ophion,' the octopus for the prosecution conveys, by oscillating between several different shades of purple, green and blue. 'You claim to have drowned every terrestrial lifeform with your godlike powers, save for one family of bipedal monkeyforms and two breeding pairs from every non-aquatic species. Do you really think that was a sensible way to behave?'

Ophion is exhausted. He doesn't care for the octopuses very much. They are immune to hypnosis, so his attempts to set himself up as their God have been embarrassingly unsuccessful. Eventually, he was arrested for being a public nuisance. The charge of crimes against reality was added after he started trying to frighten the octopuses with the details of his terrible invented history.

'They were all sinners!' screams Ophion, by turning a violent shade of red and aggressively waggling all of his artificial tentacles. 'I did what needed to be done!'

'But even if all the monkeyforms were irredeemably corrupt,' retorts the octopus for the prosecution, in tranquil shades of blue, 'and that's impossible – for their infants couldn't have had much evil in their hearts – then why did you have to drown all the other lifeforms? Couldn't you have quietly turned the monkeyforms into vapour or taught them how to be kind to each other? Why did the other lifeforms have to suffer? And, furthermore, by ensuring that all the survivors of your ridiculous holocaust were family units, or were intended to become so, did you not create a situation where universal incest was almost inevitable? Why did you force an entire planet's worth of land animals to perform incestuous acts, Mr Ophion? Are you some kind of pervert?'

'Orange Lavender Turquoise!' exclaims the judge with every inch of his skin. Orange Lavender Turquoise roughly translates into English as 'Fucking hell! This guy seems terrible! I really hope we get to put him in prison forever!'

'This might not have been a great plan,' says Ophion out loud. 'I have badly fucked this.' These are the first words of spoken language to be uttered on the planet's surface since the death of mankind. Beyond the bounds of time and space, Eurynome laughs until she can barely breathe.

Scott Ferguson

KOORA

My small brown legs swung under the kitchen table. My football socks were rolled down, and the polyester shorts had me sliding across the wooden chair, infrequently causing crackles of static. I glanced towards my older sister, who had a spoon in one hand, and the other keeping a new novel prised open. The spoon hung in mid-air, porridge starting to crust into the steel as she lost herself in whichever world she had chosen that morning. I envied her contentment.

I picked up the banana toast for what felt like the hundredth time, and forced myself to take a bite; it felt like clay in my mouth. A strawberry yoghurt sat next to the plate, with the foil still on, and the spoon balanced across the top of it. Next to that was a small plum, and a glass of orange juice. I'd maybe manage a couple of bites out of the plum, but the yoghurt would be going back into the fridge, and added to my baba's piecebox later that evening. The spoon, although untouched, would be added to the soapy water in the sink.

'Eat up Ibrahim,' my mama said, as she folded tea-towels into a drawer. 'You'll need the energy for your match.'

My sister looked up, catching my eye, and smiling, before returning to her book.

I glanced up at the clock to see it was nine a.m.; just one-and-a-half hours until kick-off. I looked out of the kitchen window, and thought I saw rain. There wasn't anything solid to see any rain bouncing off, just air, but I hoped it was raining. I hoped it was raining, and I hoped it was due to get heavier. I hoped for the heaviest rainfall of the year. A month's worth in one hour; that would surely see the game cancelled? This was the west coast of Scotland, a dump of rainfall that could cancel an under-tens boys' football game was always a possibility.

Yes, I couldn't be playing out in *that*. I needed to be back in bed, under the safety of the covers, reading one of my magazines.

The phone rang, and my hope jumped. Maybe this was it. Maybe this was the call declaring the oncoming monsoon. Flooded pitches, unplayable not only today, but for weeks afterwards, and as winter crawled nearer, possibly months.

Winter. Meaning fireworks in the estate. Like crude piles of poison, popping one by one. Volatile, and senseless, their screams silenced the house I lived in. Last year, my sister had slept under her bed for two weeks.

My mama answered the phone.

'Yes . . . speaking . . .'

Someone unfamiliar, amazing! It could very well be the coach with the news. I watched on as her face neutralised, and she absorbed some quantity of information.

She hung up. A cold caller.

I sipped some orange juice and struggled to swallow my disappointment.

The calf of my left leg found the shin of my right leg, and I pressed it into the bruise. The pain was satisfying, and I held my legs together for a few seconds.

Last week, I'd been subbed on with fifteen minutes to play. There had been silence as I'd stepped onto the field, with the exception of my baba, who'd clapped a short burst of encouragement. The other parents had stood with their arms folded, not sure how to feel, not sure how to act. Some would have been indifferent, some would have been curious, some may have thought it was nice to be giving the boy a run out. He'll probably not be back, though.

My first touch had been heavy, but the tackle on me had been heavier. It had been clean, there had been intent to win the ball, but there had been intent to win some of me, too.

I drove the tip of my tongue into the back of my teeth as I pressed down on the bruise one more time, just for luck.

Baba burst into the kitchen. He kissed my head, my sister's head, and my mama's cheek. He lay a plastic bag on the kitchen table. Within it, some satsuma peelings, and a greasy Tupperware with a licked clean fork rattling around inside. Mama threw him a plum from the fruit bowl; I really should give mine a go.

It had been another gruelling night for him. Mostly drunks. A group of obnoxious boys he'd picked up from Newton Mearns to take into town. They'd first asked to put one of their smaller friends in the boot, to save on another fare, and had tried to sneak beer into his car. They hadn't asked him how his night was going, but had asked for his aux cable. When not shouting over one another, or vaping in his backseat, their attention was buried in their phones; a phosphorescent sickness casting their faces. They hadn't tipped.

As was customary, on a Friday night especially, he would drive with at least one soul who would ask how his night had been. Who would listen to his story, ask questions of the place he came from, of the job he used to do, of the job he should be doing. They always tipped.

Baba ushered me to collect my things; we had to leave soon.

As I grasped the edges of the toilet bowl, the orange juice came first, and then the banana toast. Clumps of it, the repeat flavour not as unpleasant as I'd expected, but I'd rather not be tasting it again.

I stood in front of the mirror and exhaled. I gathered water in my cupped hands and splashed it against my face. Wiping away the sickness from my mouth, and any remnant crumbs of sleep from my eyes.

It had been the same the previous week, before my first game. I couldn't tell Baba, as he wouldn't understand. Koora, or fitba, as the Scots called it, was my passion. I would spend my time poring over sports magazines and newspapers, I would fight with my sister over the radio channel in the car, and sometimes, as a treat, I was allowed to stay up on a school night to watch highlights. I loved playing, too, but with Baba and my sister in the park.

Baba wouldn't understand, and I couldn't let him down. He had found me this team through a colleague at his work. He was coming straight off nightshift to watch me play, because he thought that's what I wanted. He should be in bed, resting before his next shift.

In the car, I sat with my cheek resting against a balled fist. I stared out of the window, silently cursing the light rainfall.

Maybe, we'd get into a car crash? Not a big one, no injuries, but enough to make me unavailable for the game. Just a shock, and a quick call to the coach to say I wouldn't make it. No, actually, Baba needed his car for work, that wouldn't do.

Maybe, the changing rooms would be burnt down? Maybe, some bored teenagers had started a fire late last night? No, there was a steel fence around the perimeter of it. I knew the changing rooms would be still standing, and would soon be full of the echoes of studs clip-clopping off the concrete.

'Have you tightened your studs?' Baba asked, acknowledging my thoughts, and the wretched patter of useless moisture outside.

I turned to look at him and nodded my head.

My bag sat in between my feet. Inside it, a pair of meticulously cleaned football boots, my second most prized possession after my Arsenal top. The boots could one day secure the top spot, but I had only worn them once before.

Last week, when I had taken them out of my bag in the changing room, I had felt the quiet sniggering and judgement from the other boys. I'd kept my face down and tied my laces, hoping my reddening cheeks could be explained by the blood rushing to my bowed head. When I'd eventually sat up, the boys had moved on to something else, and it had granted me the opportunity to look around at the other boots in the room. A variety of colours, and all branded, but a lot of money to pay for them to be caked with mud from weeks before.

As the football pitches rolled into view, I recognised some parents of my teammates standing in the goals, clipping in the nets. The game was going ahead.

I nervously sipped from the bottle Mama had made up for me, the flavour of the sweet orange diluting juice tainted by the fresh plastic.

Baba pulled in behind the coach's car. The boot was open, and both he and his son were pulling out a black net of balls, and a pile of multi-coloured cones. Our closing doors caused them to look up.

The coach beamed at me.

'Awrite Ibra son! We getting another hat-trick oot ye today?'

He shook hands with Baba, and I caught the eye of the coach's son. He also beamed at me, and pushed a strip of material into my chest.

'Man of the match from last week gets to be captain,' he smiled, letting go of the armband.

My fingers clumsily grasped to catch it.

He put his arm around my shoulder, and we walked together towards the changing rooms.

I could feel Baba's joy barely contained as he politely nodded at the coach's conversation. I could feel the parents who had doubted me shrink slightly as they saw me again. I could feel how I had felt walking back into the changing rooms after the match last week.

In this country, I realised, koora can make or break you as a boy.

How lucky they are.

Nicola Fitzhenry

THE UGLY SISTER'S STORY

AN ACCOUNT OF THE INFAMOUS BALL AS TOLD BY EUPHEMIA McGLUMPHER

I'm just out of a milky bath and I'm having a wee footer about with powder puffs and lotions. The air's all lemon and roses and I'm enjoying the quiet. This is the stuff I like; it's the actual ball I can't be doing with. My dress is laid out as if a fussy version of me has staggered and swooned backwards over the chair. Lace abounds, and ribbons drip to the floor. Mama will be along soon to check if I'm ready, which I nearly am. I just need to get my key and stash it in the pocket.

I go to my bureau and have a wee keek inside: all is good, two piles of thick creamy parchment, one tied with a blue ribbon, one with green. I lock them tight inside, and take the key – small, polished brass, a tiny pearl on the handle – and coorie it right down inside the pocket of the swoonit dress. Then I make sure the pocket's tucked into the skirt, deep inside the layers of petticoat and nonsense.

That job done, I open the door a crack and peek out to the landing. Silence reigns. The stramash is over. Above the door of Step-Papa's room, there's a fresh slice out of the plaster: in the shape of a shoe if I'm not mistaken. The smell of burnt cakes is in the air.

I pop back in to my boudoir to choose some reading material. I'll say this much for this house, there's no shortage of books. Step-Papa's got an impressive library even if the only cut books in there are those I've read and one or two that Hortensia mistakenly thought were romances. I peruse my own shelves: philosophy, obviously; some history for my research; rows of books by men. But it's the women I'm drawn to: Sappho; Julian; Aphra. And I like to imagine other women – all those whose lives and thoughts never came down to us.

I choose my book and take it into the cludgie. I say cludgie, Step-Papa says closet. We've to speak English now, he says. No more keech, no more boking, no clamjamfries, nothing lowps any more, nothing skinkles in the glisk. I can't speak it but I can think it. I light a candle and put on my spectacles.

Eventually I come out and – hoots! – who's standing there but Clara-Bella. She can sneak around this house without so much as a stair-groan or a door-creak. She's right in the middle of the room, giving off the usual grimy smell of ash and soot and an attitude of gallus skivvy. She's got twigs in her hair – a sign she's been stoking the stove again – so that explains the burnt cakes. This girl's obsession with fire has gone too far. We're all connoisseurs now: with our eyes closed we could tell you the difference between singed hair and burnt paper, scorched silk and seared cotton.

'A'right?' she smirks, as if Step-Papa hasn't spent a fortune on elocution lessons.

'I think you should be somewhere else,' I say.

On her way out she trips and gets in a fankle with my dress. On purpose. There's some mock shock, some flailing about with all the lace and ribbons; the silk's covered in cinders. It's not as bad as yon time she burned Step-Papa's letters to Mama, then took the grey dusty scraps and rolled Mama's new hair ribbons in them. But there are smears and ashes on the skirt. Of course, that's when Mama comes in, resplendent in her new head-dress. There's a wee totie second where they look right into each other's eyes. Then it's like Mama's found a fox in the hencoop. There's screeching and cursing and feathers flying.

Clara-Bella galumphs down the stairs.

'Papa! Papa!'

*

I'm not bothered about the dress. We brush it down and it looks fine but Mama is upset, Step-Papa is cross. Inside the carriage, Hortensia stares out of the window. She's been greeting all afternoon and her face is still blotchy. Poor H is wearing an old dress of mine. It's a peely-wally peachy colour that does nothing for her. She sits in misery, the dress bumfled up around her like a cake that's gone wrong. Her new dress – a deep rose pink, exactly her colour – is on the midden. All it was fit for apparently after Clara-Bella had finished with her ironing stint. No one had asked her to iron it: we wouldn't dare. That's when the stramash had happened: scorching, shouting, sizzling, screaming, objects flying through the air.

I look out at the gloaming and I think about my books. The smell of leather, the feathery pages, the knowledge and ideas they hold, the words. And next to them, my bureau with its two stacks of paper. One, with a ribbon of duck-egg blue, is the novel I'm writing about two widowed people whose love for each other is blighted by a spoiled child. Next to that, tied with ribbon in a shade of green that's like spring buds, is my finished work. It's my labour of love, my hope for the future. It's about how women are forced to primp and preen, how we're destined to be only wives and helpmeets, and how we go along with the unspoken rules, turning in on ourselves, sister against sister. I might call it *An Indication of the Rites of Women*.

'She *could* have come to the ball,' Step-Papa suggests.

'Enough is enough,' Mama says wearily, 'You have to put your foot down.'

'She really wanted to go to this ball,' says Hortensia, still staring out of the window. 'She's up to something.'

*

The ball's the usual flumgummery. Frills, shrills, fiddlers sawing, the silent parade of marriage-fodder. Much speculation about Prince No-Charm. I'm going to make my next book about men like him: how wealth and power can turn a wee nyaff into an object of desire.

Then a breeze flutters through the room as if extra doors have been thrown open. Candle flames bend, musicians hesitate. The prince is announced. He and his fantoush brigade daunder across the ballroom and pose in front of the big mirror.

The stooshie settles, twittering resumes, but before we know it there's another erumption. Candle flames bend, musicians hesitate. The Lady Clara-Bella is announced and in she sweeps, a vision in deep rose pink, glorious in Hortensia's gown.

Instant tears on Hortensia's shocked face.

Mama slumps.

Step-Papa reddens.

I'll say this for Clara-B, she plays the game to the full. Staged entrance but so douce. All eyes on her but so shy. It's fascinating. And don't get me wrong, I love a wee skoosh of perfume, a new hairstyle every now and then. But I do that for myself. Clara-Bella is all about being noticed, for good or for bad, whether it's the footman or an earl. There's a whole chapter about her in my book. I'll need to update it now.

This time the musicians have not resumed. Everyone's looking at the prince. A gallivaster like him does not like being upstaged. But he's rapt, big gawky eyes on her, wee prissy mouth agape, glittery-ringed hand on his chest. He stoats across the room on his pudgy legs, jolts a curved arm up in the air like a ham hanging from a rafter. The musicians strike up a waltz.

After the waltz, there's a Schottische. Then a Dashing White Sergeant. A Military Two-step. Prince No-Charm isn't going to ask any of the other fodder to dance. *How rude. Tut. Tsk.* It's all very predictable but I'm trying not to sneer. Mama is upset enough. She's got a fake smile stuck to her face that's fooling nobody. I reach into my pocket for the key to my bureau, my talisman, my distraction, my comfort. My fingers slide around the silk but they don't touch metal. I dig deeper. I was so careful to make sure it was safe.

I use both hands to try to draw the pocket out from my skirts. I'm doubled over to the side, frantically fishing about in my skirts when Clara-Bella simpers past me in the arms of the prince. She's scrubbed up well, no cinders to be seen, floating in a cloud of lemon and rose. The prince gives her a wee birl right in front of me.

Then I see.

Round her neck are two ribbons, one the blue of duck eggs, one the green of spring buds and tied between them is my key, small, polished brass, a tiny pearl on the handle. Round she goes again and the familiar stink of ashes and soot seeps out through the scents she's stolen from me. Her fingers are curled up on the shoulder of the prince and as she twirls away she releases them and down float some burnt scraps of paper. Paper with my writing on it. My book.

It's a few minutes to midnight and the fiddlers stop. Step-Papa's been waiting for the break – Mama's tried to hold him back but he's bealing – and he's straight across the dance floor. I'm right behind him. Clara-Bella sees us and bolts.

Out to the hall she runs.

Tugs open the huge door.

Down the stairs at a clip.

Half-way down she bends.

Takes her shoes off.

Runs on.

Swift and light, she jumps into our carriage. Shouts a command at the footman. Then she leans out of the window and throws a shoe at her father. It hits him sharp on the head and he sits down suddenly on the steps. 'The wee bizzum,' I hear him say. I run past him, I'm almost at the carriage but she shouts again, the horses take off. She leans out of the window and aims a shoe at me then looks like she can't be bothered and flops out of sight. Laughter and the smell of papery ashes trail through the night.

Tony Frame

SKIVIN IN THE FOG

The lunch bell has just finished ringin and it's time to go to ma next class, but am no goin cos it's Science and then French and ah hate those subjects. Am at the back of the school, next to the playin fields, hidin behind the PE buildin wi Josey, Doods and wee Macalduff. We're aw smokin fags like it's goin oota fashion. It's so cold that our breath puffs oot in front of us when we speak and the fog is so thick that you cannae see any further than twenty yards away, which is good, cos it means we'll no get spotted here by any ay the teachers.

Macalduff's startin to get on ma nerves cos he keeps goin on aboot how cold it is, but ah dinnae ken whit he expects the weather to be like in the middle ay January, it's no like we live in the Bahamas, this is Scotland mate, the weather is crap aw the time, especially in the winter. Ah tell him he should be wearin a big jaykit, no the crappy Hibs tracksuit top that he's got on, that he's been wearin since second year. He looks pure stupit in it too, cos the green colour of it doesnae go wi his red hair, and his red hair is more an orange colour than red, which is why we sometimes call him pumpkin heid. Skinny wee pumpkin heid.

Dinnae get me wrong, *it is cold* and am freezin ma baws off as well cos am only wearin ma Scotland shellsuit top instead ay ma coat (we aw have to wear black troosers and a white shirt and a crappy school tie as that's the rules ay the school uniform, but we can wear any jaykit we like), but you dinnae hear me moanin like a wee lassie; ah just accept it as the price you have to pay for fashion these days. So manup or shurrup.

Ah've only had ma shellsuit for aboot a week. Ah feel real good in it. It's comfy and looks the business, and some of the girls have given me compliments aboot it as well, even Yvonne Toner who ah kinda fancy. The good thing wi the shellsuit top is that ah can zip it way up to ma neck so it hides my shirt and tie, so ah look pretty good even though am still in most of ma school uniform. Ah even gave ma Adidas Sambas a spit an polish as well, so ah look like the dog's bollocks, even if ah say so maself.

The only thing aboot the shellsuit that worries me is if ah wis to drop a fag on it then there's a high probability that ah'll go up in flames like a witch bein burned at the stake. Ah've been paranoid aboot that happenin ever since Josey told me aboot a story he read in the paper. The story wis aboot some guy who fell asleep on the sofa when he wis smokin a fag and then burned to death. The guy went up in flames really fast cos he wis wearin a shellsuit.

At first ah thought Josey wis just sayin that for a joke, you know, cos he wis jealous that ah wis the first one of us to get a Scotland shellsuit, though ah wouldnae say that to his face cos he's the hardest guy in oor year; he's aboot six feet tall and he's got fists of concrete and just aboot everyone is scared ay him. But ever since he told me that story aboot the guy burnin to death, cos of his shellsuit, ah've been seein other stories in the papers aboot folk wearin shellsuits who were catchin fire easily. Ah've been tryin to find oot if they were wearin a Scotland shellsuit as well, or if it wis one of those cheap crappy ones that you get from Watties (aka Whit Everyone Wants). Ah mean, ma shellsuit is an official Scotland one. Big Roy Aitken wis wearin one when he led the Scotland team oot onto the pitch against Norway at Hampden, and he looks like he's a big drinker and smoker, so to me that's like an official seal of approval that it's pretty safe.

Ah suppose ah could try testin its fire resistance by takin it off and holdin a match against it, but ah dinnae wanna damage it, cos it wisnae cheap, especially when ah had to use some of ma Christmas money for it.

Ah turn to Doods and ask him whit classes he's supposed to be at. It takes him a few seconds to snap oot of his daydream (he's a big stoner and is half-asleep most of the time). He tells me he's supposed to be at Art and then History. Ah tell him ah hate History but ah think he's mad to be oot here freezin his nuts off wi us to skive Art. At least in Art you're actually doin somethin that's creative. Ah mean, ah've got French and Science ah tell him, they're both crappy subjects. Ah hate French, ah've no need for it, ah've no need to learn the language and go over there and mingle wi the locals and eat snails and frog legs. Maybe if it wis a cool language like Italian or somethin then ah would stick in a bit, you know, to speak like ah wis in *The Godfather*, and make those big hand gestures the Italians use when they talk, that would be well cool.

As for Science, well . . . ah hate Mr Ezzi wi a passion, the speccy twat just makes us read from books and writes borin crap on the blackboard that we have to copy doon in oor jotters. Ah wouldnae mind if we were blowin up stuff and makin crystals and usin the Bunsen burners to burn clothes and toys, that would be well cool. But that's never gonna happen wi havin Ezzi as oor teacher.

If ye didnae ken me you'd probably think ah hate school full stop, and that am lazy, but that's no the case. Ah mean, ah love PE, especially fitbaw and basketbaw, and ah'll never miss those classes for anythin, even ma Media class is brilliant cos we get to use video cameras and ah ken how to frame some ay the shots cos of aw the movies ah've seen, but Mr Miller never picks me to be the director of the projects cos of ma reputation, so it's always folk like Clusky and Chris Johnstone that are picked to be in charge, which means ah barely get a chance to be a cameraman, or somethin decent like that.

You see, that's whit ma ma and ma da and everyone else cannae understand; it's no that the subjects are crap, it's the way they are taught that makes it borin. The teachers have got no interest in makin things fun and interestin, most of them are oota touch and should be in mental hospitals wi the way they talk to us and treat us. It's crap.

Ah mean, take last week for instance, now this, this sums it up for me: last week ah had an appointment wi Craven, oor careers advisor. When ah told him ah'd definitely be leavin school this year he then asked me whit ah would like to do when ah left. Ah didnae really have a good answer to be honest, so ah mentioned to him that ah liked ma Media class and said that it would be cool to go into television, or somethin like that. But he just said that ah wis bein unrealistic aboot that cos of ma grades, so then he handed me some application forms for some factory jobs, and that wis that.

Ah mean, ah ken ma grades are crap, am no expectin to leave school and get a job as a Vice President at Warner Brothers, ya muppet. But at the very least, gimme some bloody college courses that ah could apply to, you ken whit ah mean? Courses in Media an stuff like that, somethin to just point me in the right direction. That's aw Craven had to do there, that's whit ah realised afterwards. But nope, the baldy muppet just gave me some application forms for aw the crappy factory jobs oot there.

Anyways . . . it's no worth thinkin aboot the negatives. Ah've only got five months, give or take, and am oota this dump forever. Thank God. And at least it's Friday tomorrow. Ah've got a double period of PE in the morn and then there's English later in the day, which is cool. Not cos ah like English, that's borin as well. It's cool cos am part of a special class for English. We call it the dumbo group. Ah like it cos Yvonne's gonna be there. Am hopin when we're split up into groups that ah'll be able to sit wi her, which means we can talk aboot films and music and aw the other stuff that we like. The only thing ah hate aboot the class is that Danny Keenan is part of it, but he's hardly at school these days so am hopin he'll no be in tomorrow. The group is for folk like us cos we dinnae stick in and we disrupt the others in English, so the teachers formed this group especially for us, that's why we call it the dumbo group. There's only five of us in it: me, Danny, Jaffa, Singy and Yvonne.

She's the only lassie in the group. Singy and Danny are a bunch of twats and they're thick as mince, but Jaffa's awright, ah dinnae mind him at aw, and as for Yvonne, well, ah feel sorry for her cos she's no stupit at aw, she's just like me; she's no interested in Maths or French and cannae be bothered copyin crap off a blackboard either. Ah really like her. She's no like the top girls in oor year in terms of looks, and she's no popular, but ah think she's cute wi her frizzy dark hair, and she's got really nice blue eyes. Ah wish ah had the confidence to ask her oot, but am too shy for that.

When ah think aboot it, when ah leave school for good, in five months time, ah'll probably no see Yvonne again. She lives in Whitburn, ah live in Livi. It's a shame, cos ah think we have some good banter, and if we lived closer to each other ah think there'd be a chance ay hookin up wi her. Sayin that, once ah've left school for good ah'll no see most of the folk in ma year ever again. Like, forever. Ah might see one or two people who live in Livi from ma year oot and aboot (probably doon the centre), but most of the folk in ma year live ootside Livi, so the chances of me bumpin into any ay them are slim. Not that ah care, cos am no really friends wi any ay them ootside ay school. But it's just mad to think that we'll probably never see each other again for the rest of oor lives is whit ah mean. We'll aw be movin on wi oor lives soon, goin oor separate ways. We'll be startin jobs, goin to uni or college, gettin married, havin babies, buyin hooses, havin careers and aw that crap. Ah wonder if in aboot thirty years' time we'll aw meet up for a high school reunion? That'd be mental. You gotta wonder if aw of us will even be aroond then? Ah mean, statistically speakin, some of us may die from cancer or die in an accident like a car crash or a fire, or have a drugs overdose, stuff like that. And it wouldnae surprise me if one or two folk from ma year killed themselves. A couple of them are no right in the heid already, so who knows how they'll cope in the real world as adults, or how any ay us will cope for that matter. It's mental when ye think aboot it aw like that.

Obviously some folk will stay on at school to go into fifth year, and they'll probably stay on to sixth year as well and go to uni after. But that's no gonna happen wi any of us guys at the back ay the school here. We're mostly destined for the dole.

Anyways, enough ay that. Just have to wait another minute or two and the coast should be clear; aw the teachers will be in the classrooms and we'll be able to sneak oot the back gates withoot bein seen. The fog'll give us more cover than normal. Just have to make sure we get back here for oor buses. You see, the secret to skivin is you dinnae skive the whole day otherwise the teachers notice and you'll eventually get the truant officer turnin up at yer door. Nah, you just skive a few classes here and there and you'll no be detected as much.

We're gonna nip doon to Sheila's Cafe. It's nice and warm in there. Am gonna get a chip butty and a Coke. Ah've got some spare change for *Double Dragon* on the arcade machine as well. Ah love that game. Ah can only get to level two, but am gettin better each time ah play it. If ah save up ma paper round money in the summertime then ah might be able to put it towards a Nintendo for Christmas and get *Double Dragon* wi it. John Menzies are sellin it as a bundle. Ah mean that would be amazin to play it at home. The thing is though, ah really shouldnae count aw ma chicks before they hatch. Ah just know that ma da is gonna want me to get a job once ah leave school in the summer so ah can pay some digs. It's like he says to me the other night: he says that once ah leave school ah have to *grow up*. Ah ken whit he means, but a part ay me wants to laze aboot after ah leave school. Ah feel like sayin to him that after eleven years ay goin to school (am includin primary school), ah think am entitled to rest a bit. Ma ma would agree!

Especially since it'll be the summer holidays. Ah mean, ah wanna play *Werewolves of London* and *Football Manager 2* on ma computer, and go to the pitch and putt wi ma mates, play tennis and footie an stuff like that. And then there's the World Cup to look forward to as well. Ah cannae wait for Italia '90. Scotland's first game is gonna be a piece ah cake cos we're only playin Costa Rica, then aw we have to do is beat Sweden and we're through to the second round for the first time in history. It's gonna be great. So that's ma plan for the summer. But ah'll just have to see, cos ah've got a crappy feelin that ma da is gonna put a spanner in the works somewhere.

'Let's get ready!' Josey says. We aw suck hard on the rest of oor fags like mad and then stub them oot on the ground wi oor feet. Josey peeks aroond the corner of the PE buildin to see if there's any teachers kickin aboot. Aw we have to do is head doon past the rusted chain-link fence that surrounds the bleak concrete monstrosity that are the tennis courts, and make oor way to the corner of the school building where we'll make oor crouchin run past the windaes of the Art and History classrooms, like a stealth scene from *The A-Team*. Then we'll be home free!

For some reason ah start imaginin *The A-Team* theme tune playin in ma heid, like we're on one ay their deadliest missions so far, and ah cannae but help laugh oot loud at this thought.

Josey turns and asks me whit am laughin at, but ah tell him it doesnae matter, cos he'll no see the funny side to it. He shakes his heid and peeks aroond the corner one last time as the wee cold clouds of breath continue to puff out in front of us. Macalduff starts moanin again that it's freezin but Josey shooshes him to keep schtum.

Josey's aw serious these days. The thing is, he never used to be like this. He used to be a right laugh at times. But he's no been the same for a while. Ah think he's got stuff goin on at home. Ah get the impression that his da's on his case big time aboot him gettin a job when he leaves school as well. Threatenin to kick him oot and stuff if he doesnae. It's crap. It's like aw the teachers and parents seem to ken whit's best for us but they've done nothin to help us, and they're hardly leadin a good example wi workin in crappy jobs themselves or bein on the dole, not to mention that most of them are miserable. Grow up aye? Yeah, it sounds like a right laugh. Let's get ourselves a crappy job and earn peanuts and marry some sour-faced bint and go through life pretendin everythin's just grand, all the while we'll be laughin on the ootside and cryin on the inside. Nah, hard pass on that thanks!

Anyway . . . time to focus on the present: ma chip butty and Coke and a shot ay *Double Dragon* that's waitin for me at Sheila's.

Josey turns his heid to us and says, 'Let's go!'

Tony Garner

THREE MEN IN ASSYNT

Parishes dwindle. But my parish is
This stone, that tuft, this stone
And the cramped quarters of my flesh and bone

—Norman MacCaig, 'Climbing Suilven'

Perhaps no part of the quarters of the flesh are more cramped than the gall bladder, that pear-shaped lump squashed in between our livers and the sausage-like coils of the small intestine. I was vaguely aware of its existence, but I didn't even know its location, never mind its role. I didn't know that it's a pouch for producing and storing bile, a handy pipe linking it to the small intestine, where it gets to work breaking down fats, and – not to mince words – making our shit brown.

Koji, my Japanese father-in-law, said he hadn't spotted any pastel shades in the toilet bowl. Like many Japanese, he had annual medical checks, paid for by the company he'd been employed by all his working life. A sprightly sixty-five, he'd had his first post-retirement summer all planned out. He was going to fly to Scotland and walk the West Highland Way, with me joining him for part of it. Instead, a month after stopping work, he got the diagnosis. A matter of weeks later – how long would it have taken on the NHS? – he went in for surgery. His gall bladder, whose cells had begun to uncontrollably sub-divide, was excised. In fact the small intestine can produce enough bile to get by on its own, as long as you're careful with the demands you place on it.

The week after Koji got out of hospital, my wife and daughter flew to Japan for the rest of the summer. I stayed in Glasgow, a teaching contract to fulfil, and the edits on a novel to finish. I had started writing it seven years earlier, a historical crime story set in Yokohama, where we then lived. For the last time, I had to take a deep dive back into that world, to make the book as good it could be. Lots of cuts, lots of insertions; a text under the knife. A summer of being mostly alone, when I wasn't in front of students. The sacrifices you have to make if you want to get a novel over the line.

Over winter Koji recovered his strength. Follow-up scans showed no sign of the cancer returning, and he started to make fresh plans for a visit to Scotland. This time, he had set his heart on a different location. Not the well-trodden West Highland Way, but remote Assynt, where Norman MacCaig spent his summers and about which he wrote many of his finest poems. The flights were booked for April, during the Easter holidays so that I could join him. My dad, who would turn seventy in March, decided to come along as well.

Before then, in February, my debut novel had its launch: the surreal sight of people (mostly people I know, admittedly) queuing up to buy books with my name on the cover; exhilaration of achieving something I'd dreamed of for so long. But also a sense of relief, of a weight being lifted. How many thousands of hours had I spent on that text? I was just glad for it to be finished, out there in the world for better or worse. As a writer, I was ready for something else, something closer to home.

*

I wasn't born in the Highlands, but I moved there when I was one and that's where I grew up. Like most who gravitate north, my parents were both at home in the outdoors.

When I was about seven, and my sister only five, we walked up Ben Nevis. My mum is a notoriously fast walker, and even at seventy-four and with osteoporosis, she can still notch up an impressive day's mileage. But my dad's active lifestyle used to be on a different plane.

The years he describes as his 'peak' (Mum will roll her eyes) were built around annual attempts to better his best performance at the Ben Nevis Race and the Highland Cross. When I think of him in these years, I see his gold and maroon running club vest hanging on the washing line, so sweaty that it was banned from the machine and relied on a blow in the wind and a dousing with rain. Or after his shower, hunched over a map spread out on the kitchen table, twisting a compass back and forth to plot the precise distance he'd just spent his Sunday morning running along country roads, forest tracks or mountainsides. As my sister and I got older, we started gently taking the piss out of his obsession with the average speed he held on these runs: six-minute mile pace was an oft-heard mantra, a barometer against which all runs could be judged. I remember this, and I remember the bluish ridges of varicose veins that contoured the back of one of his calves, like a 3D relief map of some mountainous region.

Maps would be the easiest topic of conversation for my dad and Koji – I could predict that even before the trip. In an email before he left, Koji told me he already had OS maps and BMC maps of Assynt, as well as a map app on his phone. True to form, my dad was bringing the OS map from about 1983 (the hills take longer than this to change, he said). I could already picture them hunched over these, plotting our possible routes, Koji's enthusiastic English just about enough, until he found himself short of a specific term and stopped to punch the Japanese into his pocket translator. They would hit it off, no doubt, but my mum was worried about Koji bringing out my dad's competitive edge: a seventy-year-old with a new hip against a sixty-five-year-old out the other side of cancer surgery. I was given covert instructions to make sure Dad didn't push things too far. 'You know what he's like,' she warned.

Writers also can't avoid competitive insecurities. How was I to describe a landscape that a great poet had already honed his finest words on? Halfway through our trip, I thought I had at least hit upon my own metaphor for Suilven. In the barren expanses of Assynt, we kept seeing MacCaig's favourite mountain from new angles. In the long flanks of its ridge, rising and widening to the craggy head of its summit, I saw the shape of that legendary enigma, the Sphynx. I could almost imagine the chipped nose, a pair of riddling eyes peering out of the rock. MacCaig was suspicious of the way his brain turned nature into metaphors: frogs into opera singers; toads into purses. But writers aren't cartographers. What means do we have of taming this ancient landscape, other than calling things what they aren't?

Like the Sphynx, Suilven sits alone. There are several higher mountains in Assynt, and if Cùl Mòr or Quinag were next to Suilven, they would diminish it. But geology, the distribution of harder rock in this land scoured by glaciers, dictates that Suilven rises out of nothing. Or not nothing, but just rolling, heather-furred wilderness, studded with erratic boulders, every scooped hollow filled with another lochan. On the fourth day of our trip, this was the landscape across which we made our long-ish approach to Suilven.

My dad and I were both feeling a little diminished ourselves. Me by a stomach bug that had hit me the previous night, mercifully passed by morning but leaving me short on sleep and energy. Dad had a crack in the skin of his heel, formed from repeated friction with the boot. As the mountain drew closer, he began making pessimistic assertions that Koji and I should leave him at the foot of the steep climb up Suilven's flank. Koji, for his part, was showing no sign of weakness. His tendency to speed up on the second half of our previous walks suggested that more arduous days were well within his compass. But we all had a common foe. Our trip had coincided with gale force winds across the country; today, our last day in Assynt, a yellow weather warning was in place. We could read the strength of the gusts in the masses of wavelets flashing across the surfaces of the lochans like flocks of rising starlings. Sometimes, sheltered by the land, we would be protected, only to round a hummock or crest a rise and find ourselves exposed, battered, sent staggering almost off our feet. If we opened our mouths our words were snatched and hurled away before they could be heard.

The last lochan skirted, we munched cereal bars in the lee of a handy boulderfield, craning our necks up at Suilven's southern flank. The path zigzags up a gully, eventually reaching the summit ridge 350 metres higher up. At least the bulk of the mountain would protect us from the gale howling from the north. My dad asked for a start, saying he'd rather set his own pace, not feel pressured into going too fast too early. Koji and I had an apple apiece. When we turned our eyes back to the mountain he'd already been swallowed in the greys and dark browns of the wall of rock. It took a while to pick him out in his red jacket, a flea on the Sphynx's back, climbing steadily. We hoiked on our packs and followed. The path felt more like a staircase, every step a different height. Sometimes you had to lift your leg high, or squeeze between a narrow gap, always looking ahead, careful where you placed your step. 'Down and down / this treadmill mountain goes' says MacCaig in 'Climbing Suilven', and with each step it truly was as if we were pushing the mountain further beneath us. We turned and the parishes below had indeed dwindled, but we could see more of them; a quick photo and back to the mountain, concentrate again on each tuft, each stone. On a slope like this everybody finds their own rhythm. Dad was faster than forecast; we were barely catching him. His heel must have healed, or maybe it was always strategic, a lowering of expectations before his big break; he always was a hustler of the hills.

At last the ridgeline was coming closer, but the path here, where the gully's at its narrowest, was just bare earth spilling between crags, crumbly and sliding underfoot. Our hands reached out for the banisters of rock, pulling ourselves upwards, onwards. I turned a corner and there he was: my dad, smiling down at us, sitting with his back to the wall of rock, the skyline just a few metres higher. He'd decided to let Koji crest the ridge first, he said. Was this a magnanimous gesture, or his cunning deployment of an experimental guinea pig? We all knew what the wind was going to do the second we lost Suilven's protection. Laughter and photos, then Koji took the lead for the final metres, the two of us hunkered tight behind him.

Maybe it was the jeopardy of the plunges either side, but the wind when it hit felt even more savage than we'd imagined. It smashed into us, forcing us to crouch low, to cling desperately to Suilven's spine; a mad lover jealous of our presence on the mountain, wanting nothing more than to fling us back where we belonged. Not being suicidal, we had no intention of going for the summit, but we did want the view of everything to the south.

Belying the answer to the Sphynx's riddle, we shuffled forwards on all fours into the gale and looked out across miles of lochan-dotted moonscape, to the rounded shoulders of Cùl Mòr; the crenellations of Stac Pollaidh. To our right, the narrow ridge rose to the summit, widening beyond the dry-stane dyke that wraps like a collar around Suilven's neck. The project, Dad told us, of some mad landowner, intent on providing unemployed locals with purposeful labour. 'Who owns the land?', MacCaig asks in his great poem 'A Man in Assynt'. The answer, up here, was obvious. This land is far too ancient and awesome to be owned by anyone. The only forces that can reckon with it are the elemental ones of fire, ice and wind, forces that make human lifespans and ambitions pale into insignificance. To climb Suilven was to understand this, though maybe deep down in our guts where the gall bladder had, or didn't have, its place, we knew it all along.

Sergey Gerasimov

THE DESERTS OF OUR GRIEF

Translated from 'Тільки не плач' by Dmitry Blizniuk
Published by kind permission of the author

a small window, an earring, and a little pot.
she feels the weight of her daughter in her arms even
 months later,
although her daughter lies now somewhere in an
 unmarked grave
in Mariupol.
memories like cobras
sway in front of her face.
at night, she groans softly, like an elevator,
like a salamander; beneath her tongue
she hides her daughter's faces, clipped from photographs,
to keep the memory intact and safe from fire,
to be reborn in the next life together,
and perhaps then her daughter will give birth to her.
this is the gratitude of incarnation, clear madness.
a bone that shines above the entrance to a pharmacy.
no tears – just dryness, and the green butter
of the silty floor; the sea has withered, evaporated,
and the heat has stripped the rainbow to ragged shreds.
these baby shoes, worn twice,
with each year,
will gradually grow in size in her head until
they turn into blue patent-leather shoes of a young graduate,
the schoolgirl of death.
our children, killed by the Russians, imperceptibly they sing,
invisibly they grow
like hair, like nails, like moire bones of ghosts,

eyes in family photographs or tails
of bluebirds.
just don't cry.
one day, the deserts of our grief
will turn into gardens for babies, cats, and cicadas.

Mirri Glasson-Darling

INTO EVELINE

Angela and I sit next to an alpine lake shaped like a wishbone. We do not look at each other. This is a part of the game. She pretends she doesn't care about me, and I pretend not to be in love with her. Which I might not be. There will be no way to tell until she leaves, because that's how she works, and how I work too. I am the kind of girlfriend with an expiration date. Angela plans on leaving me at the end of this hike – I am certain. We met up earlier in my apartment while her husband was at work. When I joked the sex was so good it felt like 'the last time,' she said nothing. That's what the last married woman I slept with did. Both of the married women I've slept with broke up with me after about six months – Angela and I have been together six months now. The women I date always have husbands, I don't know why, but at one point it just started happening and now it seems that it's something that I do. To be fair, most women around here over thirty have husbands. Sometimes, I even have a boyfriend too, though nobody seems to like that. Angela and I are not the kind of people with healthy relationships.

The alpine lake smells of water and air, which you wouldn't think smell like anything until it rains. Below us, the shower is moving away, and behind us, another one is rolling in.

'It doesn't all have to be doom and gloom, you know,' Angela says. We have been talking about us without talking about us again. In this particular conversation, we are cast as the finally and tragically receding Taku glacier – one of the last ones in Alaska advancing for years, now finally crippled.

'You sound like my dad,' I say.

'You don't have to be disappointed,' she says.

'You don't have to disappoint me.'

'You beg everyone to disappoint you.'

She's not wrong, but also, there it is.

'Don't say that,' I say and try out the words to see if they taste right. 'What if it's true? Besides, I love you.'

'If that's true, then I feel bad for you,' says Angela. 'Don't you get tired of cosplaying we're eighteen? I can't do this anymore.'

We are in our late thirties, approaching forty. We missed earlier opportunities to have healthy relationships, so now we're fucked up and we fuck up other people too. We have both lived most of our lives in rural Alaska, so the biphobia and homophobia are internalised. But this does not make us interesting – it is the most boring thing in the world. The younger queer crowd in the nearby tourist town does not have time for us, and we feel they are right to leave us behind. We've joked about it, always joking, because that's the only way Angela has a serious conversation.

There are still five solid hours of mountains between her and I getting back to our separate cars, where she will leave me. She probably didn't mean to let it on so soon.

'Do you want to go swimming?' I ask, gesturing to the lake.

'Are you kidding?' says Angela. 'We'll get hypothermia.'

She's right of course, but I would have tried anyway.

Since Angela has said she can't do this anymore, I'm supposed to think back to when we met. To reflect back on all our time together and feel sad, but the reality is this is my third secret relationship with a woman married to a man and I'm too tired. At least, with Angela, I've had a hiking partner. Those are hard to find. Mainly, because I do not like them. I prefer to hike alone. But Angela is a skilled mountaineer, and her mother is nationally ranked in rock climbing back in Norway. If there's anything I'm uncertain about or don't know how to do, Angela can show me. The ridgeline we've picked our way across so far is a smattering of rocks, hogbacked, views spreading out across a grey sea of wind blasted peaks. Alone, I wouldn't have risked today with the changeable weather. Some hikes you need a partner on, unless you want to admit you're being reckless. In between blasts of wind and rain, the views up here are really beautiful. There are glaciers out beyond the peaks towards the Canadian border in sunken dunes of white with broad, electric blue bones. It's summer, so the sun won't set until around one in the morning when we will be back at our cars. For the moment though, we are still together, and Angela is ahead of me, scrambling over boulders, tall and lean-muscled. She has the kind of definition in her legs I would kill for. A soft, feathery line along her thighs and two perfect dimples on the small of her back. When I run my hand along the prow of her hips, I can trace the line of muscle clear down almost into her. She is stronger than I'll ever be, though of the two of us, I have more stamina. I am short and squat and never thin but after years of mountains, I've found that's what stamina looks like on my body. I was thin for a while because I was running without eating and, sure, more people wanted to sleep with me then, but I didn't have the energy to care. I'm doing better now.

At this point in the route, we have already crossed our peaks. They were hard, steep, loose mouldered cones of sharp rock and sky. The top in front of us now isn't a peak, and the peak to our left on the neighbouring ridge is unnamed. There are a lot of peaks without names in Alaska. Look out at the glacial field on a topography map and you will see their constellations. Peak that is 6041 feet (1841 metres), Peak with the number forty. Peak called exact latitude and longitude coordinates. The named ones hint at mountain religion: Michael's Sword and Devil's Paw, Split Thumb, the Thoroughfare. These are the ones that people want to climb. The rest of us languish in obscurity.

Angela and I scramble single file over the jumbled rocks, and there's a view at the top again, a whole new valley full of trees and rivers needling. We can see dark cloud coming in behind us. By the time I reach the top, Angela's already headed over the other side and I have to crab-crawl down to meet her, feet first. It's a relief to see that she will wait for me. When we go climbing together and I get trapped on the mid-level routes, sometimes Angela won't let me down. She did it once until I cried.

'You make a terrible troll,' she says when I get to where she's standing. This is another joke. When we first started hooking up, the word she used wasn't troll but *jötnar*, these god-like mountain giants from Norwegian myth her mother used to tell her about. They live in a secret realm wrapped around the earth, full of mountains. Wild, chaotic, and primal – the *jötnar* are often evil in stories, but not always. They are also technically trolls, but separate from the common trolls, the lives-under-a-bridge, smells-Christian-blood, turns-to-stone kind. That's the kind of troll Angela means when she teases me now. It's affectionate, but how attractive can you really feel when someone's comparing you to an ugly, smelly monster.

'Once we're down, I'm going to grind your bones to make my bread,' I say.

She smiles but doesn't respond. Jack and the Beanstalk is more of a giant story than a troll one.

Navigation is difficult on this part of the ridge. With the cloud moving in, visibility is not great, and the broken field of scree has a mishmash of odd-looking cairns. I can't tell if they're trying to lead the way or marking out the borders of where you are about to go over the edge. Neither of us have been up here before. When I look at my GPS tracking app, a blue circle swirls and swirls. If it were me leading us, I would check the map now and do some panicky math about how many footsteps we need to take but Angela knows which way to go through without even having to check her compass. When I shuffle after her, I scrape my feet across the stones. I like the sound of that in cloud – every noise feels like its coming from inside your head. We can only see so far ahead, and it will be at least an hour until we are low enough to make out valleys again. It is easy to see how Angela's ancestors decided mountains were troll country. Both Alaska and Norway have tundra cotton and the blazing, pink-coned flowers of fireweed. Our valleys are both littered with giant, solitary boulders plopped along by receding glaciers long ago. Angela and I call them troll rocks. The boulder squarely in our way right now is one of them, it has a knobby nose and knees, curled with its thighs pressed to its chest as if huddled around some ancient, long extinguished fire.

'Does Marc know you're here?' I ask.

She laughs. 'Why wouldn't I tell him?'

Marc is her husband. We've met, and he is oblivious, which is the only thing about him that bothers me. I think a less self-assured man would have noticed by now, but Marc is one of those people who assume that their personality and sexuality are the default for everything. It would never occur to him that I am sleeping with his wife, and if he knew, he would assume that it meant nothing. It is impossible for me to threaten him. Which, in a way, is fun. He doesn't know that I could take his wife from him, that she's cum so hard before she's cried with me, that she's told me things about her childhood she's never told him. How the first girl she ever kissed wore a yellow sweater, and there was a friend of an aunt who used to take her to movies in her teens until one night, she reached for Angela in the dark car. Sometimes I wonder why she doesn't tell him, but then again, married women like to have secrets. Something about possession in a forced, shared domain maybe, a secret world you carve out for your own. It has nothing to do with who I am though, as far as I can tell, so I try not to read too much into it. When Angela and I had been together a month and I told her I was still messaging tourist girls in other towns on Tinder, she wrapped her legs around me, pinned me to the sofa and said that she forbid it. *Forbid* – flirty, joking voice, but I knew what it meant. It's not even that Angela doesn't love Marc, he isn't mean or unhelpful around the house or something. Marc is fine. I don't think much about him either way. He has dark hair with a red beard, which I suppose is nice to look at. I consider him Angela's problem.

My problem, according to a girl I was seeing last summer, is that I have never lived anywhere with a population bigger than forty thousand. She was gay, single, and from Seattle. She said that if I moved to Seattle or maybe even Anchorage, I would have no problem finding a 'real' girlfriend. But I don't like cities. People who like cities don't seem to understand that requires a personality type that doesn't happen to be everyone. When people say there are mountains in a city, they mean every weekend they drive two to three hours one way in traffic to get to the mountains, to walk on a trail full of runners, dodging families and dogs. They walk on forest tracks covered in gravel before they get to where they actually want to be. They hear their neighbours fight and fuck and play guitar through walls and ceilings at night and all hours of the day. Besides, I did have an opportunity to 'really' date a woman once. The year I spent in the Arctic I saw a woman named Danielle, ten years older than me with long black hair. She asked if I would stay there for her, but I had to say no. It was the kind of town where you can't really be 'out' and not from there. Everyone seemed to either go to church or have a drinking problem. I couldn't spend my life three hundred miles from the nearest tree – but if you made me pick between that and a city I know where I would be.

The weather moves back in and for a while as Angela and I descend, the rain is heavy. The pass feels steeper than I remember seeing on the map. My lips keep curling into a snarl of concentration and the rocks are slippery. It is still light, but also, it is getting late. We are not going to be at the cars by dark.

'If I fell,' I ask when we stop to rest, miserable and dripping, leaning up against a troll rock for protection, 'would you come back to this spot and think of me?'

Angela shouts over the rain, 'I can't hear you.'

It is deafening, to be fair.

I am worried about the route. There should have been the beginnings of a stream next to us by now that later become a river, but there is no stream. We should have checked the map when we were back up on the ridge. But Angela knows more than me. Besides, it's gone to true shit up there, and this still feels like a safe way down. The gulley is not too steep and shows no signs of crumbling.

And we do have to get down, it will be dark soon. If we end up in the wrong valley though, we're going to be out all night. It is objectively a bad idea in this weather to backtrack onto the ridge. We continue to go down the safe but wrong way and do not speak. The rain stops, and the valley opens into levels, a flat, green plateau with four more of the troll boulders down below, clustered around a circular pool. This is definitely not where we should be on the map. We are exhausted now though. On the ridge far above I can hear wind and the storm, but here on the plateau everything is quiet. We will have to stop here for a few hours to wait out the coming dark.

'I think this is Eveline,' Angela says, which is not quite the same thing as an apology. We are supposed to be in Gold valley. Eveline valley is out of the way and on the wrong side of the ridge. There will be a way to safely walk out from Eveline, it's not blocked off by a glacier or river, but that's going to add at least another twenty miles. It's that or tracking back up the way we came down and clear over the ridge again from the side. Probably, it is safer to walk out.

'This spot seems protected,' I say. That is the end of the conversation. It is understood we will stay by the troll rocks for the night. Though that really only means about four hours. It's drier by the cluster of stones, so we set up there. Usually, big rocks like these would be sitting in a ditch of mush, but these jut out from a firmer bit of glacial soil, sheathed in bright green around the pool. One looks like its curled up on its side to sleep, covered in a blanket of lichen. Another, squatting, elbows out on knees, staring at its reflection in the water.

'Your troll brethren will watch over us,' Angela says. She arranges herself in her rain gear with her back to the ribs of the sleeping troll rock.

'Suppose you'll have to wait another day to break up with me,' I say. Joking, because I can joke too. Which is mean, especially since we have a long walk out together and very little food, but that's how I'm feeling.

Angela scrunches up her face like she's driving past a landfill. 'Why would you think I want to break up with you?'

I can't tell if she means it. If I were her, I might play dumb too until the end to keep the peace through a long walk out. 'You're unhappy,' I say. 'You can't do it anymore. You said.'

'Sure, but where am I going to find another girl who's willing to stick with me when I'm married? Let alone one who lives out here and likes the same sports?' She pats the spot next to her by the rock until I am forced to sit, then puts her arm around me.

I suppose I should be relieved, but Angela's touch is cold, and I feel cold beneath it.

'There are the younger gays in town,' I offer.

'They're all twenty-three and poly. Don't be ridiculous. You're never getting rid of me.'

She leans down to rest her head on my shoulder and the light in the mountains goes from soft grey to evening blue. I try not to think about Angela or the route ahead and concentrate on how rare this view is. Eveline is not a valley people go into. It is possible that we are the only people to be in this spot this year, and it could be another, two or even three, until someone else is here again. There is a magic to that, to the soft dripping of water off the nose of the sleeping troll rock and the shifting of unfamiliar blackened shadows in the mountains as night falls. The squatting troll to our left looks especially lifelike in the fading twilight. Its reflection in the pool is a face with furrowed brows. The troll might as well be real – about to wake from stony slumber with red eyes and gnashing teeth, ready to eat us alive. Maybe that's why no one goes into Eveline. Angela works for Search and Rescue though, so we both know that no one has gone missing in this valley. One look at the map we're both carrying will show why no one comes here – Eveline doesn't connect to anything. It's not close enough to a trail or town or named peaks or of use to connect to the other ridgelines it bisects. People want views and adventure in the mountains – why bother wondering into a pathless, sunken valley?

It is very dark now, the kind of darkness that has texture and fills the space between mountains like a flood. The clouds up on the route we came down are parting, and through them I can see a couple scattered stars though the wind is still shrieking every so often. They seem so far away – eyes recessed back into a shrunken face. Angela's breathing is soft and even, to the point where I wonder if she's fallen asleep. If she is asleep, could I move her without waking? Could I lift her head off my shoulder and lean her up against the rock? She has the same map that I do. We could both walk out of here separately, safe but alone. It's not like I'd be leaving her to her death. Instead of heading around to the coast I could follow Eveline in the blackness and visit the other silent, twisted valleys it connects to – the ones where people *really* don't go. I could pass nameless peaks and waterfalls until I met my end somewhere at the root of one of their glacial rivers. Become another thing of darkness. Or maybe, I could just sit here under the weight of Angela until the rising sun turns us both to stone. A troll rock made of two conjoined women.

But I don't know if Angela is sleeping, and if I ask, I'm afraid I will find out. So, instead, I take one shallow breath after another. I wait. It is that brief, timeless place on a summer night in Alaska when there is no light. The world is safe and unknown. The dark is full, spilling into every nook and cranny between us and, just for a moment, I am only my own. Angela and I breathe in together, but out of time. There is something with us in the darkness. I am waiting for a pair of glowing eyes to appear in the valley, so I can follow them off into the night.

Mairi Griffin
WEE DIRTY

Mr Wallace owned the ironmongers. To begin with he was an unseen entity who occasionally made my mother work late, putting out new stock or changing the window display. His shop was smack-bang in the middle of the high street, his name hung in thick black unavoidable letters above the entrance: *WALLACE'S*. Underneath, painted on the brickwork: *Keys cut while you wait!* His wife was somewhat famous around town for her short body and monstrous breasts and was known locally as Jelly Bags. Sometimes she worked in the shop, but didn't wear a uniform. My mother did. She had to wear a striped sleeveless dress cut to look like an apron, with a pale blue shirt underneath, navy tights and matching pumps. I enjoyed making fun of her for this.

'A job's a job darlin,' she said. 'It's the way the boss wants it.'

On her days off, my mother bore all the happy signs of tumultuous divorce: bell bottom jeans, loose grown-out hair, cigarettes smoked at leisure. My father existed in an alternate reality somewhere, with his other wife and other daughter. I never felt I lacked him, but rather that he would have only hampered my mother as she taught me how to smoke and feather my hair.

Without the haircut and cigarettes I would never have caught Rhea Galloway's attention. We hadn't known each other before secondary school, then she sat down next to me on the first day of geography class. She was a bussed-in kid who wore boots and backpacks handed down from her three older brothers. Her mother had died when she was six and her father made the boys leave school as soon as the truant officer allowed so that they could work on the family's sheep farm. They lived fifteen miles out of town but travelled in once a week to pick up food and beer. On those days her brothers would be waiting for Rhea after school in a dirty double cab pick-up truck, her father driving, idling illegally in the bus bays and spitting tobacco out the window. Her brothers were always ribbing her, and this had made Rhea's tongue sharp. I liked this about her. She was unafraid of boys, easily dealing out insults that trumped theirs. She could turn a room blue, shoot spit and open Coke cans one-handed. Having brothers meant she also knew a lot about the things boys got up to in bedrooms and bathrooms – the ridiculous rise and look of their parts, how they went hunched and cross-eyed, feral animals just as I had suspected.

We began spending most of our time together, usually at my house because I lived on the same street as school. We would walk there on our lunch break to avoid using the girls' toilets with their shit-brown seats and locks that could be jimmied from the outside. For us it was preferable to squat by the fence in my back garden, shielded from the neighbours by our cedar hedge. One day as I was crouched there, I heard the clip of my mother's heels coming down the concrete path which ran along the side of our house, her steps uneven and accompanied by scrapes and clunks. She appeared from behind the pebbledash pushing a large metal wheelbarrow with red handles and a thick black rubber wheel. She stopped short when she saw us, out of breath. She looked like a cartoon of my mother, a joke about to begin, and we must have looked the same to her, my pants round my knees mid-flow as Rhea stood with her back to me reciting some English exercise.

'A gift,' she said, nodding at the wheelbarrow. 'From Mr Wallace.'

'I didn't want to go at school,' I replied, pulling my pants up.

'I'll get you a key cut for the back door,' my mother assured me, and promptly did, presenting it to me that evening. 'Courtesy of Mr Wallace,' she said with a wink.

From then on Rhea and I went to my house every lunch time. Sometimes my mother would be there on her lunch break too, eating tomato sandwiches and reading magazines. If she wasn't there, we would read aloud to each other from the problem pages. When we grew bored of that, Rhea would get me to open up my mother's dress cupboard. An awkward extension added by our home's previous owners had created a passage between the kitchen and living room which my mother split in half using a concertina door. Behind it she fitted a rail and hung all the beautiful things she had worn to parties before I came along. My mother's wedding dress was in there too, zipped up in a milky plastic garment bag. Rhea had never had access to such frivolous things. Cupboards and wardrobes in her house were filled with galoshes, waterproof salopettes, fishing poles. She liked to run her hands over the dresses and skirts, fingering sequins, brocade and tulle.

One lunchtime we turned into the garden to find the new wheelbarrow full of leafy cuttings hacked from the hedge. There was Mr Wallace standing on a ladder, shirt sleeves rolled up and gardening shears in hand. I could smell his body odour and aftershave mixed in with the cedar clippings, sweat spread across his back like a Rorschach test. He must have heard us coming, because he stopped his work and turned to speak to us.

'Hello girls.' Neither Rhea nor I replied, and he looked annoyed, ready to use the shears on us. 'You'd better close your mouths,' he said, and opened his own into a gape of shock, mocking us. Then he laughed. My mother came out from the kitchen through the open back door wearing her work uniform.

'Oh, hello you two,' she said. She didn't have her shoes on and walked across the grass in her tights to hand Mr Wallace a cup of tea. I felt as embarrassed as if she were naked. I couldn't speak, so Rhea did.

'We just came to use the bathroom,' she said. Mr Wallace made big bulgy eyes and pretended to choke on his tea.

'The two of you! Going together? Pfff. Suit yourselves!' Then he let out a big laugh.

'I mean we both need,' Rhea said, eyes narrowing. 'Not that we're going to go at the same time.'

'All right, all right! Keep your pants on. Or not, if you're going to the toilet!' Another big laugh. Rhea stomped off into the house, and Mr Wallace watched her go, raising his eyebrows.

'What's her name?' he asked, cocking his head after her.

'Rhea,' I said defensively.

'She's stuck up, that one.'

Both Rhea and I were in moods as we walked back to school.

'Is your mum going with Mr Wallace?' she asked me.

'No,' I said, scowling. 'Mr Wallace is married.'

'Well I know *that*,' she replied. 'I wonder if Jelly Bags knows he's at your mum's for lunch.' I made a sour face at her. Then she said: 'Did you see that he was standing in our piss spot?'

That evening my mother told me without looking up that Mr Wallace might come over for lunch whenever she was working from now on, and that was exactly what happened. I found it abhorrent that she should want to spend time with someone who always carried a set of nail clippers in his pocket, whipping them out as he rested his rear end on our kitchen counter. His grey-yellow moustache was repulsive, and it gave me chills to use the bathroom after I knew he had been in there. He was rude about my mother's cooking too, and refused to eat her boiled eggs.

'You make them all snottery,' he complained. I couldn't shake this image and never ate them again either.

He started showing up on Saturday evenings, and Rhea was usually there as well, though she stayed the whole night and Mr Wallace didn't. I soon learnt that these visits were the best time to push and cajole my mother because she wanted me and Rhea out of their way. We had soon persuaded her to pour us each a glass of sherry every weekend. Mr Wallace did not approve and made this known by tutting and sighing, then retreating upstairs. My mother would rush after him and I would turn the volume up on the television, scared of hearing them carrying on.

One evening, buoyed by the sherry and a cigarette, Rhea began needling my mother, asking if we could try on her wedding gown, an amusement on the cusp of being too childish for us. My mother resisted, which surprised me because I had always thought she kept the dress as a curio rather than a keepsake, but Rhea kept on at her until she gave in.

'Fine!' my mother said, exasperated. 'But make sure you wash your hands first.' Then she went upstairs, carrying glasses of wine and a bowl of crisps on a tray.

I took great pleasure in releasing the dress from its dust bag, holding its translucent layers up to the light where they almost disappeared. Being my mother's daughter, I had rights to first try. I stepped into it, keeping on my little lace-trimmed vest and bra so neither Rhea or I had the discomfort of seeing my breasts. The dress was not white but a very pale rosewater pink with leg o' mutton sleeves that kept slipping away from my shoulders. The bodice came to a point just below the waist, taking aim at my groin, and the train got caught under my feet when I moved. We were hysterical at the ridiculousness of it. Then Rhea tried the dress on and I stopped laughing. She looked like an adult in it, and so beautiful that I ordered her to go out to the hallway and behold herself in our full-length mirror.

My fault then, that Mr Wallace saw her. He stopped on his way to the kitchen, watching Rhea watch herself. She didn't notice, so impressed was she that she could pass for a fully grown woman. I saw him, a glazed look in his eyes, and I rushed to Rhea and stood close behind her, fussing at the skirts and sleeves, guarding her with loud phoney giggles that made her frown at me. Mr Wallace bumped past us, poured himself more wine and went back upstairs.

Then I suppose he must have waited. For our wedding dress game to end. For the wine to reach his head in such a way that it could lend itself as an alibi. For my mother to take her evening shower in the ensuite upstairs. Then he came back down, made noises in the kitchen until he saw Rhea go along the hall to the little bathroom under the stairs, and followed her. From our living room I heard some kind of commotion: a metal rattle, wood being forced, Rhea shouting. Then Mr Wallace's voice booming, full of false joviality. My mother must have heard all this too because the next noise was her light footsteps rushing downstairs.

'Sorry! Sorry!' Mr Wallace shouted as he came through to the living room. He held one hand theatrically over his eyes and waved the other around as if groping in the dark. Some big joke, a misunderstanding. I heard soft soothing sounds from the hall, then Rhea and my mother appeared. Rhea's face was red, angry.

'The lock's gone on the bathroom, girls,' my mother said.

'Don't worry,' said Mr Wallace. 'I know where you can get another one!' He laughed, though no one else did. 'I'll use the upstairs loo,' he said, and waddled off.

My mother made the unusual effort then of fussing over us, rolling out our sleeping bags, fetching pillows. Once she had turned all the lights out and left us in the dark, Rhea and I lay side by side on the living room floor and she told me what had happened. She had heard a scraping, a definite prying from the other side of the bathroom door. She had shouted out, thinking at first it was me, joking around, a strange joke to play when we both knew the tender privacy with which we held our bodies. Then the door had shunted open and there was Mr Wallace, eyes bulging. *You wee dirty*, he had breathed at her as he watched Rhea clinging to her pants and stretching down her t-shirt, stunned into silence as she tried to cover herself up. She burst into a fit of giggles when she finished telling me, and not knowing how else to respond, I began giggling too.

'He's a creep,' Rhea said.

'He is a fucking creep,' I replied. 'Wanky Wallace the key-cutting creep.' We laughed again.

'I should have told him to fuck off,' she said. Then we fell into silence, but didn't sleep. A little while later I heard Mr Wallace coming down the stairs. I moved my hand on to Rhea's back in case he entered the wrong room again, but he found the front door and it opened, then closed.

Next school day Rhea wouldn't come home with me at lunch, so I stayed with her, my bladder cramping in solidarity. When I got home that afternoon I found my mother fitting a new lock on the bathroom door. Her t-shirt was damp under her armpits as she mounted the sliding bolt. The little paper bag that it had come in was stamped *WALLACE'S* and lying on the floor.

'That should do it,' she said, as she turned the last screw.

After that Mr Wallace stopped coming over, and my mother began working less and less. The new Woolworth's opened in town and she got a job there. She never had to work evening shifts, and her uniform was a pair of sensible navy slacks and a collared t-shirt. I kept on asking Rhea to come over, assuring her whatever had been going on wasn't anymore. Eventually she relented, and the three of us operated psychically to ensure Mr Wallace was a subject never touched upon.

Rhea's father started picking her up from my mother's work on the days they did their family trips to town. We would walk to Woolworth's after school and buy Coca-Colas and peppermint creams to share with her brothers, and I would sit in the truck and wait with them while their father finished his errands. Sometimes we would see Mr Wallace, and he would cross the road and pretend not to notice us, even though the huge old pick-up was impossible to miss, parked up on the kerb over double-yellow lines. Her brothers would roll down the windows when they saw him coming, leaning out to clean their fingernails with sharp Swiss army knives that glinted in the light for everyone in town to see.

Kate Hendry

SONNETS FOR MY DAUGHTER

Her Room

She says, *you hurt my feelings every day.*
Her room's a tip: trampled tissues, lipsticks,
lids off, stuck to the floor. *In little ways,*
she adds, as if my rough-edged nails will rip
her skin even when we hug. There's that book
I bought, still unread. Why did I buy it?
I'd complained. One of those questions that hook
her into guilt, a feeling she unclips
and tosses back to me. I let it fall
among the dirty mugs, shattered make-up
palette and discarded socks. Our fight stalls
while she's away at school. I brood all day.
Then hometime – her key's in the door. My heart,
as messy as her room, strains to stay hard.

Mondays

Oh my God, I can't do this! from her room.
I cower in mine. Thumping boots, the door slams.
She's gone to school. That hour she rails and fumes,
I keep myself apart. Whisper – *I am*
writing! Stare at my computer screen. Wait
for the house to empty and you'll never
catch a word, I warn myself, each Monday.
Quit complaining, woman. Pick up your pen.
Then all's quiet, except for cars slowing
at the crossing and laughter at the chemist
on the corner. Pansies at my window
toss and throw their tattered purple petals
at every word I scrawl, hard won. I'm like
her – my God, I can't write a simple line.

Prothesis

The role of women in caring for the dead
is the subject of her essay on life
in Ancient Greece. At the moment of death,
daughter, sister, mother or wife would tie
shut the mouth to stop the ugly drooping
of the jaw, as if the dead might yet spit
out some final cruel words. When muted,
the body's wholly subdued. *Prothesis*
is the word I read in the book I bought
for her: the first act in the funeral rite.
She's not written a single word. I'm caught
between a bandaged silence and a fight
without any end – essay unfinished,
Antigone still can't bury her dead.

Angel

All evening she's been at her boyfriend's house
to decorate their Christmas tree. Ours waits
outside the front door, tender branches bound
to its trunk by plastic net: darkness tamed.
At last she's home. We free it from the mesh
and heave it to its station to be trussed
with tinsel, lights and baubles, each branch tip blessed
with red and gold. Our year of fighting's hushed.
One catch – how to grace the top of the tree?
Last year's white star? Its glued-on wire has snapped.
She claims her boyfriend's gaudy angel gleamed.
I search for ours. Old and grey, she carries
a bent steel star. Her tinsel hair's gone wild
but it can't hide her shy and homely smile.

Tom O. Keenan

DUCKS AND DONKEYS

I'm in her house. It's to be cleared. Died a week ago. Cash Cow. Smells like her. Sixty years' Capstan, Woodbine, Players Navy Cut, Senior Service, Benson and Hedges. Menthol for her health. OCPD is everywhere. Curtains, bedding, clothes, carpets. Compared the number of cigarettes consumed in her smoking life with the number of breaths she had in the same time. It was in a notebook by her bed. Cigarettes at sixty a day for sixty years, that's 1.3 million breaths, twenty thousand a day for sixty years, 433 million, divided by 1.3 million, 336.9 million. One cigarette for every 336 breaths. She settled for that. A draw, a breath in, followed by a cough. One cigarette equalled 168 breaths and 168 coughs. She settled for that too. Justified her smoking. A book keeper, a statistician, then . . . a mother. Dad was an American, an academic, then a . . . . He left and went back to Boston. I got an occasional cheque from him. He died too. Carers came in at the end. From Nigeria. Did their best. Didn't like the way they cut her bread. Salvation Army comes in tomorrow. Left her stuff to me, only. Nothing worth keeping. Not even me. For free? Might be something. Baubles, ornaments, photos, books. She collected books. I've to have the watch, photos, the books. The rest to Great Western Auctions. Her money in cash, savings, accounts, proceeds of the sale of the house, all to the Donkey Sanctuary. Credit's running out on my electric metre. She liked them in Blackpool. Donkeys. In the summer, every summer. Some photos of me. Wee, digging to Australia. Dad, his trousers rolled up, hankie knotted at the corners on his head. Her on a deckchair, smoking. The books are the years of my life. *Kidnapped*, aged four. *David Copperfield*, aged seven. The whale in *Moby Dick*, aged ten. Gulliver in his travels, aged twelve. Benjamin in *Animal Farm*, aged fifteen. Winston in *1984*, aged seventeen. The watch, Amaryllis, rolled gold stainless steel from Embassy Coupons. Stacks of fives. It was on her arm. Like a bank teller giving me my daily tenner. Cash Cow is dead. The Bank Teller goes in my coat pocket. The books and photos go in a cardboard box, no gaffer tape. I don my armour against the world, my black Crombie, a black woollen scarf up around my mouth, over sore ears, dark glasses on scared eyes, a black fedora, my helmet. I leave the key in the key safe, 1206, her day and month. A life of birthdays. Next one doesn't happen.

Hi FJ, I hear, turning the corner from Great Western Road to Byres Road.

Francis Joseph, I say, inside the armour. There'll be more. There's the paedo, bounces off. I need to go to the library. I need to. To want to is different, can mean you don't want to, you can change your mind. Needs are different, you can't not need something, when you need something, you need it. I need to go to the library. I also need to take this box home. It's not taped at the bottom, only folded. I'll go to the library first, I need to.

Hi FJ, the guy in the library says.

Francis Joseph, I say. I don't know his name. I didn't ask.

He looks into the box. Bringing these back?

I growl at him over my glasses. I ordered *Ducks, Newburyport*, a paperback, one thousand pages. Guess I won't see you for a while. Guess I may be gone some time. I open it. There's a proviso in it. This is a work of pure supposition, it says. Pure supposition. Can you believe that? Look up supposition and tell me what it says. I want to be sure.

He looks at me as if I am stupid. Goes to his desktop. The fact of believing something is true without any proof.

Why would you believe this is true without any proof? I put *Ducks* in the box and head out onto Byres Road. I keep my arm under my life, to stop the bottom falling out of it. It's heavy, my life. I'll walk down the road to Partick Cross, turn right, go along Dumbarton Road, to Hyndland Road, turn right, then left into White Street. Number 52, on the right. I could cut off Byres Road where White Street meets it. Going around the Cross offers more chance of running into someone. I carry a bundle of *Socialist*

Workers in my coat pocket. Papers not people. Take a pound for each of them. Ten makes me five pounds. Even more from a donation. Donkey Sanctuary. I measure the Hi FJs by whether they are a hit for a paper or not. I ignore the nots.

Hi FJ, Tam says, standing outside the Aragon.

Francis Joseph, I say. Want a paper?

Aye, suppose. Another pound. I go inside. Two more on the way to the toilet. I pop into Davy's, the uni barber. Tells me I'm looking old. Gives me a haircut. Electric clippers.

You look younger now.

Thanks. I head down to the cross, turn right and walk along to the Lismore. I get a Coke. Alcohol affects my medication. She takes a pound. Just what I have. I sit in the corner near the fire. Put the box on the seat beside me. Pull out *Ducks*. Could've got it on the internet, if I had a computer, if I could use one. Recommended by a guy in the pub. Professor at Glasgow University. Creative writing. Said I need to read it. I need to again. Not that I want to. Got two weeks to read it, then take it back. Could keep it out though. I open it and read the proviso again. A work of pure supposition, it says. Okay, I think. I'll see. I eke out the Coke as I read the first passage. Starts with a lioness and its cubs. Not ducks. All my life is recoil and leap. Leap and recoil, it says. Mine is rise and fall. Fall and fall. Then it starts. The fact that. Lots of the fact that. I see that it is one long monologue. One long sentence. Interspersed by the fact that for one thousand pages. Read a few pages. Reach into my pocket. Pull out her watch. She was wearing it at the time, the Bank Teller, when she died. It connects me with her. I put it to my nose. Smells of cigarettes. Means death. Used to mean money. The Cash Cow. Put it back in my pocket. Get the armour on and pick up the box. The bottom bursts open. The books and photos spill out onto the floor under the table.

Story of my life, I say, putting the box back together.

Let me help you, this guy says. His girlfriend gets up. She's heading in my direction. Oh, Jesus.

Thank you, I say, I can manage. They're on me, before I can get my armour on. Get a few books in the box before they're picking some up, looking at the titles.

Oh, *Moby Dick*, that's about a whale, he says.

No, it's not, I say. An allegory for human's search for meaning.

Looks at me and picks up *Metamorphosis*. Oh, I liked that one, she says, an allegory for the dehumanising effects of modern society.

Aye, it is, I say, also metaphorical for the changes that occur in an individual's life.

Yes, I know, she says. Like she knows.

1984, big brother, he says, putting it in the box.

A warning against totalitarianism, she says. I nod.

Doctor Jekyll and Mr Hyde, he changes into a monster, he says.

The duality of human nature, she says.

Extinction, he says. Murau gets the family estate and gives it away. As if I don't know that. Donkey Sanctuary.

Would you like a newspaper, I ask. *Socialist Worker*, one each? Two pounds for the metre. Get the armour on, arm under the box, head out passing them. They smile. I go along to the paper shop. Get five pounds credit on my card.

Want a bag for your books? she asks.

No, I like them in a box, I say. My life shouldn't be in a plastic bag. I go outside. It's raining. I'll use my bus pass and go along to the Galleries. It's dry in there. I get on the bus. Right away I hear who the fuck do you think you are, Quentin Crisp? These guys behind me start singing if you hate the fucking poof clap your hands. Pull my helmet down over my eyes.

You leave him alone, another guy says.

Want a newspaper? I ask him. Get off at the Galleries and go in. Find a bench upstairs at Expressionism. Take a few books out of my box to rearrange them, to rearrange my life now she's gone. Had I loved her? Naturally, my mother. Why would it be natural to love her? She didn't love me, wee me. Gave all her money away, Donkey Sanctuary. She always referred to me as a charlatan, a blatherer, a parasite. Don't know when I stopped loving her, or she stopped loving me, if she ever did, and started hating her, and her me. Just happened. She wasn't a natural mother, a statistician. Measured her love in her daily handouts, an extra ten on birthdays and Christmas. Cash Cow. Everything else was rationed: food, clothes . . . love. She saved a lot in her life. The solicitor said over a million. Donkey Sanctuary. Always good for an aphorism. A penny saved . . . he who pays the piper . . . all things come . . . give a man a fish . . . better being feared than loved. The priest said a lot about her devotion to God, at her funeral. To the church. To donkeys? To what she had done. The bookkeeper, church's finances. She loved the church, he said. Naturally, when's all said and done, there's more said than done. I walk along the Gallery rooms. Get to *A Man in Armour*, Rembrandt, 1655. Sit down opposite it. I study it often. I fashion myself on it. I like to be pretentious, but safe in my armour, just me. Next, *A Lady in Black*, Francis Campbell Boileau Cavell, 1925. She always wore black, unpretentious. I like I'm pretentious. She wasn't. Time to go home. Armour on, box in hand. Head out and get a bus. Get off at Partick. Three and a half minutes and I'm at the door of my flat. Put my box down. Take out my key and put it to the lock. Doesn't fit. There's a voice behind me. O'Brien from the Landlords.

We've changed the lock, he says. I've a warrant from the Sheriff Court. You got the eviction notice, registered post. It's time to take a walk, he says.

I'd prefer to sit tight, I say.

You didn't respond. You had twenty-eight days. A month's notice.

It wasn't February, I tell him. Can I get some things? He thinks for a minute, not normal for him. He puts his key in the lock, pushes on the door, opens only enough for a wee body to squeeze through.

We've been in, he says. We'll be clearing it out tomorrow.

Why?

Well, you're a health and safety risk. Health, rats in there. Safety, your books are floor to ceiling in every room, including the kitchen and toilet. It's a fire risk.

I like to read, I say.

You like to read, he repeats. And?

And what?

I have to tell you the other residents don't like you.

Don't like me?

No, they find you . . . pretentious.

Pretentious, me?

They want you out.

They want me out?

I'll give you five minutes. I try to close the door behind me. His foot stops it. I go into my bedroom. Sit on my bed. Open a holdall and think about taking books.

Have you got your stuff? comes from the hall. I don't answer him. What do I do? I don't know what to do. All I have is my books and the armour I wear, won't protect me now. Hear other voices.

Is Francis Joseph in there? We found his library card, and a letter, an eviction notice. It had his address on it. It was on the floor of the pub, where he was sitting.

He's in there, O'Brien says. Who are you? he asks.

Just two friends from the pub, one says.

Francis Joseph, she calls from the hall.

I call back, I'm in the bedroom. She comes in. It's you, from the pub, I say.

Aye, we found your library card and letter on the floor. She hands them over.

I'm being put out, I say.

I know, we'll help you, she says.

How?

We're social workers. We know the law, she says. She looks around the room. Francis Joseph, you can't live like this.

It's the only life I know. Her friend comes in. I've only a few minutes to put some books in a bag, I say.

I spoke to him, he says. I told him we need time to get a lawyer involved. We'll go to a sheriff, explain the landlord is acting unfairly, making you homeless. He agrees to come back tomorrow. We'll fight this.

My box?

He goes out and brings it in. The bottom has fallen out of it, he says.

Aye, I know, my life.

What are we going to do to sort this out? she asks.

I've got my books, I say.

Your books won't sort this.

Cash Cow died last week, I say. She looks at me. My mother, I say. She puts her arm around me.

I'm sorry, Francis Joseph.

Like to buy a *Socialist Worker*? I ask.

We've got one, he says.

We'll be back in the morning, she says. I've to get something to eat, some sleep, to try to think about what I can do to get out of my predicament. They leave. I add the credit to my metre and make some toast and tea. I push back my books to clear a place to eat. I've to think about how to get myself out of my predicament. I'll read a book, have my tea, set about finding a book that'll help. My world is disintegrating before me. Cash Cow is gone. Corporations and Rachmans rule over people. Thugs rule our streets. Society taken over by corporate, political, organisational thugs. They don't control my mind. They want us to be like donkeys. Put us into sanctuaries. No one looks out for anyone anymore. Money before people. Profit before need. Corporate thugs control lives. Make people homeless. Leave them without a place, light, cooking, warmth, books. Individual thugs control the streets. I'm just a donkey. A donkey with a brain. I reach into my box for *Animal Farm*. I'm just Benjamin. A symbol of apathy and cynicism, accepting organisation and individual brutality. Best be wise and intelligent in the face of tyranny. That's what I'll do. I reach in for *1984*. My fatalism equals Winston Smith's. I'll be Winston. I need his rebelliousness. What good's that in the face of impending doom? Will it stop O'Brien? I reach for *Down and Out in Paris and London*. Glasgow, I add. I hear claws scratching, jaws chewing, paws running. I look up to see the bluebottles on the window. That unbearable buzz. I reach for *Metamorphosis*. I'll become vermin, an insect. By the morning, they'll not see me. I'll hide under the books, survive by eating my kind. I'll be free from society's changing norms. I'm alienated anyway, isolated. My life has no meaning. An insect or vermin. I haven't decided which. My life will have meaning. To survive. I'll go into the water at Stobcross Quay. Become a white whale. They can't control a whale. I'll seek my meaning of life. To be free. I look at the book. *Moby Dick*. The human condition. Ahab's hunt for understanding. His own existence. I'll rely on *Extinction*. Murau, like me, loved and hated his parents. Mine died on me too. Why did they die on me? I needed their money. They were clever, but not intelligent, like me. They despised me. There's no book that'll get me out of an existentialist crisis. What is my life? It's in a box. I read some *Ducks* and have a very fitful sleep. I've to think about what to do to get out of this situation. What can I do? Next morning, the social workers and the lawyer come in. She introduces herself.

Mary Prentice, solicitor. Pleased to meet you, Mr Moore, she says.

Francis Joseph, I say.

Francis Joseph, please call me Mary.

I'm sorry, I don't know what will get me out of my predicament. I was asked to think about this. I just don't know.

That's okay, she says. I kind of know what we need to do.

Oh?

Yes, we need to go to court, have the eviction notice overturned. At least until you can get some sort of agreement with your landlords.

The thugs? I don't think so.

What was the grounds of the eviction?

Hadn't paid my rent in months.

Oh, she says.

I'm also a health and safety risk.

Can you pay anything, even start to pay rent again, bring down your debt gradually?

No, I say. Rent went up to eleven hundred a month. Only have six hundred in benefits.

Oh? she says, really. Could you get the house tidied, cleared a bit?

Give my books up? No, I don't think so.

We could get you a flat through the homeless section of the council?

I'm not going into a high-rise in Lincoln Avenue, among the druggies.

We can go to the tribunal, get you more time, two months before you could be evicted.

I'll still be evicted?

Yes, if the grounds are met.

I need to pick up my *Socialist Worker* papers, I say.

What are you going to do?

Pick up my papers, I say. They look at each other.

We'll go the tribunal. It'll buy you more time.

The lock?

We'll get your old lock refitted.

O'Brien?

We'll ask them to leave you alone through the process.

Thought police?

Them too, she smiles kindly, not cynically. You're a reader, she says, looking at my books. Can I look? She picks up *Moby Dick* and looks inside. Her face changes. Francis Joseph, this is a first edition.

I know, I say. Cash Cow only bought first editions. She collected them.

They're worth a lot of money, she says. She reaches for others. *1984*, *Animal Farm*, *Treasure Island*, they're all firsts, she says.

I know, I say.

You have thousands of pounds here, she says. Maybe a hundred thousand pounds worth? They're looking aghast now.

I know, I say.

If you sold them, all your problems are over. You could buy a wee flat.

I know.

Well?

Well what?

Sell them, buy a flat, your own, no more thought police.

I can't, I say.

Why not?

Don't sell my books. Only sell newspapers. They look at each other again. I need to pick up my papers, I say.

Okay, Francis Joseph, we'll—.

Aye, you'll do your best. Thank you.

Francis Joseph?

What?

Please think about it. Your books?

I have done, thank you.

The next two weeks pass. They come back, the eviction is put back. Two months. But they say it'll happen. I need to go to the library. I need to. I take *Ducks, Newburyport* back. I want to, you see. I didn't need to. I was told I could keep it out longer. Takes it from me. Stamps my card.

Did you like it? he asks.

It's a lot about facts, I say.

And that's a matter of fact, he laughs.

Aye, I say. I don't laugh. The fact that I'm all fact out, the fact that I just realised the narrator said when this monologue in my head finally stops I'll be dead, or at least unconscious, the fact that it is stream of consciousness, the fact that when the stream, the monologue, stops, so does the consciousness, hers, the fact that this blew my mind, the fact the proviso says this is a work of pure supposition, the fact that this supposes, not the fact that this is the case. The fact that I'll never read books in the same way again. And that's a fact. He looks at me.

Thanks, FJ, he says, I guess you've read it.

Francis Joseph, I say. Silence has fallen at the busy counter. Did I say something wrong or upset anyone?

No, he says, we'll see you soon.

Do you want a *Socialist Worker*? I ask. For free?

Áine King
WEATHER WARNING

Splish!

Whoosh!

Wheeeeee!

Mara presses the flush button and squeals with delight as Dolly swirls and spins in the cascade, then disappears.

Mara! Where's Dolly? Did you— Oh no! You flushed her! She's gone in the pipe. To the river. To the sea.

Mara is almost five. Super bright, says the Class One teacher. Can't-take-your-eye-off-her-for-a-second, says everyone else.

Dolly, now heading seawards is, or was, a small, grey, bottle-nosed smiling toy dolphin from the Children's Zoo gift shop. For months she's been Favourite Toy, carried everywhere, sitting beside Mara at mealtimes, tucked under her pillow at night. Now, she's another bit of plastic flotsam heading for the ocean.

I brace myself for Mara to miss her pal, but she's busy. Drawing.

Look, Mum.

That's great . . . is it . . . a giant snake? The inside of a monster?

It's a map, silly! Toilet, pipe, sewer – stinky-poo! And river.

Mara's river flows in fattening loops of blue crayon to the sea. A bean-shaped smudge drawn in my eyeliner, is Dolly. In the sewer.

Holding her nose, says Mara.

I magnet the map to the fridge while Mara draws sewer-rats with bullwhip-tails and teeth like dragons.

It's okay, she says, Dolly knows the way to the sea. Dolphins are super bright, too.

Bath-time, Mara says the water's too hot, though I checked it twice and she's happily splashing. As the bubbles drain she leans over the plug-hole, calls, Good luck, Dolly, see you Saturday.

Saturday?

The river gets all the way to the sea, on Saturday. We'll go to the beach and bring Dolly home.

By Saturday the sea and Dolly will be forgotten, and we'll be shopping.

Monday our wee flat fills with fish. A riot of Rainbow Crayon trout, Lego lamprey, Stickle Brick sticklebacks, Mega Bloks minnows, a plump plasticine pike.

I don't think jellyfish live in rivers, I say, catching a fluorescent yellow Slime-blob in the sink.

She's lost, Mara beams, Dolly will help her find the sea.

I rescue the wobbly dollop from the waste disposal and hunt for old tights to make an octopus.

Tuesday's too wet for the park so we scoff fishfingers and go river-rafting across the lounge on a flood of blue bedsheets, our box-boat shooting the rapids of Granny's rag-rug. Mara wild camps on the banks of the sofa, waiting for dragonflies. Torchlight flickers inside her sleeping bag as my glowworm-girl tells the beam-faced moon-lamp how Dolly is befriending beavers now, on her Important Mission, somewhere downstream.

We're going to get Dolly back on Saturday, she promises her bedroom night-sky.

There are more luminous pale stars on the ceiling than there are pounds in my account to spare for seaside trips. Dolly is far from forgotten.

Wednesday we bake starfish biscuits and take some, on a Little Mermaid plate, to Mr Bahari on the ninth floor. Below us the city is spread like a play-mat. The river wanders away to the sea, too far to see, even from up here. Mr Bahari praises the biscuits, mist-eyed in memories of his sun-dried war-worn home. Mara presses her nose to Mr Bahari's blue-lit fish tank and chats to the swordtails, Dolly's in the river now, whooshing down waterfalls, breaching beside boats, speeding to the sea. We're going to bring her home on Saturday.

Thursday we walk home along the sluggish, slug-grey river, the city rumbling on over our shoulders. Ducks are ducking-and-diving around a half-drowned bike. Pond-skaters skuttle and skim in the scum. Spiders silver-thread the dipping willows. Unseen creatures make ripples and splashes. The water moves as it has forever, slowly seawards.

A heron clatters upwards suddenly from the weeds.

Dolly's going down the river, Mara tells him as he wings up over the car park. We're going to the beach on Saturday to bring her home.

A swan draws up its gorgeous, graceful head and looks me in the eye as I try to re-budget the week ahead, daring me to disappoint a child.

Friday there's a new smudge on the map as Dolly dolphin-leaps river-to-sea. Mara writes a welcome-home song, teaches it to the plasticine pike. Her backpack by the door is loaded with wellies, water-bottle and Tunnock's Wafers, ready for the beach.

Watching evening TV. Turbines and gannets and whale-pods stranded. Droughts and hosepipe bans. Swirling storms and flash floods. Mara in her penguin pyjamas, sleepy against my side, blinks as a glacier calves and crashes.

She says, It's a Red Weather Warning. That's why Dolly's gone to the sea, to weather-warn all the fish. The water's too hot, but Dolly will tell everyone. It'll be okay.

How did I let it get this far? Why didn't I stop it before now? What can I say to her? A tap at the door. Mr Bahari returns the Little Mermaid plate with shy thanks.

And train tickets tucked under the tea towel.

Saturday, the train rattles us seaward. We're going to the beach to get my dolphin, Mara tells the conductor as he scans our ticket, hoists an eyebrow and chugs along the carriage.

In the deeps of my pocket a new gift-shop-dolphin is hiding, waiting to be found among barnacles and bladderwrack just as hope begins to ebb.

There's a small, sad knot in my chest for yet another chunk of plastic in the world . . . but . . .

Our days to come will be full of tall tales of Dolly's river-swim from toilet to tide. Full of dolphins and ducks and pike and pebbles, crabs and cormorants, orca and octopuses, sharks and seals and seahorses, whales and walruses and whirlpools. And a wee girl who knows she can save it all.

Pippa Little

LAMMAS GOLDFISH

for Ray

Men slapped the ponies from pit bank to field,
slammed the gate shut and left them to their fortnight
but it rained solid so their poor backs turned black-sodden
as old carpet.

Told not to, the boy went out with brown apples and
endearments,
dug his nails into their manes, gave each one a Sunday name.
Then
saw it first, flickering, inner-lit through the gloom of their
trough,

strange discarded thing from a drunken homecoming
the night of the Lammas fair, won for a kiss perhaps,
beautiful, the word hurt in his mouth.

And kept watch day after day as it swelled in its pink-gold
pomp, memorised every curved samurai scale,
its secret flowering. Until one morning early

he came to the field to find it gone,
the water numb and calm and grey
and every beast led back inside the earth.

Màrtainn Mac an t-Saoir

A LEABHAR BEAG DUBH SA CHAFAIDH

'S e leabhar beag,
meanbh, dubh, fosgailt'
an fhir thapaidh aoig,
dhan tug mi an aire –
sa chafaidh chòmhraideach chumhang thrang:

Eadailtis, Albais,
gràdh daonnda
gan sadail an ear is an iar
mun cuairt air,
is gan glacadh le craos gàire
no glaodh lasganach àrd:
'*Pizza* idir, *amore*, no *lasagna*?'

Sin,
agus a bhriogais dhubh
an lèine gheal is
a ghiùlan balbh sòbarra,
ach na gathan cràiteach
a thigeadh air,
an lùib gach aoibhneis dhripeil
is e leis fhèin leis –

na shuidhe tarsainn bho dhithis òga
ri spògadh is pògadh a chèile,
triùir thall a' seinn gun chùram
nan aona chinn
ceòl binn soirbh an cuid saorsa.

Agus mar a ghreimich iad e,
an dà dhòrn mhòr
rinn trom-ruamhar tric roimhe
eadar talamh ruighinn is teàrnadh –
is mar a thionndaidh fheum-san is acras
na duilleagan tana, tana, ud
gun tacsa caraide no cobhair.

Agus mar a shocraich earrann
– no bloigh earrainn? –
fa dheòigh, bu choltach, e
mun do dhùineadh Am Facal,
is gun tug An Gàidheal goirt o shean
nam cheann an saoghal air.

HIS LITTLE BLACK BOOK IN THE CAFÉ

It was the pallid well-built man's
open, tiny black book
I noticed –
in the bright tight chatty café:

Italian, Scots,
human affection
being tossed all around him
and caught with a wide smile
or wild raucous laughter:
'*Pizza, for you my darling,*
or are you lasagna?'

That,
and his black trousers,
white shirt,
mute sober deportment,
bar the pain spasms
midst the joyful hubbub,
and his sitting alone with it –

across from a young couple
pawing and snogging each other,
the three behind singing in unison –
not a care in the world –
the easy, cheery, music of their freedom.

And how firmly they gripped it –
his two large fists
ones that had often dug heavily

between unyielding land and salvation,
and how his acute need and hunger
turned those flimsy pages
without succour or a friend's support.

And how a passage –
or was it part of a passage? –
eventually settled him
it seemed,
before The Word was closed
and the Gael of old in my head
confronted the world.

AIG UAIGH SEANN CHARAIDE

Mìos a bhios ann, a-màireach,
bho chaidh innte do chàradh,
is na sìtheanan sgaoilte fhathast
an ion 's mar a chaidh an càradh –
ach air crìonadh.

Air seacadh:
gu sireadh na tìre
a chinn iad,
ach a-mhàin na ròsan dearga
anns a' bhlàth-fhleasg as fhaisg' ort
tha sìnte.

Is an-siud is an-seo
rin lorg nam measg
tha briathran:
od chloinn is o chloinn do chloinne-sa,
an dubh a tha air thuar sìoladh –
pàipear chuir aghaidh air na siantan
ghleac ri grèin mar a b' fheudar
mar a b' fhìor èiseil

airson 's gun leughte iad
le duin' thig le chogais
no na èiginn –
meud an gaoil, dhut fhèin, nach trèigeadh
dh'aindeoin dhùbhlan
dh'aindeoin ciorraim
dh'aindeoin truimead goirt an cuid èislein.

AT THE GRAVE OF AN OLD FRIEND

A month it will be,
tomorrow,
since you were lain –
the flowers still arranged
much as they too were lain,
but now decayed.

Withered:
in pursuit of the soil
that grew them,
except the red roses
in the wreath placed nearest to you.

And here and there
can be found among them
words:
from your children
and your children's children
in fast fading ink,
on paper that faced the elements
confronted the sun, when necessary,
when absolutely vital

so a visitor with a conscience,
or at a time of need, might read:
the scale of their love for you,
that will endure
despite the challenges
despite frailty
despite the weight of their own infirmity.

FÈILL AIR SANT PERE

Naomh Peadar
as riatanaiche
dhan bhaile seo

is dhan ath-bhaile
agus dhan ath-fhear,
ged nach do ghlèidh
iad-sin ainm.

Tha fhios nach b' urrainn
dhan a h-uile baile san sgìre
is iad cho mòr an crochadh air a' chuan
a bhith air an aon ainm –
a dh'aindeoin am feum air cobhair.

Ach bidh na h-eaglaisean
ga chur an cèill nan glagan cianail,
bidh agus na daoine –
a chuireas lìn nam fàilte
is a roinneas an toradh eatorra
nan ùrnaigh theasairginn
ron chàradh chùramach.

SANT PERE'S POPULARITY

Saint Peter
is most important
in this town

and the next
and the next,
though neither of those two
retained his name.

Every town
in the area couldn't –
however great their dependence
on the ocean –
be given the same name,
despite their need of his support.

But the churches
sound him in their longing bells,
as do the people:
they cast nets in welcome,
divide the catch between them
like a rescue-prayer,
before commencing heedful mending.

Donnchadh MacCàba

DÌLEAB NAM MARBH

clàran loisgte
cànan seargte
cultar sgàinte
gun eòlas
gun tuigse
chan eil
air fhàgail
ach criomagan
ar n-eachdraidh
bratach phrìseil
leabhar nan deur
clachan snaighte
teachdaireachd dhìomhair
talamh nam beò
ri thorachadh

LEGACY OF THE DEAD

records burnt
language withered
culture fractured
without knowledge
without understanding
nothing
remains
but crumbs
of our history
a precious flag
a book of tears
sculptured stones
a secret message
the land of the living
to fertilise

BEANNACHD

Lorgan-coise aosta fo do chasan
gad threòrachadh air do shlighe,
seachad air gach duilgheadas,
gu saoghal ùr, làn dòchais,
a tha gad fheitheamh air fàire.

BLESSING

Ancient footprints below your feet
guide you on your way,
past each and every difficulty,
to that new world, full of hope,
which awaits on your horizon.

AN CÈITEAN UD

D' aodann cho bàn ris a' cheò air na mullaichean,
làn-àrd, is sluaisreadh nan tonn na mo chluasan,
coltraichean nan suidhe, buthaidean air bhogadan
a' feitheamh ri rud air choireigin.

Aodann na creige, 's gun sgur, na faireagan
bho nead gu muir nan cuairteachadh,
agus a-staigh san tìr sna doireachan,
air tilleadh bho h-imreachd, cuthag a' ceilearadh.

Bu bhòidheach thu:

cuailean a' sèideadh sa ghaoith air a' bhàta,
do ghuth a' fannachadh thar suail na mara,
nad eilthireach a' falbh, agus mise, a-cheana
gad ionndrainn, air fhàgail nam aonar air a' chala.

Wendy MacIntyre

HAIRCUT AL FRESCO

Until I looked out and saw my neighbour
playing barber to her husband
at noontime on their patio,
he seated, facing outward,
and she bending by him, with the scissors,
neatening his temples,
until that unexpected glimpse
of a scene that seemed too intimate
for me to gaze at longer,
I had forgotten that I used to cut your hair
which was not at all like my neighbour's,
straight and dark and sleek,
but wide and high as a lively bush.

You would sit at the kitchen table
with a towel draped about your shoulders
and at your feet,
a sea of newspapers I spread out
to catch the clipped curls.
I believe you often sipped a beer
while I worked
and that sometimes I had to ask you
to keep still.

The wonder was that I could do no wrong.
I snipped an inch away, all round,
top, back and sides,
and your hair sprang back,
irrepressible and sturdy.

I cannot remember the last time
I gathered up the newspapers
with the fallen curls.
It must have been long before my leaving.

Your hair grew higher and wider,
its red the colour of your rage.
Let it be, you snapped,
if I suggested cutting it.
Let it be.

THE RIVER WIND

After you died, I affixed to the side porch of my house,
facing the river,
the Tibetan prayer flags a well-travelled friend had given me.

I cannot read the script on the square flags
or make out which deities sit in their enclosing circles,
although I see clearly
the god at the centre rides a fine horse.
The colours of the flags repeat
so that there are ten in total,
five blue, white, red, green and yellow,
and then again,
each barely attached to the other
by a supple white thread.

For three days the prayer flags
caught the wind from the river,
belled out and fell back,
belled out and fell back,
in the kind of gentle movement
one imagines the soul of the earth having,
if all were peace above.

I sat sometimes at the little table on my porch
and watched them wave as they would.

It was their ease of motion I thought you would relish,
the naturalness of their rising and falling,
I would have given you such breath in your last years
had I had the power.

And on the evening of the third day, I took them down.

Iain MacLeod
THE BOOK OF DEER

'Bed Déar a anim ó shunn imacc—'
'Let Deer be its name from this on—'
(from Note 1)

'Given in
freedom til Doomsday, you are to know
that we, the Deer, strictly enjoin that no
one shall dare harm on them or to their goods,
quit and immune from all lay service
or improper exaction, as is written
in their Book, proved by argument and sworn
at Aberdeen.'

That that, this Book of Deer, *an Leabhar Dhèir*
named for the aber, from the river
mouth where this book of saying speaks to us
now, this book of *déara*, book of tears—
the Bede's salt of grief and then cleansprung
from Drostán's lacrimal wells as the monk-
saint passed the blessed monastery on—
that it sings here from thanksgiving, children's
healing from Old Deer to Maud to Buchan
and back through the stained hands of Columba

is a miracle. And in this dear book
is a language first recorded: Gàidhlig
in the margins and spaces found beneath
the Word of God, in St John's undergrowth
taking root in the written down. Latin
scribed by just one, illuminations
on vellum in the brown ink of oak gall

and umber and madder conjure gospels
like blaeberries lure a hart to the wood.
By dim light, the book's kell scribe takes a reed

or swan feather maybe, their handheld wand,
and japs onto calfskin, tattooing and
knotting that Celtic interlace like box
hedge bordering or the shore of a lough;
peripheral and central to the end
like tree rings of oak Columcille was fond
of. So the heartwood beams of Iona's
first abbey. That Irish oak: *daire*, *darragh*,
straight from the Ogham alphabet, a book
of stone planted in a field four davochs

worth and wide. This is a small space though,
semantic, marginal, a tongue with no
possessive, less plosive. I have no earth,
let the land be 'at' me, transcendent, 'with'
me, in transience. And do no harm.
A roe deer sleeps there in its hollowed warmth,
in the quires of the wheat's sea gold, lost
to us but safe to itself in its toast
coloured safety in the unseen wade.
Like a nesting bird in a farmer's field

given time by the old timers to make
the long grass by their whispering scythes, weak
with effort to cut from the middle out.
If something's lost, how do we care for it,
call it, with what word. That world of buck deer,

of corncrake and curlew, may disappear
and in their silence witness. Once happy
in the babble, once and for all, it's we
who need a clearing; quit and give Eden
back for a bit—the forests imagine

it, the fields and 'as far as the great
pillar stone at the end of the thicket,'
the rivers, the hills and their corries—
land given, but we'll fuck it as always.
And back to the Book, tinged with biblical
inaccuracy, begats fallible,
historically wrong but an open
space where five Gaels' nibs have conversation
with kings, high priests, sons' sons, toísechs, mormaers.
Yet spare a thought for Ete ingen, daughter

of Gille-Micheíl, MacDuff of Fife, witness
to the consecration 'free of impost'
and all in bond; first woman written down
into Gàidhlig but as wife/child of thanes.
Like the four Marys and sister Martha,
St John's well woman of Samaria,
we are that what we do and who we are
as tattooed Latinate in books of Deer.
Let Ete speak into this commune, decreed
by more than 'Woman' and a line in sand,

let burns let bourns let their waterways talk
through sluice gate through aqueduct through tear duct
open up sun so pass down through new soil
roots and to the moons on our fingernails
witness silently if need be or in

that spoken realm of good old tradition
witness without possession as Gaelic
does—'*Bed Déar a anim ó shunn imacc*'—
and Irish too wherein their books of elk
melt out of the ground to warn our step back

to amaze and astound us, if not kill
us with anthracis. To our eternal
future, til freedom's Doomsday imagine
it better if the Deer move in downtown
as we moved in, their libraries immune
from human thought or word and our gardens
their garden again to bed in. Namely
primum non nocere, and lastingly.
Take this Book as read, as map, as gospel,
an unwilful misreading of title

perhaps
that nevertheless brought me here, my heart
to high land where farewell mountains covered
with snow, farewell the forests, wilderness,
our parliament gone; and so come torrents.

We're a book being written by writing.
Like the tract of Deer, three voices singing.
In its fictions, there in the colophon:
'Be it on the conscience of anyone
who reads this that they say a small prayer
for the soul of the wretch who wrote it.' Here
where words are blown into, life. The patient
wait I suppose that this time seems now right
and word from books becomes deer everywhere.

Robbie MacLeòid
LASRACH

Sinn a' dannsadh san t-sabhal, 2022. Cuimhn' a'd?
Nach can thu gu bheil? Cuimhnich
an t-àile: fàileadh an t-seann fhiodha,
an duslaich, an uisge-beatha dòirte,
an fhallais. An talla tais, stampadh nan cas
's bualadh bhas, faram is fuinn a' fàs,
a' sìor-fhàs, seadh, is thusa
thusa, ri toinneadh, cuailean buidhe bàn' a' bogadaich
anns an àile ud.

Thug mi rudhadh air do ghruaidhean le droch chainnt gun
nàire,
is nach binn do cheòl-gàire, is mi air mo bheò-ghlacadh
danns' às dèidh danns' às dèidh dannsa chur seachad leat.
Sheall sinn dhaibh uile mar a bha còir, an dithist againn
air ar deagh oideachadh on a bha sinn òg,
gach geamhradh san sgoil, gach banais on uair sin, seadh,
's iomadh turas a chuir mi na ceuman seo
ach cha b' ann leatsa roimhe. Ach seo sinn,
dà chuairteag a' teannadh air:

mo làmh chlì nad làimh dheis.
Mo ghàirdean mun cuairt ort.
A h-aon, a dhà, a trì, up-down.
Do dhà ghorm shùil mheallach,
's do bhroilleach geal bàn laste,
's na gruaidhean fhathast cho ruadh,
agads' is agamsa, bualadh
bhas is eil' a' fàs. Seadh.
Sinn an cunnart
sradag chur ri sabhal.

Thàinig madainn, is sgar sin, a' stampadh
diofar cheuman thar chuantan, cèilean
is cèilidhean eile, leantainn dannsa dol air n-adhart
na cruinne. Ach thug an dearbh chuairt
air ais còmhla sinn, is tha mo ghruaidhean
fhathast ruadh, is mar sin:

nach teannaich thu rium aon uair eile,
nach teann thu nall? Nach cuir sinn Glaschu
na lasair? Mu dheireadh thall, nach seall sinn
dhan bhaile seo air fad
mar a nì iad waltz?

YE DANCIN?

Mind us dancing in the barn, back in '22? Won't you say
you do? That you mind the air, that scent
of old beams beneath our feet,
the dust we're kicking up, the whisky
spilt, the sweat the same. That humid hall,
fit to catch a spark, stamping feet and
clapping hands, percussion and perspiration, and you
spinning there, your gold curls bobbing
in that air.

I rouged your cheeks with smut, aye,
and sweet your laughter, I was enrapt
and dance after dance after dance
we danced. We showed them all how it was done,
both of us well-schooled from childhood,
every winter in PE, every wedding since, aye,
many's the time I've danced these steps
but never before with you. But here we are,
two turning towards:

my left hand in your right.
My arm round your side.
One, two, three, up-down.
Your roslyn blue eyes, your chest flushed,
and those rosy cheeks,
both yours and mine. Aye. Us in danger
of burning that whole barn down.

Then came morning, and we split,
stamping our way across cities and seas, finding new dances
and new dancers, following the world's progressive dance,

but we made our way round the circle
and here we are again:

won't you come here to me,
one more time? Let's put Glasgow
to the torch. Let's you and I
show this whole town
how to waltz.

Fiona Mossman

THERE IS NO SUCH THING AS A CREATURE THAT EATS YOUR MEMORIES

or at least that's what you say when she tells you about her creature. She explains it all on the day she gives you the sarangi and asks if you can fix it for her. It is a beautiful instrument, hand-carved from tun wood with great skill – squarer than the violins you'd usually get in the shop and with three resonance chambers. She tells you that it was her grandfather's, taken over with him from Uttar Pradesh, that she had dug it out of storage during her recent move, that the chambers were called *pet*, *chhaati*, *magaj* – stomach, chest, brain. Like a person, she says with a sideways smile. Together you listen to YouTube recordings of sarangi-playing. The sounds are more like a human voice than an instrument's, and full of loss and longing.

'It will depend on how bad the damage is,' you tell her. 'But I'll do my best.' You know her well enough to understand what she's giving you: one of the few remaining links to her heritage, a past that's mostly inaccessible to her and yet still part of her. You'll handle it with care.

As you walk along the canal together after the lunch she treated you to as a thank you, and you ask how she is, she repeats the words *it's fine, I'm fine* just enough times for you not to believe her. Overhead the sky withholds rain, and everything is too dry, choked.

The creature, she eventually tells you, is always with her. It must have been there the whole time; but now she's figured it out, what it does.

It lives off memories. Her memories.

You don't know what she's talking about. 'What kind of creature? What do you mean, it eats your memories? How is that even possible?'

She can't tell you what it is – something not quite mammal nor insect nor bird, but a little of each. It scurries like a spider but is furry like a vole or a squirrel, and about that size. It seems to live in the walls, to follow her from place to place. It might lay eggs: papery, fragile things that she finds every now and then which dissolve if touched. Sometimes she hears what could be the fluttering of wings.

You listen sceptically, worriedly, as she tells you how its feeding results in forgotten keys, unbrushed teeth, missed appointments. 'But you've always been like that,' you protest.

There's more. She has also lost her oldest memories to it – when she first learned to tie her own shoelaces, learned to swim. Her most treasured memories too. So many of them, gone.

'I don't understand,' you tell her. 'It's normal to not remember everything from your childhood, you know. We're not meant to remember everything, our brains wouldn't be able to cope. A little forgetting is good for you.'

She asks if you remember how you met. For her, it's an eaten memory. She knows it was in a seminar at university, but nothing else.

You feel a jolt in your gut. That wasn't how you had met, and you almost say so, but you can see how her hands are twisting and her voice is shaking and you think twice. But doesn't she remember that you met on a subsidised outdoor adventure weekend arranged by the university for what they'd charmingly called underprivileged students? And you'd laughed about that terminology, bonded over it, the otherising assumptions of it.

You tell her as gently as you can that her memories aren't being eaten, because there is no such thing as a creature that eats your memories. You'll bring her the sarangi to her new flat next week, if all goes smoothly.

The workshop at the back of the store is a place of peace, of concentration and wood shavings and resin, of broken instruments being remade. The smells enfold you in their comfort and your tools are all lined up on the bench, precise and well-cared for.

You cradle the sarangi, feeling its heft. It is lighter than it should be. You begin to take the instrument apart, figuring out as you go how it was put together. You'll have to learn about the design, talk to an expert or get a book out, you decide. But first, you need to see what the damage is.

Perhaps she has gone mad. She's always struck you as someone a bit too open to the weather of others, her own reality slightly in question. But you remember her downcast eyes, her sadness, her fear. She didn't seem crazy.

What are memories, really? Your mind playing tricks on you? Shadows of real experiences? Stories you tell yourself? You remember things, you know you do. Even right now, the smell of the tun like the smell of cedarwood, the feel of the grain under your fingers with its ever-so-slight grooves and nicks: these remind you of other instruments you've handled, other memories. Your music teacher who noticed your fascination with the way that different designs led to different sounds; your first attempt at whittling a whistle.

What if you were to go poking around in the attic of your memory and find nothing inside the boxes there?

But there's no such thing as a creature that eats memories. You know it can't be real, and you repeat that to yourself, just enough times to not believe it.

Your hands busy with the sarangi, you distract your mind by thinking about woodworms. They aren't really worms but beetles. You've spotted the tell-tale frass-lined holes at the base of the sarangi already, and as you turn it over, loosening the pegs, you see more of them along the sides and back. Not good signs.

Woodboring beetles prefer damp wood, so where there's beetle-eaten wood there's also likely to be a ventilation problem – the wind getting in, or the rain soaking through. She'd shown you the padded bag her grandfather had stored it in, told you about the cupboards, the basements. Dampness must have got in at some point.

You prise off the final strings and the bridge and lay them to the side. Inside the hollow chambers, the holes made by the woodworms proliferate, riddling right through the body.

*

With the sarangi still on your workbench a week later, you go to visit her at her new flat. You've not heard from her since that conversation at the canal.

The sky has finally opened and the rain is pouring when you reach her place. She lets you in on the second buzz, looking worn. She leads you to the kitchen and puts on the kettle. You tell her that you're working on sourcing some materials for her sarangi, to replace parts, but you're not sure how far you'll get. She nods, and you can see that she's upset. She's probably thinking of how little she knows about her grandfather, about her family's past, as she's told you before.

You hesitate, then ask: 'So, how about this creature, then? Still here? Still eating your memories?'

She takes you through to the living room and you both sit down, the downpour outside half-forming rhythms, drumming on a bucket left in the grass. She takes a deep breath and a sip of her tea.

She is afraid, she says. People are made up of their memories; if your memories are disappearing, is your self disappearing, too? So she has tried it all. She's tried to escape the creature, moving home so many times, and always it has followed her. She's tried to kill it: there's mousetraps all over the place, all untriggered. She's asked for help, asked animal shelters, talked to the police, to her therapist. Asked the witchy woman she used to live near to sage her home. None of them were any use.

She's tried to starve the creature out. Not going anywhere, not doing anything. But it's impossible. Even slowing down to a crawl, the world spins on: the weather, the news, reading a book, playing a videogame. It's all fodder for the creature.

So, she tells you, she's accepted it. If memories make people who they are, she has the creature. The creature makes her who she is.

Her eyes challenge you over the cup's rim, and you cannot read their depths.

Discomfited, your eyes dart to the corners of the room, your ears prick at the sound of scratching in the walls. You see something then, a flash of fur and teeth, there and gone.

'Did you see that?' you leap to your feet, upending your half-drunk tea. She's staring at you. 'I'll get it,' you say, feigning fearlessness. 'It's probably just a big rat.' You advance upon the dark corner of the hallway that it had scuttled off to.

You feel her pushing you away. She's pushed you halfway to the door before your instincts dig in and you hold your ground. Then she's yelling at you: *you can't have it, you can't hurt it, it's mine. It's me.*

You want to stay, you want to protest, you want to help her calm down but everything you do seems to be making her more upset and so you do as she says and leave.

You hope that it's the right thing. The rain soaks you as you head homewards, your hands deep in your pockets, your heart feeling waterlogged.

You think back to that first meeting. What was it that you said, that she said? Can you remember how you felt, what you thought? The time of day? Was it in fact at a tutorial, not a hillwalk?

The reassuring weight of the door against your palm, the relief of taking off your sodden clothes, pulling on a jumper: well-kent, groove-worn actions. You stand for a moment in your bedroom. Outside the rain beats down, rhythms forming and dissolving against the roof tiles. Have you done the wrong thing? Should you not have left her?

*

You find yourself drawn to the mirror beside your wardrobe. There's your room, reflected; the same messed up bed, the pile of books, the pile of clothes. There's your own reflected self. Would you know your own body across a crowded bar? on the street?

You step closer, until you and your reflection are eye-to-eye. There's your laughter lines, there's that frown line between your brows. You trace those tiny marks on your skin until you lose them. Your eyes are familiar too, the same colour they have always been. Your nose. Your eyebrows.

You stare. You stare so long that time stretches out and you begin to lose yourself, those features that you know so intimately, so unthinkingly, now the face of a stranger; there is a challenge in those eyes and you cannot read their depths.

Then the stranger blinks and the semblance shifts and you reassemble yourself.

There's still a residue of that moment as you watch yourself pull away in the mirror. The drumbeat of the moment echoes like rain on a forgotten metal bucket. It reverberates as you leave the room, make dinner, watch TV; it's there as you lie in bed and it threads its way through your dreams. The question of it, the challenge, the fear, the freedom.

The rain falls all night, and in your workshop an instrument with a human voice is the only one that remembers the man who once made it sing. Across town in her new flat the instrument's keeper listens to the scratching in the walls and wonders if anyone knows who they really are. Waking, you wonder too.

The rain dampens everything, working into every crack and groove. Soon you'll walk to your workshop, and you'll get soaked again, and you'll look up before you go in, head tipped back, throat exposed. The rain will keep racing groundwards, without past or future, without memory.

As if it will never end, as if this is all there is: the moment, and the movement, and you.

Chris Neilan

HOT RICE AND COLD WATER

Early morning, early winter, and I am on my way. What will they think of me? So early after check-in and baggage scan and the stagelit wander through the Duty Free grotto (perfume agent crouching in front of a foot level mirror to touch up her make-up, Leith girl with a tray of plastic shot glasses – *wid ya like tae try some gin*?) that the airside windows over the other side of MacDeardry's Brewhouse and Kitchen are – it surprises me – still dark. The darkness surprises me, but I am on my way, and what will they think of me? I sit with two cups of tea made from one bag, one brown sugar in each, and I write in my notebook. Jonny used to say I was too British, back when we first met, taking all my little rituals as humorously emblematic – everyone else screws up their nose (brown sugar in tea? Two cups from one bag?). Jonny has always had a habit of acting like he knows everything, and dragging along in his wake all those who believe him – which, I suppose, at one time included me.

I sit with two cups of tea from one bag and I write in my notebook. I write about my heart. I look inside and write what's in my heart. I write what I think I am like now, what I think I was like in the past. I write about the overpowering guzzling thirst that lives always inside me. I write about Jonny. I wish to fuck with all my wishing heart that my fucking heart would stop telling my pen to do that. But still I write. Early morning early winter gloomy beyond the airplaned glass.

*

We met in the middle of a snowstorm by the East China Sea. In Busan, to be precise, in the university district. A beer bar had been turned into an art gallery for the evening, then into a rock club, and a group of Dae Woo's Kyungsung Uni buddies were blasting their way through a set of Korean surf-rock: twangle-dangle

Ramones covers and so on. Appropriate, in the California of Korea, and weirdly refreshing in the chill. Busan doesn't hit the frozen, twenty-below-zero heights (depths?) of Gangwon-do or, on a bad day, Seoul, but it can get close, and this particular year – 2013 if you must know – it was giving it a go. There'd been October typhoons, November frost, Christmas snow on Haeundae beachfront. Twenty-six and partnerless, I'd spent Christmas with a group of other expat teachers in some American boy's apartment in Gwangali, eating 7/11 ramyeon and instant ddeokbokki and playing soju drinking games, watching YouTube videos, playing ironic Christmas playlists, karaokeing in a nearby noraebang (closed at Christmas? Pull the other one), wandering the streets, nailing Jägerbombs in one of the foreigner bars. There'd been an Irish girl and her Australian beau, and Sunny – my best Korean friend from the language school. She gave the American boy head in the bathroom, back in his apartment, with the door kind of open, as I snuggled with a Canadian (clothes on, everyone there, boner against my thigh). She quit before the New Year classes and I never saw her again. She got a job in Seoul, she told me, in one of the twelve IMs I got from her before she completely removed herself from my life.

Dae Woo was a sweet guy. Round-chinned, stout and smiley, thirty-ish. He tutored the kids in maths and science while I tried to teach them the past participle. He had no wife, no kids, lived with his ageing parents, and he embraced friendships with foreigners with an enthusiasm rooted in a desire to improve his English but which felt disarmingly innocent, as if a beaming child in the playgroup had come up and taken your hand and told you to come and play. It took a while to come to terms with the kind of friendships I was able to have with Koreans. Married couples would lavish you with generosity, family dinners, camping invitations with the kids, and the younger unmarrieds would whisk you out on the town, pound soju in food tents or drive you to edge-of-nowhere seafood joints (and pound soju). They'd teach you Korean drinking games (who knew the numbers printed on the underside of soju caps could provide such fun), beam and joke in blunted English. Then the inevitable discarding – and the realisation that no bond had existed at all. Transaction complete. So it goes. It makes as much sense being irked as it does yelling at the rain – which I'd seen more than one hammered office drone doing at eight p.m. on a mucky Wednesday night in the gusts around Gwangali.

But if I had to put my money on anyone, for genuine warmth I mean, it would be Dae Woo. He was bopping in his best Hawaiian, arm draped platonically around his best friend's bob-cutted monolingual wife. They are good! I are – ah, I they are – ah, I sink: very good! His sentences would often start and restart as he realigned his grammar cogs. They are good, yeah, I said, modelling the correct form, as I'd learned to do when teaching. I think they're good too. There were a whole lot of people there that night who I'd never seen before and would never see again, college kids, local hipsters, a cluster of the worst kind of expats, the kind I avoided like the plague: caterwauling drinkers who murdered the three words they'd bothered to half-learn and treated Koreans like mildly amusing labradors. The band's singer-bassist was junky-skinny and Patti Smith-haired – no Korean women looked like her, but there she was, rounding off the consonants to a Beach Boys Blitzkrieg Bop as the mop-haired guitarist, Dae Woo's buddy, chimed in with his off-key back-up. Outside it was really coming down – there were voices in the doorway, the stamp stamp stamp of snowboots – and this power chord twangle was bouncing around inside me like laser beams. I hadn't been sleeping. There was this awful nighttime pageant that had taken on a life of its own. I squirmed away, through the head-nodders. The snow was falling in sheets, falling like kisses, like wrapping paper – fat quiet gobs that darted and shunted in silence. I hadn't been a happy person, I would realise later, but at this point I was still locked in situation management. Slaying the dragon in front of me, with smirks, and denial, leather jackets, and ballroom twirls in the snow. I heard Spanish voices, and saw two men in the doorway: the one with the eyes was Jonny.

Hold it – future me says. Hold up there kiddo, madam, put the brakes on there snowflake. Eyes? A doorway? A snowstorm waltz? Cut the crap, past me. See things as they are. A moment is a moment is a moment, no? And what was there to this moment? A twenty-six-year-old woman at sea in a country she barely understood, running from one she understood all too well, in seven kinds of pain, all of it pushed down deeper than the Sewol, three bottles of Korean beer, and a buyer who knew a bargain when he saw one. Fuck off, future me.

*

It was a photography show, I told him, in the alcove under the stairway, over very strong rum and cokes, the music muffled enough that if we held our heads crooked to each others' ears we could just about hear. Before the music started I mean, I said. Uh-hgugh, he said, with that guttural Madrileño vowel that I would later cease to notice, but which then, five inches from his generously lashed eyes (there go the eyes again), bordered on the erotic. Some of the work was on the wall behind us: a triptych of nicely composed black-and-white studies of a Korean guy in bed. Naked under the sheet, his face was mostly hidden in the pillow, under his arm, but you could see the dark scrags of his pit hair, the paleness of uncreased lines on his raised arm's belly, a Vaseliney light, white as paper, diffusing from the apartment window beyond, and through it the blankness of a monochrome sky. It was Dae Woo's underarm, Dae Woo's pit hair, his pale unfolded skin, and the name on the card underneath the second piece, Koh Soong Geum, belonged to the best friend's bob-haired wife. I'd helped to hang them.

Jonny looked at them, leaning into the wall, a sideshow solo dribbling in the din. His neck was slim, and though he had a composed, groomed quality, the hair behind his ears was soft and skewed in little messy tufts. He said something that I couldn't hear very well.

What's that? I said.

He turned his handsome head back toward the music. Yeah is good, he said. I like fotografía. He used the Spanish, as if he'd forgotten not to, and I wanted to swim around in his long o. Iss a real art form. I have a ca-meh-rah, and he gulped at his mostly rum. I could tell you about the rest of the night. I could tell you about the shots I made us drink, and how eventually, when we'd drifted again into discussing the work on the walls, I pointed out the two pictures that were mine. You might like to know what the pictures were of, or how he reacted, but I'm not going to tell you. I don't want to. I don't want to remember that. You can make that bit up for yourselves. But I'll remember for you how he bit my lip on the subway train as it took us toward his part of town, Nampo-dong, and how there hadn't been any ajoshis or ajummas around to glare; how his room had smelled of recently sweated clothes and exotic things I couldn't name, and hash, and how we'd smoked a joint on his bed as he played Manu Chao through his phone. How his body was leaner and different to the other bodies I'd had, and how he drank plum wine from a clear plastic tumbler throughout, and how the East Asia beyond the window seemed to meld with Madrid.

Photography hadn't been much of a thing for me before – a passing interest only, left over from a single first year undergrad course, and the days of film studies, of analysing frames. When my grandad died I got his Olympus reflex, and when I left Scotland I took it along like a friend. Constructing pictures made me feel less alone. Displaying them on walls made me feel stupid. Jonny made me come twice – no other person had for a year, more. I never collected the pictures – for all I know they're still there.

When you live with emptiness inside you, the tendency is to fill it. With booze, for example, or dicks. Jonny moved into my apartment in Yeonje-gu on the fourteenth floor of a block above a pharmacy, three weeks after the snowstorm. His landlady, he said, was a psycho, and he preferred to stay at mine. We moved some of his work shirts into my Formica wardrobe; his backpack found a spot next to the bed, between my piles of semi-clean clothes and half-read books (care-worn second-hand things that made their way from ex-pat to ex-pat: Alex Garland and Harry Potter and Orwell and Le Carré). We drank with his friends in the foreigner bars – other Spanish speakers, Americans, a cluster of cackling British boys, the kind I'd left the UK to avoid. We watched videos in bed, he played his guitar (nylon-stringed, always out of tune), we gobbled up each other's bodies. I stopped learning Korean, started on Spanish. He made me thirsty. We bought the cheapest bottles the 7/11 had: fifteen thousand won for a bottle of Casillero del Diablo but only four thousand for a plum wine, two thousand for soju. We made mixers out of Fanta, Sunkist, Dr Pepper, ate Cheetos and slimy packaged sausages and triangle kimbap for tea. Went out to the bars, sopped up with two a.m. bibimbaps with Kaolan and Carly and Joaquin in the orange restaurants that stay open as long as there are hungry drinkers in need of hot rice and cold water.

Okay, future me says, all right. I'll take it like that if that's how you wanna throw it. If that's the game you wanna play, I'll strap on my pads. But tell it like it is girlie. See if you can do that. Clutch into the memory pond and see if you can wrap your hands around a fish. Not as easy as you make it seem. Give us a for instance.

Like what, future me?

Some details. What did he taste like?

Like flesh and blood and saunas. Happy?

What did his ears look like, his feet, his neck?

His Adam's apple bobbed as he swallowed. He was long and lucid, like a dream that isn't.

Were you drunk all the time?

No, just lots. On his birthday for instance. You want that one? It's a classic. We went up to Sokcho to climb Mount Seoraksan, with Kaolan and Carly, but we got too drunk instead, stayed up to gone four howling power ballads in a noraebang, went back to the one double room in the shoreside love motel we'd chosen to share to save money and I made out with Carly while they watched. Happy now?

Are *you*? Take us back to the orange restaurant. You're sobering up on hotplate bibimbap. How is it? Tell us.

The rice is crisping and sizzling on the bottom of the heated bowl. The metal cup is cool and wet.

And?

And my body knows its hunger and its thirst are about to be quenched, for a bit, for a while, until they're back, in the morning, with a headache and a gasping throat etc, but for a while there's hot rice and cold water.

And?

Jonny's talking to Kaolan about why Asians make crappy students.

And?

And I don't want to play this game any more.

So don't. You're in an airport before dawn. What can you see?

I can see the girl with the gin. She's wearing a branded apron, carefully folded, and a thin black cardigan over a polo shirt. She's holding the tray in tired arms as she talks to a stout coffee-skinned guy in high-viz overalls – maybe a baggage handler. Outside the favourable lighting of the perfume grotto she has dark rings encircling her eyes.

She puts the tray down once the stout guy has left, sits. She looks over her left shoulder, over her right, and necks one of the gins.

I look down at the paper in front of me. On this page, I have written

What I Think I Am Like Right Now

Underneath that, I have written what I think I am like right now. I won't bore you with the details, but the findings are, at best, mixed.

A tannoy announcement calls for the family Mahmoud to make their way to gate twenty-seven.

Underneath what I think I am like right now, I have written

What I Would Like To Be

and under this I have written

Happy

There are other things too, but that's the headline. The tannoy implores the family Mahmoud to make their way to gate twenty-seven.

So I ask myself if sitting here with my coffee is making me happy. I ask myself if the choices I ordinarily make have succeeded, generally speaking, in making me happy. I approach the gin girl.

Hi, I say, mind if I sit here?

She looks surprised and confused as I sit at the table next to her. I was watching you from over there, I tell her. I saw you drink one of those gins. I'd join you, only I'm an alcoholic, so. Not my thing anymore. She looks, now, less like she's about to call me a psycho and walk off. She looks a bit like an exhausted little girl, which is almost exactly how I feel. I'd like to take your picture, I say to her. I'm a photographer, see? I show her the camera. And if you don't mind, I'd like to take your picture.

It is seven twenty-four in the morning and still dark, but edging from black to blue. The screens with the departure gate updates say I should await information. The gin girl's name is Deb – Deborah.

I told her, looking at her through my camera, that you don't meet a lot of Deborahs these days, and she shrugged and looked over her shoulder as if a duty manager or nosey traveller might be watching her.

Through my camera's digital screen I framed her. The overhead strip lighting exaggerated the dark rings under her troubled young eyes, so I asked her to turn to the side, to look away from the camera. I took a stream of images, the yellow of the airport signage creating a faint glow around her hair as she looked off towards the strip of brand outlets lining the path to gates 11–18. She looked nervous. As if life had been quite hard on her, and taught her to expect the worst.

Yer an alky? she'd asked, once we'd finished. Yes, I told her. An alcoholic is what I am. One of the things that I am.

Ya dinnae look like one, she said, fiddling at the hem of her polyester skirt.

What do they look like? I asked. But she didn't seem to like that, seemed to take it as a rebuke, and she went back inside her shell, started saying she had to get back to work.

I'm sorry, I told her, I didn't mean to sound short or whatever. I just meant that lots of different people can be addicts. That we don't necessarily match the image people have in their heads for us.

Right, she said, standing and straightening her half-apron.

That was part of what made it hard for me to see what I was, I said.

So why wis you an alky then? she said. She sounded even younger than she looked.

Because I was sad, I said. She left, with her tray of gins in plastic shot glasses, back to the perfume, but not before letting me see, through her expression, through her shoulders, and her breathing, that she understood very well, and not before sitting back down and exchanging some nice words – some for me, some for her.

Not before asking what I'd do with the photos of her, and not before asking me where I was flying to, and why.

To Madrid, I told her.

Holiday? she asked.

No, I said. Well, yes, but – no. I'm going to see someone I haven't seen in a while.

She didn't seem to need to know more than that, and I didn't seem to need to tell her. It is seven-forty-six in the morning, and the black has started to blue, out beyond the parked planes and the very flat grass and concrete beyond them. Still early morning, still early winter, and what will they think of me? I have eighteen photos of her in my device, and I look at them now, one after the other, even though the screen with the departure gate updates is now telling me in green font to go to gate. Her name is Deborah, and I magnify the images so I can look more closely. Her name is Deborah, and I told her I would send her her photos by email. Her name is Deborah, and you don't meet many of them these days. Her name is Deborah, and angled away the dark drifts under her eyes can barely be seen.

Niall O'Gallagher
***MISE* AGUS PANGUR BÁN**

Mise agus Pangur Bán
– cat mo sheanar sa Chreagán –
bhitheamaid a' cluich gun sgìos
mise 's Pangur, nar dithis.

Cliste agus luath na spòig
rinn e snaidhm nam shreangan bròig'
ach gearain, cha tuirt mi smid
– b' e Pangur mo dhlùth-charaid.

Coma leinn is sinn a' cluich
na bha tachairt taobh a-muigh;
bu bheag fios gille no cait
air cogadh, fòirneart, àimhreit.

Chluicheamaid, leis nach robh cead
an taigh fhàgail, falach-fead;
ghlacainn Pangur Bán fo cheal
oir dh'fhàg e 'm follais earball;

is dh'fhalbhadh Pangur na dheann
mar sheabhaig, fiadh no bradan
is ruithinn tron taigh le tlachd
air mo dhòigh is aighearach.

Nuair bha Mam aig an stairsnich
dhèanadh Pangur siosarnaich
gus nach toireadh i gu ceann
ar cuid spòrs is dibhearsain.

Cat is gille, gille 's cat,
leth-aona dìleas, leam-leat
gaisgich an dèidh na Fèinne
ann an saoghal troimh-chèile.

On uair sin tha iomadh là
ach tillidh mo mhac-meanmna
don taigh san robh sinne slàn,
mise agus Pangur Bán.

Kailee Parsons

THE LAST DYING EMBERS

Cate held the laundry room door open for Delia, pressing the heavy wood against the broken hinge so it didn't creak. When no one appeared, she poked her head inside and found the last member of their group applying rose-coloured chapstick in the dusty mirror above the sink. 'Hurry up,' she chided. 'They're leaving without us.'

It was unlikely that any staff would appear in the laundry room so late at night, but Cate thought the chapstick could wait until they made their escape. Ahead of them, a line of girls made their way up the drive to the forest. Delia clicked the cap into place and Cate closed the door gingerly behind her before they hurried to catch up to the group.

The girls carrying torches switched them on, swinging the beams of light along the muddy ground. They let themselves out through the gate and climbed the hill to the forest that bordered the school property. They could hear voices now, the soft strains of laughter and conversation of students already at the fire.

A fallen tree marked the entrance of the clearing. From the right, a group of boys passed in single file, carrying more firewood down from the hill where it was hidden. Campfires were not allowed on school grounds, but the sweet smell of sun-dried grass promised summer, and the boarding students wanted to break one last rule before they left.

There were already thirty students gathered around the makeshift fire pit, a little hole in the ground marked by the remains of burnt kindling from October, the last time there was coursework little enough and weather dry enough for a fire. Fallen logs were dragged closer for seating, and groups of friends were gathered around them, four or five students to a log, with another two on blankets in the damp dirt, leaning against the bark for support. It was conspicuous to say the least, but the groundskeeper rarely ventured into the woods, as evidenced by the fact the Deputy Head had not reprimanded anyone over dinner.

One log was unclaimed, with only space for two and positioned several feet from the fire. As the other girls joined their friends in the dirt or shimmied closer to boyfriends to create room, Cate brushed her fingertip against the log and, finding that it was dry, took a seat.

Delia sat down and began to play with the zipper of her coat, the plastic scraping up and down in a high-pitched squeal. Cate shot her a sidelong glance, but she didn't seem to notice. Delia scanned the crowd. 'Where's Isaiah? He told me he was coming.'

Cate watched the flames lick up a marshmallow left too long in the embers, turning it red, blue, black. After a moment, there was a chorus of screams and laughter, and the boy holding the stick shouted and flung it into the fire, where it crumbled into ashes. Cate was jostled to the side as Delia's hand shot up and began to wave. The rough fabric of her winter coat scraped against Cate's shoulder as she bounced to her feet.

Cate averted her eyes, not wanting to give her friends the satisfaction of seeing them together. Or perhaps she didn't want to see Isaiah in his black corduroy jacket for the last time. They would say goodbye tomorrow in the warmth of day, but she preferred to remember the jacket draped over her own shoulders where he had placed it on a walk some weeks ago. It was nothing more than a kindness between friends – it was late afternoon and she was cold; he saw a need and filled it. That was fine with her. Now that Isaiah and Delia were dating, however, his kindness was reserved for Delia alone.

In turn, Delia lavished her attention entirely upon him. It had been weeks since she last appeared in Cate's room hours after curfew, the light from the windows reflecting off her blonde curls, and beckoned Cate to the back staircase. There, they could climb into the wide window ledge, knobbly knees bumping, and talk at full volume, about divorce, ailing parents, sex, music, French philosophers, and the trysts and breakups of their classmates. Now, when Delia talked to Cate, she talked about Isaiah.

There was a piece of broken glass near Cate's foot, the remnants of a bottle discarded at the last campfire. She traced its shape in her mind to keep from thinking, but it failed to block out the grating sound of Delia's high-pitched giggle when Isaiah whispered something too quiet for Cate to hear. She chewed the inside of her cheek and waited until she heard their voices dissipate, the crunch of their footsteps growing softer as they retreated the way she and Delia had come.

She wondered if he had even seen her, realised that by taking Delia he was leaving her alone. Surely it bothered Joey, too, even if, on the surface, the fourth member of their friendship quartet appeared unmoved, following Delia and Isaiah around like a bumbling dog, tail wagging, oblivious to the fact he was unwanted.

'Hello, everybody.'

Cate glanced up at the sound of a German accent, surprised to find Joey standing before the fire, beaming. A few heads swivelled to face him and there was a weak chorus of polite greetings before the group lapsed into previous conversations.

Cate was used to this lack of reticence. Joey believed he was universally loved, and as a result, he loved universally, or perhaps it was the other way around. In either case, he was too earnest for subtle British sensibilities, and speaking English as a second language created a further divide. They became friends as outsiders in a cold country, along with Isaiah, the Canadian, and Delia, who liked that they were different. Joey pointed at the log. 'All right if I sit here?'

She answered in the affirmative, but the sound was drowned by the raucous laughter of a group of boys now burning marshmallows for fun, heaping them into a bubbly, ashen mass. Joey sat down. Cate glanced over at him and watched strange shadows cast by the fire climb across his face, distorting his features. But it was still him, just as he always was. She looked away.

'After six years you really think you'd be sick of a place, eh?' he said.

She picked up a stick and prodded the dirt with it.

He heaved a sigh. 'Or maybe I love it more than ever.'

'I'm ready to leave.'

He looked at her sharply. 'Really? Do you mean that?'

'I miss home.' Cate finished drawing a cloud around the green glass bottle with the stick.

Joey admired it briefly before surveying the group around the fire with a small smile. 'For me, this is home.'

'Joey' was short for something she had once tried to pronounce, which started with a 'J' but sounded like a 'Y' and contained several syllables that required Cate to make a hissing sound at the back of her throat, the kind that sounded nice when spoken by German girls but made Cate sound like a snake with a cold. After a week of this, he ditched the German and rechristened himself Joey, a name he regarded as all-American because he'd heard it on *Friends*, surely possible for her to pronounce, but which sounded to Cate like a baseball player from the 1950s.

Delia had recently changed her name to Cordelia on all her social media accounts. It had not caught on as fast as Joey.

'Cut it out,' she said. 'I mean it. Really.'

'What?'

'I can't take any of your melodramatic philosophical crap tonight.'

'I wasn't—'

'No, I know, but I can tell you're going to get all sentimental and say you love the *at*mosphere of the school grounds at night or something, and I'm really not in the mood—'

She glanced up at him. Although she couldn't see well in the dark, she was sure there was a trace of hurt in his freckled brown eyes, like the time he had offered to go to the shops for her and she had turned him down, not wanting to owe him a favour in return. He pulled back. 'All right.'

'No, I'm sorry, I didn't mean that,' said Cate. She looked back at the fire and the people with whom she had spent the better part of six years. 'Maybe I will miss it.'

He was silent, so she bumped her shoulder against his. 'Don't listen to me. I'm a mess tonight, honestly.'

Cate looked away again. Her eyes stung from the smoke and tears pricked the back of her eyelids. There was a slight breeze, unseasonably cold, and the smoke trailed to the other side of the fire pit. A couple of girls shrieked, there were a few theatrical coughs, and someone said, 'Smoke follows beauty.'

Joey leaned closer to the fire hugging his knees. 'So cool about Isaiah and Delia, right?'

She looked sideways at him. 'You're joking.'

He laughed, but it was throaty, forced. 'What do you mean?'

'You're honestly happy about the situation?'

'I'm happy for them.'

'That's not the same thing, Joe,' Cate said.

His smile faltered. 'You're not?'

'I think it's a huge mistake. They won't even live in the same country next month.'

Joey considered this. 'Is that why you don't hang out with us any more?'

Cate said nothing, but jabbed the dirt again. It was true that she had become friends with the girls in her English class quite suddenly, and had spent the whole of the previous afternoon in the library, scrolling through the Boston University website, her mind firmly rooted in plans for the following year.

'I don't think it's a huge mistake,' Joey said. 'I just hate that it's the last week of us all being together. It's the last week of my life, and I'm spending it alone.'

'It's not the last week of your life,' she said, but she knew what he meant.

She leaned the stick against the log and picked at a splinter in the palm of her hand. When she looked up, Joey was staring at her with a dopey look on his face. 'I'm going to miss you, you know.'

She knew. It reminded her why they had stopped talking, just the two of them, and she felt self-conscious. The splinter removal was a messier affair than anticipated. She wiped the blood on her jeans.

Beside her, Joey wrapped his arms around himself. 'Doesn't this feel strange without Isaiah and Delia?'

'Not really.'

He looked over at her with big, solemn eyes. 'Do you think I'll ever forget what they look like? Once we're gone, in the future, I mean.'

'I wouldn't worry. You're going to see pictures of him all over her Instagram as soon as we leave,' said Cate. 'Except they'll be old ones, the ones *you* took, until they're on the same continent again.'

Joey smirked. She remembered him saying he loved the way she said whatever was on her mind, as long as it was true. He liked it less when she said she only loved him as a friend.

'I know it's important they spend time together before we leave, but it seems so selfish,' he said. He made a sound somewhere between a laugh and a groan, and rolled his head into his cupped palms. 'And it's selfish of me to think that.'

When he looked up, he wore a sheepish smile. If the night sky were any brighter, Cate would have seen the colour in his cheeks. 'Plus, I'd started to like Cordelia,' he said.

Cate looked away, past the broken glass to the knobbly line of trees. She knew he had, which was a funny feeling. She was grateful his childish crush on her had passed and they could go back to being friends, but the substitute was disappointing. There was not a single moron not in love with Delia. She could slander a boy to his face and leave him enchanted, swearing he had never seen such a goddess. At least she was relieved to find she wasn't the only one feeling silly right then. She almost said the thing she wanted to say about Isaiah but stopped herself.

He continued. 'I knew it would never happen, but—'

'Why?' she snapped.

Joey blinked. 'Why what?'

'Why did you know it would never happen? She's just a girl, for God's sake.'

'Because Isaiah really liked her,' said Joey. 'For almost the whole year.'

'He *lied* to me the whole year,' she said. 'He's such an asshole. I asked him if he liked her, and I knew he was lying, but—'

Joey let out a nervous laugh. She still couldn't believe Delia had waited twelve hours to tell her about she and Isaiah, and Cate had actually had to confront Isaiah before he spilled the details. They were friends, weren't they?

With Delia, she could understand. She was closed off, mysterious. They were friends, yes, but Delia only divulged personal information on her own time and Cate never pressed her. But Isaiah was always asking questions and answering them in return.

There were so many times he could have mentioned his feelings for Delia. While they were watching a movie, for example, or during one of their night-time expeditions to the staff kitchen to steal hot chocolate or, on one lucky occasion, alcohol leftover from a Christmas party. He could have told her on any number of weekend day trips on the 61 bus – could have removed the earbuds they were sharing and told her before she fell asleep on his shoulder on the way home.

She had seen the way he looked at Delia, of course, and had asked, but he always waved her off with a reminder of the pretty girl he had left waiting in Winnipeg. 'He sent Morgan a love letter a month ago,' said Cate. 'He told me they had a date when he got home. It makes me sick.'

'They were never really dating, though, were they?'

'They were doing more than flirting, Joey. They sent *love* letters. In the *mail*.'

'But he hasn't seen her lately. He's been here for three years, excluding summers.'

Cate put her chin in her hand. She wanted to cry or kick something and hated herself for it. The question which had plagued her throughout the week resurfaced in her mind. As if reading it on her face, Joey said, 'Why are you so upset about this?'

He had that dimple between his eyebrows that appeared whenever he was worried. She could not bear for Joey to worry about her, so she fumbled for an answer, not knowing whether it was correct. 'I thought he could tell me anything.'

Joey shrugged. 'He was embarrassed, I guess. What if she didn't like him back? You've never done that?'

Cate felt a pang in her heart. 'It was a shitty thing to do to Morgan.'

'She was a sure thing, in case Delia didn't work out.'

Cate shook her head. 'Why can't people like each other enough to tell them or care enough to say when they don't?' A blonde girl from their Latin class was staring, so Cate lowered her voice and attempted to steady it. 'Fuck, I did, Joey, and I'm sorry I hurt you, but it's better than leading you on, isn't it? Morgan is a human being. Isaiah is our friend, and he kept her around for *backup*.'

Joey looked down at his palms. The blonde resumed her conversation with the girl next to her, and for a while, the only sound came from the crackling fire and the chatter of other students. Joey stopped looking at his hand and ran it along the damp moss of the log.

'I liked you the whole bloody year.'

He had picked that up from boarding in Scotland. *Bloody.*

Cate leaned her chin in her cupped palm. 'But we're fine now, right?'

'Yeah, we're fine,' said Joey.

She hoped that was true. Funny, she had spent the past few months avoiding being alone with him, and now he was the only one of the three she could picture writing to her at college. Cate picked some moss off the log. 'Do you think they'll get married?'

'Maybe.'

She nodded. 'Do you think you'll forget me?'

He grinned. 'Definitely. The moment we leave.'

She shoved her shoulder against his again. He laughed and pushed her back.

The embers of the fire were dying. Most of the students remained, but there was no attempt to save or revive it. A cool breeze tickled the back of their necks, and Cate shivered.

Joey stood. 'Let me walk you back.'

She thought about it for a moment, how annoyed she would be if anyone caught them walking together. The boarding school was small, and everyone knew something of each drama but never enough. They had seen him touch her back in the dining hall, but had missed the private conversation afterwards where she raised her voice and reminded him they were not a couple.

Why had she done that? He had chosen her over Delia. It would have been perfect, two and two. Neither of them would feel forgotten; neither would have to leave so tragically single. Yes, they would be miles apart, but she could brag about her German boyfriend the way Delia would surely talk of Isaiah . . .

She didn't like him, though, not like that. She loved him as a friend. She remembered a time when Delia chided Isaiah to wipe some crumbs off his face, and another when she had swept his brown hair just so to cover the part that was thinning, and doubted that she loved him. But maybe Joey was right, it wasn't her place to be upset.

Joey was still waiting for an answer. She thought about the branches and rocks and mud and the darkness, and how she hadn't brought a torch. She realised she didn't want to say goodbye to him now, not yet. 'Sure. Thanks.'

He flicked on the torch. They walked through the woods and down the hill to the old, stone building. They came to a halt around the back of the school, where the only unlocked door to the girls' dormitory hung off its hinges. Joey thanked Cate for letting him walk with her and she thanked him for his torch.

'I should let you go,' he said.

Cate hesitated, thinking about the morning. There would be luggage bumping down the carpeted steps of the grand staircase of the girls' house. In the quad, people hugging, crying, laughing – a mess of emotions she could not unravel. Coaches would be parked in front of the main entrance, waiting to take departing students to train stations and airports, away from each other indefinitely, or at least until plans were made, tickets were booked, and time was set aside to see each other again. She could already hear Delia and Isaiah promising to visit – after all, she was not so far from Canada! – but she couldn't see it happening. For the first time, she let the truth settle on her like softly falling rain: she would probably never see them again.

Cate threw her arms around Joey and hugged him tightly. She felt his back stiffen. When he recovered from the surprise, he hugged her back, and for several moments, neither let go. He was good at hugging, felt solid and warm in her embrace.

Eventually, she let go. She turned toward the door without looking back, opened it carefully, pressing the broken hinge to the wall so it didn't make a sound. As the door closed, she heard him say 'goodnight' on the other side. She slipped around the corner through the dark and up the stone steps to bed.

Martin Raymond
REQUEST STOP

The bus was late. Or early.

Early was worse. When it was early you turned up on time but had no idea whether it was still to arrive or was long gone. You could only be sure if you hung around for the next bus, an hour later. The timetable was on the shelter wall, behind much abused perspex. In the small print, which I had often read to fill in the long hour, it stated you had to be there *ten minutes in advance of the stated time*, just in case. It was unfair, gamed towards the operator.

In this village I was often the only person waiting. There was one other today, standing back a little from the shelter. I'd seen him before. But that time, a week or so previously, he'd been speaking to another irregular passenger, a woman in advanced middle age, who always gave off an air of polite contempt for her fellow travellers. Polite for me at least. For him she jumped to contempt, and his slurred greeting had been crushed underfoot like a brittle insect.

Today it was just him and me, so I studied my phone carefully. I'd lived in this village for more than two decades, so I knew how to deal with drunks. No eye contact, but if addressed don't ignore, stay cool, non-committal and all will be well.

'Damp conditions.' His voice seemed to come from another person. Or from another time. Clear, authoritative and what my mother would call 'educated.'

He was right, it wasn't actually raining, but the pavements and the stone church across the road had leached the wetness out of the air. The steeple would have been glistening, if there had been enough light.

I looked up at the sky, as a way of not looking in his direction.

'It might brighten later though.' I said. Just enough animation to be friendly, not enough to invite anything more.

'These buses,' he said. The statement hung there. I did loathe commuting. The hour in a bus either icy cold or overheated, eerily empty or even more scarily full. But I did need a break from working at home with my mother noisily downstairs. There was no shame in living with my mother still, at my stage in life. It had become normal. I didn't go to the tiny Edinburgh office for company; it was rare to find a colleague there. I went occasionally to feel I hadn't become completely inert. The job involved buying tons of tiny chopped up bits of wood for a Swedish multi-national. It was what was left after the actual timber had been carefully extracted from the forest. When the mulched debris became available, I pounced electronically and bought it up. The bit that couldn't be algorithmed yet, was the negotiation of dates and transport. Stimulus. Response. Completion. It wasn't much different from the evening games I played with my friends all over the world. Or my relationship with transactional porn sites. I was barely twelve months ahead of AI.

'Yes,' I said, 'the buses.' I bounced his enigmatic tone right back. Confident the bus could not be too much longer, I risked a look. His shoes were black dress Oxfords, still with ghost of a shine but scuffed all over and only one was loosely secured with grey string. There were no socks. I passed over the stains on the suit trousers quickly. The jacket was from another suit altogether, a blue one, fastened with the bottom button only, over a sweatshirt of no colour at all. I avoided his eyes, but his face was frosted with white stubble. Thin and with no sign of a stoop, he was carrying a bag of shopping – limited shopping – just the Special Brew cans, fresh from the chiller cabinet, wet and visible, stuck to the filmy plastic.

I looked back down the main street. It's the position we travellers all took. A yearning to see the blue and yellow bus swinging round the junction at the end of the street.

There was a movement in the cool spring air and I turned to see him go down like a felled tree, so straight and tall that his head arrived on the pavement first. The noise was not like a tree. More like a dropped item in the frozen fish aisle. Blood spread out over the pavement, slow, thick and relentless, like lava.

On my knees on the wet ground, I looked round. No one. The sibilance of passing traffic. I looked down, his eyes were wide open. A beautiful grey-blue. I was all for eye contact now. But there was nothing doing from his side, just a long stare towards the distant clouds.

'Don't be sick. Don't stop breathing,' I said. Out loud, though I wasn't sure which of us I was talking to. His cans lay corralled in the bag. I could see one at least was extravagantly dented. And then a voice behind me:

'Is he breathing?'

'I think so.'

I had no evidence one way or another. He wasn't blue or gasping, but there wasn't much movement. There was a woman behind me wearing a white coat. God was not indifferent after all. She had a blanket and an air of calm. She handed me the blanket. I wasn't sure what to do with it and made to put it under his head. In the blood.

'No, no, no.' Her charity had limits. 'Cover him up – he'll be in shock. Keep him warm. I'm the pharmacist. Round the corner. I've phoned for an ambulance, it'll be here soon.' I turned to thank her. It was such a relief not to be kneeling there, alone and responsible. But she'd gone. Then the screaming started.

It was a mum with her primary-school-age daughter. I'm not good with children's ages. The daughter was doing the screaming, but the mum looked at me as if I might have knocked him over.

'Oh,' the girl wailed over her shoulder, as she was hustled down the street. 'Was that blood mummy?'

I didn't need that level of drama. His eyes were still focused on the distant grey sky and there was a faint stirring under his sweatshirt: hardly animated. As if he had accepted his fate. There was even the trace of a smile around his dry, cracked lips. Wet seeped through my jeans at the knee. But I was locked here, an incompetent supplicant until the ambulance, please God, arrived.

But it was the bus that turned up. Growling up to the stop. There was a sharp intake of air as the doors opened. No one got on, and no one got off. I turned to the driver. He looked down, a lofty spectator with a schedule to keep. He raised his eyebrows. I shook my head. He took in the scene a second longer and with a last, gasping breath, the doors closed.

I was alone again. Even the traffic seemed to have thinned. Were people taking a longer route to avoid the sight? The few pedestrians were all on the opposite pavement. An occasional blink and the tiny twitches round his lips were encouraging. He did look like death, but then he had looked that way when he was still vertical.

'Are you okay?'

It was a woman, thirties maybe. My age, more or less. She wore neat little black boots, black leggings and a dark grey jumper that was slightly too big and asymmetric at the neck. Normally that lack of symmetry would unsettle me, but I could see her collar bone and a gold chain so fine it was like a faint glimmer of sunlight along the contours of her neck and shoulder.

'Well, I think he's breathing still.'

'No, I meant you. Someone said you'd been here for ages with him.' Her hair was pulled back into a sort of twist impaled by a wooden peg thing. But pulled back like she'd done it with her fingers – not that she'd caught it in something. 'I'm just back from taking the kids to school or I'd have come along sooner. I just live down there.' She nodded towards where the street ran out of the village. 'I'm a nurse.'

Thank fuck, I thought.

'Thank God,' I said.

'I'm a paediatric nurse, though, so this isn't really my specialty.' She was hunkered down on the other side of the old boy. Unlike me she hadn't put her knees down in the wet ground. Perhaps it was the extremity of the situation, but I looked her directly in the eye, more than a glance. They were green and looked as if they were lit from inside. I even kept looking in her eyes as I said:

'I'll settle for that. I've really no idea at all what I'm doing.'

'He looks okay.' She looked down and gave him what I imagined was a professional appraisal. 'Ish.'

'Should I put him in a recovery position?'

She pushed down the blanket and patted his hand. They were crossed over his chest like an effigy. Had I placed them there? Her nails were the colour of nails, but each a perfect luminescent oval. 'Not if he's conscious and responding. I think he'll be fine.'

The blood had stopped its advance over the paving slabs. It was darker than before, with a skin forming. His thin white hair was attached to the mess. I thought of Gulliver tied down on the beach. Still my favourite story. The awkwardness of never fitting in.

'There's a lot of blood,' I said.

'That's not a lot of blood.' She laughed. Like bits of ice falling into a stream.

'Call that blood!' I said in a voice that was supposed to be a bit like Crocodile Dundee – the scene with the mugger and the knife. She blinked and I was about to explain but she saved me by laughing again:

'You should see what I've seen in training. Gallons. We were slipping about.'

We were hunched now, both of us, over his long body, just a skeleton apart.

'An ambulance is coming. The woman in the pharmacist called them,' I said. 'It's her blanket.'

We were quiet for a bit. The three of us, but strangely, it didn't bother me at all. After a while the ambulance came into view at the end of the street. There was no siren, no light. It was travelling at bus speed towards us.

It was operated by two middle-aged men. Their green jumpsuits had been designed for much younger, more athletic colleagues. I told them about the fall, the head on the pavement, the breathing, while they bustled about the doors and the wheeled platform apparatus. I didn't expect thanks exactly, but I did anticipate slightly more interest. I suppose a fallen drunk wasn't high on their priority list.

'This yours?' said one of them, holding the bundled-up blanket. As I took it, the old boy reached up and took my other hand. With a surprising strength, given his pipe-cleaner frame, not to mention his recent experience, he pulled it towards his mouth. I resisted. Was this a final flourish before the ambulance doors closed on him? Was he going to sink his teeth into me?

She was at my side now. 'He wants to thank you,' she said. 'He wants to kiss your hand.'

His nails were like those of a woodland animal who'd just finished digging out a den in stony ground. I felt his scaly lips on my skin. He squeezed my hand. I squeezed back.

And then he was gone. The pharmacist woman came for her blanket and brought a bucket of water for the blood. It made little difference. The nurse and I stood there awkwardly. I looked away – at the timetable. *This is a request stop. Passengers should signal to the driver if they wish the bus to stop.*

'Is it this exciting around here all the time?' she said.

'Not usually.' I felt something surging in me. It must have been a delayed reaction of some type. Shock, or adrenaline or something.

'I've just moved in here. I'm not sure I can take this level of drama.'

'How long?' I made this bold move – asking a question. There was an odd gathering of energy inside.

'Less than a month. Just me and my girls. They love it. The school's great. This is only the third day off I've had here. It's quiet though – normally. Don't you find?' She was looking right into my eyes now. I was looking right back. Reckless.

And then the bus was there. I hadn't put my hand out, but it stopped anyway. The doors were about to open.

'Would you,' I said, 'like a coffee sometime?'

'Or even a wine. They sell alcoholic beverages out here?'

'Of course.' I'd forgotten what this was like. The excitement of it.

'I need some warning for wine – a babysitter. Give me . . .' She mimed with her lovely nails, tapping on her palm.

I don't hand over my phone, ever. I dumb-show patted my jacket down, then took off my bag. It contained my notebook and the sandwich box my mother had prepared. I handed her the notebook and pen. I felt the driver's eyes on me.

'There,' she said and handed it back. 'That was a good thing you did.'

Then I was on the bus. I didn't want to risk her not waving, so I sat on the outside seat, but she'd crossed the road already and smiled as we swept past.

On these rare commutes, I made a positive effort to not look at my phone. To get away from the screen – advice my mother was keen to give. And the novelty was interesting. I always took a window seat so I could look out on the world, the villages and traffic, with my bag firmly on the outside seat in case anyone was tempted to sit there. Today I looked at my notebook. Many times. I flicked past my neat lists, colour-coded and diligently ticked off, to where her name suddenly appeared on an otherwise extravagantly blank page. *Jennifer.* Her handwriting big and stylish. This was better than having it typed into my phone.

All that day I went back to my notebook – in between the ten texts from my mother. A record even for her. Word travels fast in villages. That night, after a long and in-depth interrogation, where it seemed my mother knew more about what had happened than I did, I went upstairs to my room. To my notebook. I didn't call the number though. I wasn't scared, I only wanted to draw it out.

*

The next day I was up and back at the bus stop. The prospect of all day with my mother, and even the possibility of some of her friends dropping by to milk the drama of all its tiny nuance was too much to bear. There was a passenger waiting already. The middle-aged woman I'd seen before with the old boy was there. She was wearing a coat with a print from an animal I didn't recognise. We both nodded, eyes down. I couldn't see any trace of the blood. It was raining gently so we stood under the arc of the shelter. Both of us turned towards the corner at the end of the street where the bus would appear – like stone monoliths gazing to sea.

'Have you heard?' she said.

'No,' I said.

'They didn't let you know?' She shook her head. I now assumed this was a build up to a big reveal – information only she possessed.

'No,' I said, 'they didn't take my details or anything.' If she had the final paragraph of the story she was making me wait. 'Have *you* heard?'

There was a long silence. Maybe she knew no more than I did. The traffic hissed past and the drops fell from the edge of the shelter.

'He wouldn't thank you.'

We were both now fixed at forty-five degrees to the road, staring out into the thickening rain, less Easter Island now, more fisherfolk on a sea wall, peering into the grey mirk.

'I couldn't leave him,' I said.

'No. Maybe. But he'd probably rather that had been it. Out cold on the pavement. For ever.' She paused, shuffled closer to my shoulder so she could lower her voice. 'You know his story?' She assumed I didn't, and went on. 'He was a big lawyer in Edinburgh. Retired and bought thon house on Harvester's Crescent last year. And then his wife died of cancer. Sudden. She was away in two months. He fell to pieces completely, poor old sod, and he's been killing himself with drink ever since.' We looked at the rain for a second or two. 'He's banned from most of the pubs, only the Polecat will still take his money. Shame.' She sighed. 'Shame. But there we are.'

'Poor man,' I said. I thought about the feel of his lips on the back of my hand and nearly told her. It might not have been gratitude. The bus appeared, and we got on. She sat at the front, I went to my usual place five rows up on the pavement side. She got off at the next village and I went on to town.

*

That night, after we'd eaten, I went upstairs and very carefully cut the page out of my notebook, tore it up thoroughly, put my headphones on and settled down. I reduced it to such tiny pieces that some fell through the bottom of the wicker wastepaper basket and my mother said, didn't I know that she had better things to do than hoover up after me.

Tracey S. Rosenberg

I WANTED TO SEE A WAR

There's a photograph I saw from Bucha.
Two people are lying on the pavement near a stack of
        wooden pallets and a pile of bricks.
They're curled towards each other, almost facing.
I can't tell from the photograph what they mean to each other.
Maybe he fought to protect her and died in rage at his failure.
Maybe they were strangers, unlucky in the same place.
The woman's hands are tied behind her back with a white cloth.
Her fingers are bent over her palms.
Her wrists are bound so tightly, her fingernails are blue.

I want to know why your ex-girlfriend cheers the dictator
        who demolished your city.
I want to understand how she still thinks he's the good guy
even after he tattooed her body with shrapnel scars
and starved you down fifteen kilos.
I want to know why you loved her but you won't love me
and why I feel compelled to walk into your country at war
three years after you walked out.

I don't understand why it's not enough
to be a compassionate spectator in a rubber bracelet,
why I need to step off a train and be in this place –
air raid sirens screaming through the night,
town square memorials with new faces added every day,
flags and flags and so much glory
every other ex-soldier I see
has a metal pole where half his leg used to be.

I want to bind my wrists with shreds of white cloth
and apologise for not knowing what it means to starve.

I want to stand in that space near the pallets and bricks
and know those two people were respectfully buried –
together, if that's what they would have wanted –
then light candles for them in the crypt of a tall white church.
I want you to know how grateful I am that you weren't left
            to die.

I want to know what any of this agony is for.

I want to understand why I want to see this war.

K. H. Ryan
LIBERTY

I remember the shock of finding Da's girlfriend, Selina, seated at our Formica table. And Ma across from her, awkward as a teenager as she smoked one of Selina's gold-tipped Sobranies. I remember how small Ma looked and how straggly her perm was, and how I wished she wasn't wearing the gingham tabard she wore to do the housework. But, of course, I know now she would have been wishing the very same.

Selina was smiling at me. 'You and your sister are going to spend every second weekend with your father and I. It will be a regular thing.' She gave a soft clap, silver rings on every finger, even the thumb. 'Isn't that exciting?'

'That's right.' Ma was putting on a voice. The same voice she used with bank tellers and the insurance man. 'Isn't that exciting?' She glanced at Selina, biting her lip.

The hunting lodge where Selina and Da were living was on the Ayrshire coast at the end of a secluded glen that sloped into hard scrabble and met with the Irish Sea. On a rare clear day, you could see Ireland and the hump of Ailsa Craig always, squat and grim in a constant lash of waves.

Before we went inside, Selina handed wellies to me and my wee sister, Midge. 'The boots are a necessity because of the cats. Some of them are dreadful scratchers. Though do watch out for rats too. Because the cats are terribly lazy.'

The whole estate from Carleton to Lendalfoot belonged to an English laird who was living abroad. He'd lent the lodge to Selina because she'd helped him out of a sticky situation, but what that was, she wouldn't say. The locals were taking the new laird to court because he refused to let them walk through his fields. The court case was nothing to do with her, Selina explained to the butcher, the grocer and all the others in the village. Soon enough, parcels of pheasant, rabbit and dented cans were left on the doorstep. Selina would blow the shopkeepers kisses from her twenty-year-old Lotus on her way to the supermarket in the next town.

The lodge was weary with damp from centuries of rain and sea fog. In some rooms, the wooden beams were swollen and split and water pit-patted into tin buckets and enamel basins. Now and then, a thrust of pale mushrooms would sprout between the floorboards in a foetid vegetable sweat. Other rooms were out of bounds because they were filled with junk: shipping crates, animal traps, ancient perambulators embossed with the Duke's family crest. Da's plan was to clear one of these east-facing rooms and use it as a studio. He was going to paint grand landscapes in the style of Samuel Peploe.

We hardly saw Da. He spent most of the time in the outhouses or in Galashiels learning husbandry at the college, sitting with ripe lads half his age, he said. The plan was that Da and Selina were going to save up and buy a farm. When he was home, he talked a great deal about sheep: the rearing of sheep, the breeding of sheep, the slaughter of sheep and the general ministering of sheep. Selina would ask him questions about his day in the fields or in the classroom, only to leave the room as he was mid-sentence. *I've had an idea*, she'd say. *I must capture it before it fizzles*. Her cigarette would be left smoking in the ashtray and whatever meal she'd concocted from the dented tins in the cupboard congealing on the table. She was writing a great book, the subject of which was a secret unknown.

We two girls weren't meant to step foot in Selina's study. Though, when she and Da were down at the pub, I always made sure to have a good root around. Midge was too feart and kept to the front room, kneeling by the fireplace, praying for my soul. This was around the start of the terrible piousness which would end with her becoming a Carmelite nun at Craigton and cleaving our mother's heart in two.

Selina's study had a tall window that looked out over the swim of sea caught in the mouth of Tarbet Bay. As well as stacks of hardbacks sent up from London, there were Chinese vases, Moore figurines, and Italian etchings on the shelves. Selina would take us to the charity shops in town and while all I could spy were worn versions of the checked shirts and wax jackets Da had taken to wearing, Selina would somehow unearth French mirrors and Russian dolls and Royal Copenhagen that had, she said, belonged to someone with actual taste.

One afternoon, she turned up in a borrowed van, the back filled with tins of paint she'd bought for pennies off a local farmer. He couldn't understand why she would want limewash as it was for barns and outhouses and poor people but by the time the last tin was brushed on the walls, a friend had come up from London to take photos for *Home and Garden*. And the magazine paid too.

'See, my sweet Joseph? Something always turns up.'

No one ever called our Da sweet or even Joseph, for that matter. Not even his own Da who was a church warden, and the only man allowed to polish the priest's shoes before Mass.

In Selina's study, there was a framed photo of her three blonde boys on her desk. Her ex-husband had won the custody case because he'd used devious methods, Da said. The boys stayed on the weekends we weren't there. Family time is so precious, Selina would say, sighing. That she felt this way was why Da had started up seeing us again after not bothering for over a year. No one told us that outright, but we knew it just the same.

The boys had their own room with bunk beds and we girls had the room across the hall with a rash of mould on the ceiling that Midge swore looked like Our Mary, Mother of Christ. Sometimes, I'd sneak into the boys' room and examine their things: rugby balls, ice hockey sticks, the Beano and the Guinness Book of Records with the page folded at *The World's Strongest Man*. I left a note for the eldest in his schoolbook: HELLO NOAH!! I'd used my special strawberry-scented notepaper and decorated it with Fyffes banana stickers. But the following week there was a lock on the boys' door, and I didn't dare say a peep in case my rooting around was the cause.

*

'Don't swear,' Selina said to me one afternoon when we were walking in circles around the garden. 'It's vulgar.'

'I didn't swear.' I crossed my arms and put my nose in the air like I'd seen her do when she was annoyed with Da. 'I said tush, Selina. That's French, you know.'

Selina laughed and laughed. The crows in the dark pine cawed along. 'Tush is an American word meaning buttocks. *Touché* is what you mean, darling.' She rapped my forehead with her knuckle, wooden bangles clacking down her arm. 'Say it like this: *touché*. No, no, not like that. What's wrong with your ears?'

Selina was going to show me how to glide through the world successfully. She gave me her old peasant blouses and patchwork skirts that smelled of patchouli. She gave me books: Shakespeare, Sagan, Thackeray. 'That dreadful school doesn't appreciate her,' she told girlfriends visiting from London. They wore wrap dresses and knee-high boots with silver buckles and spoke about Martin and Teddy and darling Stella. They told Midge she was sweet and told me I was clever and claimed I was going to make quite the splash, but then Selina spoiled it all by telling them about that *touché*. I had been listening behind the door in the hall and I stood there as shame burned me hot from ears to toes.

Later that evening, I decided I was going to read Selina's diary after all. I'd found it in her desk drawer a few weeks before but put it back without more than a quick look inside. This time, I decided I didn't care about doing the right thing. I waited until Selina was out with her friends and while Midge was busy staring in the lounge mirror, hands pressed in prayer, a black tea towel draped over her head, I snuck into Selina's study.

> *If only he would stop that hideous clearing of his throat. I stuff my ears with cotton wool and can still bloody hear him.*

His politics are utterly naive. He has no understanding of how power works yet insists on holding court. Anu came for a flying visit and after listening to him for just five minutes, she hissed into my ear: 'Have you gone quite mad?'

His poor girls are head over heels in love with him, but they'll soon learn. I'll eat my hat if he ever starts a painting. Of course, he's an absolute beast in bed which does help rather.

Selina drove us home as usual the following day. She told Midge that if I was going to be so moody and silent, then it was best just to ignore me. The next weekend when we were supposed to go back to the lodge, I said I felt sick and wanted to stay home. Ma was over the moon. According to Midge, Da was determined to let me stew until I changed my mind, but when I refused to go to the lodge a third time, Selina phoned to ask what was wrong.

'It's her decision, Selina,' Ma said down the receiver.

I'd shaken my head when Ma had tried to get me over to the phone. I would stay home. It didn't matter that home had become dark and narrow, the furniture ugly and that no one came to visit and nothing ever happened.

After a bit more talking and then when I was sure I heard Selina say goodbye, Ma took a breath and said: 'Now listen, ya posh cow. She's no going and that's that.'

Afterwards, Ma made out to the neighbours that she'd said this when Selina was still on the phone. I didn't let it be known that I'd heard Da's girlfriend hang up. Sometimes just to look at Ma was enough to make me weep.

Six weeks later it was all over anyway. Selina had gone to London to settle her boys into their new prep then she phoned and told

Da she would not be returning. The laird was though and so Da had to pack up his things quick smart and come home. Only he didn't have a home anymore because he'd given up his council flat to live at the lodge with Selina. He had to move into the box room at Grandda's, who soon took against his eldest son staggering home from *The Rob Roy*, howling sad songs and beating his chest.

Da eventually moved into one of the condemned flats on Thornhill Road. Ma said I wasn't to visit because of needles in the stairwell and stabbings in the street, but I did now and then, for a time. His checked shirts were more worn with each visit, yet still he spoke about buying a farm in Ayrshire. Sometimes I'd hear him talk to his pals as if he'd actually been a farmer and not just studied husbandry at the college. Becoming an artist in the style of Samuel Peploe was no longer mentioned. As he went on about fields and drainage, I'd see him as Selina had in her diary. Before long, I stopped visiting.

Instead, I took to visiting the library in town. How I loved that building: solid sandstone you could trust, a vaulted roof that didn't leak, radiators ticking with warmth, the carpets thick, the librarian ready with a kind smile, and all drama kept safely between the covers of those neatly numbered books. It was here on a wet Wednesday that I spotted Selina's photo on the cover of a broadsheet. Our corner shop didn't sell that kind of newspaper, so it was chance that I even saw it.

> *Her detailed rendering of the eighteenth century is exceptional. Yet her true achievement is characterisation that is three-dimensional to the point of pain. You rage against the boorish Robert Burns and root, powerless, for the brilliant, long-suffering Jean Armour.*

I ordered her book from the library, but they already had a copy due. When it arrived, I sat in the children's section under a poster of a rainbow – *Reading Takes You Places!* – and ate my way through that book until the streetlights turned pink and the kind librarian was cashing up the fines in the till.

Robert Burns talked a great deal about sheep: the rearing of sheep, the breeding of sheep, the slaughter of sheep and the general ministering of sheep. And if he wasn't speaking about sheep, he was winking at barmaids and milkmaids. I recognised too the views from the Burns farm – Ailsa Craig, Ireland on a rare clear day. I recognised the rats, the cats, and how Burns was forever clearing his throat as if about to make some great speech. And the children: I recognised them too.

Da wrote to the publishers demanding Selina's address. Of course, the publishers never replied. The newspaper review had mentioned that Selina was living in Italy and engaged to a Viscount like a story from one of Gran's Mills & Boons. Years later, when the internet became a thing, I searched for any mention of her but all I could find were old copies of what seemed to be her only publication. She had disappeared. Gone to ground. It was difficult to believe that Death would have been permitted to inconvenience her. If he had dared loom, Selina would simply call someone, arrange something, get someone's father somewhere high up to do something. Death would be sent off with his tail between his legs.

When Da died, I was working in Edinburgh as a college librarian. As Midge wasn't permitted to leave the order, it was left to me to clear his flat. At the bitter end, he'd been living in a tiny one-bedroom in a high-rise the locals called Heartbreak Hotel because it was where divorced men drank themselves to death.

His brown coat was still hanging on the living room door. His tobacco tin was on the black-ash table, along with betting slips and a torn scrap of a shopping list: *Baxter's soup. Stork. Plain loaf.* The furniture was the kind social workers source from budget wholesalers for people in need: a striped sofa that if it had been any smaller would have been a chair; that black-ash table; and a two-bar electric fire with only one bar in working order. There were no curtains or blinds. Pigeons were nesting and shitting in the balcony, sheltering from rain and wind that beat against the building without end the whole time I was there.

I left clearing his bedroom to the last. It smelled of feet and fags and Paco Rabanne. It smelled of my father. The red-and-white striped duvet cover had been mine when I was wee. Faded, bobbled and now more pink than red, it lay atop a single bed that sagged as if in mourning. I took it all in – the wire mesh on the windows, the Styrofoam sandwich box used as an ashtray – and thought of prison cells.

I was nervous about clearing the boxes jammed under his bed. For who knew what magazines and such like a daughter might find? But what I did find didn't shock, it only saddened: an easel, folded up and dusty; three blank canvases, still wrapped in cellophane; and, by the bedpost, a Sunblest bag of brushes stiff with ancient paint. There were shoeboxes filled with detritus: plectrums, shells from the beach, Jobcentre cards, yellowed maps of Ayrshire farmlands. There were birthday cards we'd made for him and stiff photo albums of us as girls. There were no photos beyond our teens because by then even Midge had stopped visiting him.

Right at the back, I found a cardboard box of Selina's things: a silk scarf with a repeating peacock design she'd bought in a shop in Dalrymple; an empty perfume bottle – *Boudica*; old bills from the lodge and bank statements showing a huge overdraft; and books too – *Vanity Fair*, *Crime and Punishment*, *David Copperfield* – awarded when she was deputy head girl at St Paul's; and, at the very bottom, three black-bound diaries written before she met Da.

> *Went to an awful meeting at the 2-4-6 Club. Oscar was quite right: socialism takes up too many evenings. Yet one must try. Afterwards, we all tumbled along to Lou's. Her cook had made the most delicious Portuguese pastries, so that rather sweetened the deal.*

Something must be done about all this trouble in Brazil. I shall write to the embassy.

Had lunch at S's. He pointed his fork straight at me and in that magnificent Shakespearean manner, declaimed: 'The problem with you, my dear, is that you haven't found your subject yet. You must hunt it down. You must take it by the throat. Sink your teeth in. Do not let go. Immerse yourself fully. Leave behind this fluffery you get so caught up with and then you shall triumph.' Of course, he tried to get me into bed, but I wouldn't. Not after the last time. The horror, the horror!

Yes, I used the diaries as inspiration, but I believe my long literary career speaks for itself. No need to waste ink detailing what was fiction and what was fact. There was just enough of both. Yet despite the brave face I put on for the sales team, the truth was I expected that first book to sink without trace. Until the reviews came in, of course: *Razor-sharp, relentless satire*; *Minty is a horrendous yet utterly compelling character*; *Run don't walk to your nearest bookshop* et cetera et cetera. Some critics were agog that I, a lowly librarian from Glasgow, had managed to capture 1970s literary London in such vivid detail.

The letter arrived a few weeks after I won the French book prize. I recognised the handwriting immediately. Inside was a single sheet of pale-pink notepaper, a sprinkling of cigarette ash in the crease, and one word:

Touché

Finola Scott

THE MAIDEN SAYS AWA

1679. Scots Juistice

Come awa in. Dinna be feart, thon blade o mine's
anely shiny airn. Gaither roond, A've mony tales
tae tell. Frae ma blithe name and fame ye'll ken
A'm a douce sowel wha aye sorts oot wrang-daein.
If yer hairts are ill-less, ye'r siccar here wi me.

Mony bethank me fir the enterteenment, the divert
at the Tollbooth. Ithers are gratefu when A lichten
thaim tae thair deserred end. But A'm no ettle
for the rochle and rauchle yins. Drunkarts, limmers,
fornicators. A strang hemp's guid eneuch fir thaim.

Ma skeel wis fordelt fir the Persons o Quality, fir noble
Lairds and Lassies wha ferdit their wey. Fir thaim,
nae coorse axe wagit by a deft bruit, nae neck
mangled lik a fermyaird hen, nae repeated bangs.
Ma way wis certaint, ma cut wis swith and pintit.

Aye A'm prood. A Maister craftit ma mervelous frame
o dark beams tourin heich. Thon blade hystit up,
sae heavy, sae sharp, sae humane. Doon it slams,
gleg as saumon leapin. Bluid, bricht as a cock's comb
aw sookit up fest wi fresh gowden straw.

Ane A mind weil wis Adame Sinclair. At Scallowa
A took his rotten heid, strukin it fra his bodie,
dung it fra his shoulder, severed neat and true.
Sic a fine act exemplified fir ithers, that slauchter
o yir neebours juist isnae richt.

A mind tae Lady Christine. Kilt thon wickit philanderer,
hir luver, Lord James wi his ain sword. Curled weegs
and beggar bowls thringit roon the Cross aiverin
tae ettelt her deith. Mindin the juidge's lang-heidit wirds,
thay rairt *Murtherer* oer the clatter o the knabberie's
    carriages.

Shameless adultress, she cast aff hir white taffetie hood.
Whit she thoucht naebody kent, but ilka body saw
thon bare shoulders, gleamin white as muinrise
abuin hir black silk goun. Hir bonnie brent neck wis saitin
saft as she set doon her heid tae kiss me, her ain Maiden.

Note: The Maiden was the name given to the guillotine used in Scotland to execute Royalty and members of the ruling class.

Shane Strachan

THE ROARING OF THE SEA

O gin ye shoud kill him Fa'se Footrage,
You woud do what is right;
For I wot he killd your father dear,
Ere ever you saw the light.

Gin you should kill him Fa'se Footrage,
There is nae man durst you blame;
For he keeps your mother a prisoner,
And she dares no take you hame.

—from Anna Gordon Brown's rendition
of the traditional ballad, 'Fa'se Footrage'

Ye bide deid still, back flat on the grun, airms raxed oot, legs straight and stiff. Ye keep yer een open, staring up at the same spot on the plain, white ceiling. Ye darena blink the hale time – ye jist let yer een prickle a bittie then ging numb, but nivver ivver blink. Ye barely breathe – jist wee shalla breaths that mean yer belly disna rise and faa. One by one, the ither soldiers are found tae nae be deid enough and are made tae stand up at the side o the room. But they winna catch you. Ye learnt lang ago hoo tae switch aff fae the world aroon ye, hoo tae fade intae the backgroon.

You can stop now. You win . . . You are too good at this!

Ye finally blink and feel yer eyebaas moisten. Ye stand up and yer heid furls a little. The ither bairns fae the kids' club are pittin on their yalla caps wi the flap o material at the back tae hide their necks fae the sun sae ye dee the same. The kids' club leader heids oot the room and aabody snakes ahin, doon the hotel corridor and oot intae the midday Spanish heat bi the poolside. Aa the ither bairns have paired up and haud haans, but ye trail alang at the back alone.

Oi! . . . Hey min! somebody shouts fae a balcony above. Ye look up and see yer stepdad Zander wi the videocamera in one haan and a fag in the ither. He's tapless, his torso beamin white compared tae his tanned face and reid tattooed airms. Ye gie him a smaa wave. The rest o the kids' club sneak glances back at ye, smirks on their faces, but ye'd raither be doon here than ony closer tae Zander.

The home video says it is mid-June 1996, a couple o wiks shy o the official school summer holidays. It's the start o yer wik in Alcúdia, Majorca. You, yer sister Charlene and yer half-brither Jamie are aa smiles on the balcony, yer skin peely-wally apart fae yer flushed chiks. Ye aa sing snippets o Zombie for the camera, afore you and Charlene pipe up, *Mr Lover Lover!*

Sing Shaggy, ye say tae Jamie.

Shaggy, Shaggy, Shaggy.

The video constantly chaps and changes.

Filmed fae high up on the balcony, the camera zooms further and further in until only Jamie can be seen runnin aroon the poolside wi a little reid flotation vest on. He leans doon at the pool edge and scoops up some watter in his haans then throws it at somebody's heid in the corner o the screen – yours. Zander's high-pitched snicher can be heard.

Yer mam sits on the balcony by hersel, drinkin a tamata juice. Zander is filming her fae the cooch inside.

Oi! . . . Smile!

Yer mam turns tae face him, but at the sight o the camera, she turns awa.

Why ye filmin me just sittin here? she asks, still lookin awa.

Anither shot above the pool. Charlene's lang, dark-blonde hair is dreepin weet as she helps Jamie open a bottle o Tango afore pourin some intil his moo. He drinks it like a dog suppin fae a runnin tap.

Cut tae yer mam and Jamie in the hotel room. Yer mam's skin is already darkenin, makkin the white shorts and bikini top she's on glow in contrast. She's showdin Jamie in her airms, his face reid and his hair slick wi swiyt.

Ye sulkin? Zander says fae ahin the camera. It's nae clear fa he's spikkin tae.

Tell daddy ye'r too hot, yer mam says.

I'm too hot. I'm too hot, Jamie peeks.

Cut tae aa o yis in a horse-draan carriage. Palm trees slide alang the sides o the road as the horse's hooves rhythmically clip-clop against the tarmac. Under the glare o the sun, aabody sleepily squints at the camera then looks awa. Naebody says a word.

Back in the hotel room, Zander opens the toilet door tae reveal yer mam sitting on the lavvie wi her shorts and punts doon. She covers her face and laughs afore throwing a toilet roll at the camera.

Oooh! Look at the butterfly tattoo on her bum! ye say.

Jamie runs intae the toilet tae point at the tattoo below yer mam's left hip.

Get oot! yer mam shouts in atween bursts o lauchter.

Oh, what a smell! That's honkin, mam! ye say.

Right, that's enough. Oot!

Cut tae you lying on the beach, Jamie slowly burying you wi sand.

Shane, mak angel wings, Charlene says.

Ye start flappin yer airms up and doon on the sand, a dark circle formin aroon ye. Jamie gets mad that the sand he's been piling on ye is faain doon yer sides. He kicks at yer airms tae stop ye moving then scoops up mair sand in his little bucket tae start burying ye again. Ye lowp up and the sand flees doon aff ye. Jamie screams. Ye run under the ootdoor shower and rinse the sand aff ye.

Mannie! Ye caa oot Jamie's nickname wi a wee smirk on yer face. *Stand here!*

Ye pynt at a patch jist in front o the shower, the button grippit in yer hand, ready tae be pushed back on.

No! Zander baals fae ahin the camera. *He'll be soakin!*

The camera cuts oot.

Aifter, ye aa made yer wye back alang the beach taewards the hotel, the sun still beamin doon. On the edge o the beach, a black mannie stood next tae a blue beach toowel covered in different gold and silver watches.

Real Rolex. Good deal for you, he repeated ower and ower in a Nigerian accent as yis neart him.

Yer mam tried tae keep walkin on, but Zander knelt doon and picked up a chunky yalla-gold watch, turnin it roon and roon in his haans.

Och, ye'r nae needin ony o that, yer mam said.

Zander kept at it, pickin ither eens up and pittin them doon, before gan back tae the first een he'd picked up. Yer mam huffed through her nose.

How much? Zander said, haudin the yalla-gold watch up in the air.

Six thousand pesetas.

Nah nah nah! Zander put the watch doon and got up ontae his feet. As the seller started tae bargain wi him, yer mam pushed Jamie's buggy onwards. You and Charlene trailed aifter them, leavin Zander ahin.

Oot the front o a restaurant facing the beach, yer mam smoked the hale wye through supper that night, her sunglaisses kept on. She barely said a word in atween each fag as Zander fichered wi his new watch, twistin the crown roon and roon. Ye watched flakes o yer mam's fag ash get caught in the breeze and drift doon intae her half-eaten bowl o paella and the near-empty glaiss o sangria that Charlene kept askin for anither a taste o aifter she'd been allowed a wee suppie tae try.

The waiter came ower.

Mr Moneybags is pying, yer mam said, pyntin her fag in Zander's direction without lookin roon at him.

Nithing new 'ere.

Right then – you bide at hame and watch the bairns and I'll ging oot and work, yer mam said. She forced a grin.

You gan tae ging tae sea, like? Cuz yer fuckin pocket money fae Avon winna pye the bills.

Yer mam stubbed oot her fag hard, the tabbie near splittin in two. She stood up and bunged Jamie intae his buggy then started walkin awa.

The hame video starts again. Smaa yachts in a marina can be seen, the camera gliding back and fore across them. The camera bobs up and doon wi each step Zander taks, like a boat rearin ower waves oot at sea. The camera turns awa fae the marina and focuses on the street – up aheid, yer mam pushes the buggy at speed, you and Charlene traipsin aifter.

Cut tae the hotel room at night. It's dark ootside the balcony winda. Jamie and Charlene are dancing in the living room under the saft orange glow o the lamplight. Charlene has one lang pink braid threided through her dark blonde hair wi beads stitched intil it.

Face! Get . . . outta . . . my . . . face! she screeches at the camera. *I wanna be a hippy! . . . I'm nae drunk.*

You are sut drunk! ye say, appearin in the corner o the screen, a shorter blue braid danglin fae the side o yer heid.

I'm nae!

I can smell sangria!

Charlene goes ower and kisses Jamie on the chik afore walkin up and blockin the camera.

I'm filming Jamie, yer mam says.

Grandma and Granda are gan tae be watchin this, ye say.

I dinna care, Charlene replies.

Aye, yer grandma's gan tae see it!

No! Charlene skirls.

Ye were sent tae yer bed nae lang aifter then, but ye remember hearin a glaiss smashin and then shoutin.

Calm doon quinie! Zander shouted. *Fuckin hell, there's ayewis summin wi these bairns.*

Well, you shouldna'v kept giein her sangria. I telt ye nae til.

You're the een that gied it til her first.

Aye, I gave her a taste o it. Nae mair than that. She's only ten!

. . . It's aye my fuckin fault.

The video cuts aheid tae the next mornin, up on the balcony again, lookin doon. The date is visible in the corner: 12 June 1996. The sky is cloudy as yer mam can be seen walkin fae the pool back taewards the hotel. Zander mumbles summin under his breath and then tuts.

The taxi tae the beach later that mornin wis silent as ye pressed yer face up against the half-opent windae tae let the wind blast through yer swiyty hair. Below the wisps o creamy cloud driftin in the blue sky, ye could pick oot folk skiytin aboot on jet skis. Oot o the car, ye could hear the buzz o their engines, rising up tae a squeal fan they sped up, and then faain tae a low hum faniver they came in tae land on the weet, glisterin shore.

Ye'd wanted tae ging tae the kids' club instead, but the beach was too far awa, and the rest o them widna be back in time tae get ye fan the club finished at dennertime.

Ye stuck close tae yer mam as ye aa churned through the haet sand, yer sandals sinkin in, near hault aff by the sand's grip.

Zander bargained wi the sun lounger mannie tae get three loungers for the price o two.

You eens can share, yer mam said tae you and Charlene. *You'll be busy paddlin onywye.*

I'm nae gan in the watter. Nae wi ma cut, Charlene said, pyntin at the plaster on her fit far she'd stood on broken glaiss the nicht afore.

Och, the seawatter wid dee it good I'm sure. I'm nae gan.

Well, I want a shot on the seat an-aa, ye piped up.

Yer mam pynted her finger up at yis, the ither airm haudin Jamie in her bose.

Can you eens jist behave for one bloody day?

I ken, Zander said as he pit his toowel doon on his lounger. *Tell ye fit, Shane – you could come dee the jet skis wi me. That nae better than biding here fechtin wi yer sister aa day?*

I'm too little.

Och, come on! Dinna be a wimp.

Zander, he's nae gan tae be allowed tae dee that, yer mam said as she sat doon on her lounger wi Jamie. Charlene lowpit up and claimed the last seat ahin her.

Come on and we'll see, Zander said nudgin ye in the shooder.

Ye looked oot at the jet skis on the watter. A stream o watter shot up oot the back o each een like the metal poles on the back o dodgem cars, sparkin wi electricity. Ye liked the dodgems at the fair, sae surely it couldna be that bad.

Okay, ye said. Ye trailt aifter Zander ower tae the rental stand.

As expected, the aul, stoot Spanish mannie workin the stand said you were too smaa tae ging on a jet ski yersel, but that ye could sit on the back o Zander's. It wid be cheaper tee.

Zander wis noddin his heid afore you had a chance tae say onything, and you were seen being passed a thick blue flotation vest tae shove on. Ye had tae wyde oot intae the watter a bittie ahin Zander tae get tae the jet ski. The watter wis cauler and choppier than ye expectit, the waves tuggin ye aboot. Zander had tae help ye up ontae the jet ski, grippin hard ontae the tap o yer airm until ye got yer leg up and ower the seat. Ye looked aroon for haanles tae haud ontae, but there wis neen. The mannie signalled for ye tae pit yer airms roon Zander. Slowly, ye placed yer haans on his sides and held onto the front o his hips. His flotation vest was rubbery and slippy, but ye were too affrontit tae grip him ony tichter, yer belly aaready pressin up against his lower back and the tap o his bum. The engine started up wi a high-pitched roar and ye were quickly flung backwards, almost losing grip o Zander's sides. Ye had nae choice but tae haud ontil him tichter as ye attimpted tae reach yer haans roon tae get a haud o the ither, but yer airms werna quite lang enough.

The speed soon levelled oot and it felt less choppy as ye wheeched alangside the waves, side-on wi the shoreline. Yer mam and Jamie waved taewards ye. Zander waved back wi one haan, but you were too feart tae let go, jist in case it suddenly jolted forward again.

You could hear the engine startin tae ging higher and higher, the speed pickin up. Zander taen a sharp turn right, heidin further oot tae sea – the waves caught ye baith aff guard as the jet ski went heid on intil them and yer were flung back like ye were on a buckin bronco. Yer airms slid aff Zander and ye slipped back taeward the edge o the seat, almost tippin ower it afore being flung forward again.

Waatch! ye shouted. *I almost fell aff.*

Zander roared wi lauchter as he twistit the haanlebar again and the jet ski started speedin alangside the shoreline eence mair.

Anither couple o jet skis appeared ahin ye at each side, a teenage loon on each een.

Think they're it, eh? Zander shouted as he revved the engine up. He started zig-zaggin the jet ski fae side tae side, pullin oot in front o the loons. Each time he turned shairply, ye were tossed tae one side. Ye kept picterin yersel fleein aff the back intae the water and een o the jet skis driving straight intae ye.

Stop it! ye couldna help but scream.

Zander lauched as he kept at it.

Please stop! I'm gan tae faa aff!

Ye were aboot greetin, but ye clinched yer jaa hard tae stop yersel screaming again – the funnier it wis for Zander, the mair he'd keep deeing it. It wis like that time fan ye were six and yer uncle kept shakkin and swingin the cage ye were suspended in at the tap o the Blackpool Ferris Wheel – the mair ye screamed, the harder he shook until the mannie workin it had tae stop the machine and shout up tae him tae quit it. Or the time he'd hung ye upside doon ower the bridge tae the Peterheid golf course and at the first sign o tears in yer een, he started swingin ye fae side tae side sae that ye scraiched even mair. Ye'd learnt then that the mair ye showed ony signs o weakness by screamin and greetin, the mair the men in yer life wanted tae torture ye.

Zander widna let up. Ye went quiat and closed yer een, hoping that it wid jist aa stop, but he kept at it, faster and faster, showdin ye side tae side sharply.

There wis a thud at the front o the jet ski and ye lost yer grip on Zander and were flung backwards, aff the seat. Ye hurtled doon intae the sea ahin, disappearin under the waves, the roar o the ither two jet skis approachin.

The flotation vest pulled ye back up tae the surface. Ye keeked yer heid up oot the watter, hoping if they saa ye, they would turn the jet ski awa, but een o them kept straight on taewards ye. Ye ducked yer heid back doon ablow the watter as the jet ski engine got louder and louder, closer and closer. . .

The buzzin noise faded.

Ye tried tae look aroon, but the seawatter stung yer een as ye gaspit for breath. Though the saatwatter kept stingin, ye evintually saa Zander makkin his wye back ower tae ye – he wis grinnin like it was aa a joke.

Come on then, get back on.

Ye bid put.

I could have been hit by them, ye said at the tap o yer vyce.

No, ye widna'v! He snichered again, but wi a darker tone tae his vyce. *I kent fit I wis deein.*

Ye wanted tae keep arguing wi him, but there wis only one wye ye were gan tae get back on shore.

Can we go back tae the beach noo? You can keep gan if you want, but I dinna want tae, ye said.

Aaricht, but dinna bother gan greetin tae yer mam, Zander said as he hault ye bi the airm back up ontae the jet ski. *It wis jist an accident. A wave came oot o nae wye.*

I winna, ye said. Zander started up the engine again and the waves helped push ye back taewards the shore quicker.

As soon as the jet ski slowed doon tae land, ye let go o Zander and leapt aff the side. Ye paddled until ye could feel yer feet on the grun and sighed wi relief. Ye didna look back as Zander sped aff ahin ye.

As much as ye tried tae stop yersel, ye couldna help bit burst intae tears as ye made yer wye ower tae yer mam.

Fit's happened noo? she said as ye stumbled doon next tae the side o her lounger and grut intil her side.

He made me faa aff and I almost got run ower by anither jet ski. He did it on purpose.

Och, dinna be silly. It will have been an accident.

He kent fit he wis deeing. He didna care if I got hurt. I sweer.

Yer mam sat up and looked up the coastline. Zander wis nearly oot o sicht. She huffed through her teeth.

I'll spik tae him later.

The video cuts tae us aa at a watterpark. A wave machine has Charlene jumpin up and doon in the pool, Jamie squealin in her airms wi fear and delicht. You're on yer ain further up, vanishin intae each wave crest tae then pop back oot in the trough afore being swallaed hale aa ower again bi the turquoise watter.

Yer mam turns the camera awa fae yis and ower towards Zander fa's lying on a lounger further awa, his een shut and face set hard. There's a pale patch o skin far his new watch had been strappit tae his wrist for a couple o days.

It's nae working onymair, he'd said at brakfist that mornin. *The crown's broken.*

I telt ye, yer mam had huffed.

The camera turns back tae focus on you, Charlene and Jamie. The waves are higher noo, pullin yis aa under. They morph intae waves o grey and black fuzz that rolls across the screen wi the hiss o white noise.

Lynn Valentine

CHRISTMAS MORNING

Rare for her to lay the table,
white cloth over dark mahogany,
sole decoration a star of poinsettia.
This would normally be pub time,
joining the band of males
in the family, their *Merry Christmases*
toasted in the snug; whisky reeking
its warming work of three full rounds
then back to the house. This year
she is alone with the table, counting
settings, silvering forks to their spot.
She will toast the males in their absence,
pour a drink for herself. Jesus watches
her from the corner, his crown
of thorns as dark as her wine.
She waits for strangers to fill
the table, lift their heavy knives.

Augustijn van Gaalen
LETTER TO CALLUM

The veins of a sycamore leaf, he said, are exceptionally strong. He brought his hands together to illustrate this to me, how the stringy stems and veins could hold together congealing debris until, like a throbbing mass of rats, it became one solid, impermeable thing. A rat king, I think, such a phenomenon is called – or Rattenkönig in the original German. Looking this up later I was both horrified and intrigued to learn that, upon finding a rat king comprised of seven rats in the Netherlands, subsequent x-ray imaging revealed broken tails and worn-down nails, the result of forced efforts to pull and claw their way free. They had been like this for a while, it seemed. I found myself, in the seconds it took for Callum to bring his calloused hands together, imagining them not as fingers but as tails, squirming irredeemably for supremacy. It was the sound, apparently, that alerted the farmer to their presence. A high-pitched squeaking, which rats only ever emit when they are distressed or in pain, a sign of acute, even unbearable, discomfort.

I'm so sorry about all this, Callum repeated time and time again that morning. It was clearly a genuine apology, suffused with regret and guilt. I told him not to worry about it, and he said insistently, no, really, it's my duty. His duty – that was what he called it. It was a strong yet fitting word, and it captured him perfectly. Although he had enlisted the services of an estate agent, it was clear that the agent's involvement – friendly and helpful as he was – was reserved purely to the administrative legalities of allocating the property. Once allocated, Callum intended to be a hands-on landlord, if you could call it that, for the way in which he offered his assistance bore no hallmarks to previous landlords we had encountered in our many years of renting. It was his duty. Unperturbed by the simple fact that the maintenance of a drain could feasibly (and perhaps legally, if one bothered to read the lease) be considered the tenant's responsibility, he acted as if the drain itself was an extension of his body, a limb whose very movements and existence he was responsible for.

He took a great deal of pride in that house, in the careful running of it, its appearance. He had come to own it, you could say, out of pride. It was an impractical decision, taking on the croft and the house that came with it, but when his uncle died, Callum could not stand to see this land – the land his forefathers had fought so hard for – fall into a stranger's hands, could not imagine a world in which he and his wife and children drove past the house that once had borne his family name, exclaiming ruefully that once upon a time that house had belonged to them, the way they had belonged to it. So he took it on, the land, and the house, which I imagine must have been falling apart, and he built it up to what it is today: the clean, white render, the fresh paint, the new carpets, the sheep-wool insulation, the three-piece bathroom suite, the cooker, the central heating system (uncommon for island homes at that time, I'm told), and the rows and rows of neatly lumbered pine for the kitchen, which made you feel at all times as if you were in the belly of a ship. It's a good house, he told me when we met him, on his third drive by the house, that first weekend, late May. Always he had rented it, or so it always seemed to me, at a reasonable price to good, upstanding folk. Which meant that we were now good, upstanding folk. We had become so, simply by moving in. But would, I ask you, good upstanding folk have allowed such a thing to happen to their drain? Would they have allowed the water to come billowing out in steady streams, the grass by the drain turning brown and then, finally, dying as it sat, unaided and forlorn, in a never-ending puddle of watered-down detergents which, no matter how natural they proclaimed to be, seemed to destroy all living things. But even then, Callum's eyes remained kind and warm, and when I asked him whether previous tenants had ever encountered such a problem, he merely said, no, I don't think so, but you never know with these things, do you? And I suppose that was how he thought of everything: you never know, you reserve judgement, you do not judge at all, you merely wait until you are called upon. Because it is your duty.

Perhaps he used an estate agent only so that he would not be badgered by the many, many people who would want to rent his house, which was in good shape and located in what we discovered was a desirable town on the island's eastern coast. Good links into Stornoway, a regular bus service, with a post office and a petrol station serving the cheapest fuel on the entire island. People travelled not just for fuel, but also for haircuts, it seemed, with a barber so well rated that she was often forced to send people away when, late at night, the queue inside her tiny pebble-dashed building was so large that she would no longer have time to cut the men assembling patiently and silently on the benches, waiting to be called. I have clients all the way down in Harris, she told me once, smiling proudly.

The easterly winds, Callum said, were coming earlier this year. Every year for many years now they were coming earlier. Speaking with great certainty, he had a way of conveying calm and assurance. He could have said anything, claimed anything, and I would have believed it. But some things you did not want to believe, could not believe. When he said those things, he did so without melodrama and self-pity. He owed her a duty too, it seemed. When he spoke of how difficult it had become – taking care of her – he did so merely to illustrate the physical and mental toll of vigilance, the unrelenting, never-ending nature of care that comes with dementia. And there were good days, but also bad days, he admitted. Such was life. Sunday, and Monday too, those had been bad days. And I knew before he told me – about Sunday – for it was Sunday that we saw him, driving slowly and aimlessly past our house without any urgency at all, stopping occasionally and suddenly – the sort of slow-paced driving that people normally employ only when sightseeing. But Callum was not sightseeing, for he had seen it all before, knew the land, the houses, and the people better than anyone else in the village, and besides, it was the Sabbath, and Callum respected such things, even if he did not always attend church himself anymore. I understood clearly what I had seen that Sunday: that Callum was looking for Jan, that Jan had gone missing, that he had had to do this once or twice before, that things that once felt surreal and almost cinematic were becoming by the day more ordinary and mundane. It was the Tuesday after the Sunday and the Monday that I messaged him on his mobile, asking whether he'd managed to find the handpump that he'd mentioned to me before. And the response, hastily written and containing an uncharacteristic number of errors, apologising profusely for the delay, stating that it had been difficult, of late, to leave Jan alone, but that he would make time if he could later today.

Callum brought, in his black hatchback, a diesel-powered water pump and a small handpump capable of applying, he told me proudly when I respectfully questioned its usefulness, up to 100 PSI of pressure. A hundred pounds to an inch of pressure, he reiterated slowly, and all I could think of was what would happen to your head if you applied that amount of pressure to it. I helped Callum unload everything and attach a long, green hose to the pump. He pulled the cord and it gurgled loudly. Removing the grate from the drain, he proceeded to jab the pump into the viscous sludge. It was immediately clear that the blockage would not be fixed by an above-average injection of water; no, it required serious pressure. To my great shame, remnants of sour-smelling food began to emerge: carrots and shards of spaghetti from our weekly vegetable bolognese, yellow specks of canned corn, and large clotted balls of couscous. Leaves too, from the barren tree behind our house. Callum graciously did not comment on the smell or proliferation of food items in what should ideally be a food-and-oil-free drain. Several metres to our left stood the three sheep that grazed in the adjacent field. I noted that Callum did not acknowledge their presence, despite the self-conscious way they stood by the fence, their thin black heads bent downwards as they watched us. Occasionally, they would sprint with remarkable speed across the field for no reason at all.

Callum took out the small, cardboard box that held the hand-pump. He made his way back to the car and brought out a white sheet, which he dropped carelessly on the grass. Already, somehow, he was bleeding, a scrape on his right hand that must have occurred when removing the grate or pulling out debris. Mind your hand, I told him, but he simply shrugged. I doubt he noticed it, even though it continued steadily to bleed for another hour, mixing in with the dark-grey sludge. I watched him, feeling rather hopeless, but feeling too that to go inside was to abandon him entirely to this impossible task. He pumped up the handpump using just one hand. I had my hands in my pocket – it was cold, and I was grateful that I had slipped on warm socks and my boots when I saw him pull up in his van, and that I'd remembered to grab a hat. Still, with my thickest jumper on, I was freezing, whereas Callum looked impervious to the chill. Under his jacket, which wasn't even zipped up fully, I noticed he wore an overshirt without a jumper.

Callum motioned that I should step back and inserted the pump into the hole. He then wrapped the sheet around the edges of the drain. Placing his left foot on the drain, he arched his back from the hole and released the trigger. The sound was remarkably loud, and despite his best efforts, some of the water spurted out beyond the sheet onto Callum. I was standing some three metres away, but still, I had to jump back to avoid the splatter. Callum repeated this process half a dozen times, and after each detonation he tried to see if water flowed smoothly, but it merely filled ominously back to the top of the drain and into the large pond beside our propane tank. He was unperturbed by this, despite my suggestion that perhaps we needed to call someone – who that someone was, I still don't know – politely resisting what must have been an unbearable urge to tell me off more forcefully. He merely smiled and used the hose to clean the mud off his glasses.

It was at this point that he walked to the adjacent field and began digging in the soil, lifting up a large slab to reveal where the pipe ran from the house into the nearby public system. Where the two pipes met, there was a small chamber. See that, he said, pointing down. No flow at all. It must be properly clogged. And I realised at that moment that I could have been helping with the pump all along. I finally suggested this to him, and my immaculate hands emerged from my pockets. The pumping was much harder than Callum – who must have been in his sixties – made it look. I could barely get it to about 70 PSI, but Callum said, that'll do, and detonated a smaller blast. Eventually I managed to get it up to 100 PSI by placing the pump between my shoes and pumping with both hands. Callum began rapidly detonating after that, passing me the pump back while he flushed the drain. After a while, Callum asked me to go back to the drainpipe in the field to see whether the water was flowing through at all. I told him it wasn't, and he asked me to stay in the field while he detonated a few more blasts.

Then, three immense balls of leaves and food and gunk flowed through the basin and into the public system. Huge, solid, meaty things they were. I think we've found the culprit, I shouted at Callum, who was making his way over the fence and into the field. But by the time he'd arrived, all the gunk was gone and a steady stream of water flowed. The water gradually became clearer and clearer. He went back to the house, smiling modestly, and power-washed the area around the drain. We talked for a short while as he packed up his tools and the dirty sheet, ignoring the rain that was beginning to fall. He seemed relieved more than anything that valuable time away from his wife had been worthwhile, that the task had been completed. I watched him drive away and went inside to take a long, hot shower.

When we eventually moved out of Callum's house, we left a small print of a cottage on the beach with a short note of thanks. It felt appropriate, somehow. Callum responded just as we drove off the ferry, informing us that he intended to frame and hang it so there would always be a piece of us there, in that house. It was an act of sentimentality I did not expect from him, or myself for that matter. I doubt he'll ever read this story, although I did not change his name. I think about him often, still. How are you, Callum?

Katie Webster
FUCKINSTUCK

There is a wee squad o kids from ae village at ae door, and ae one wi ae sweetest voice is lookin up at my mither and sayin,

Is she comin oot til play?

And I canna hurt my mither's heart so I nod and I say,

Oot til play, oot til play.

Now ae gaggle o kids is swarmin doon ae hill til ae harbour, and I am wi them. One o ae big kids slings an arm across my shooder, pulls me in close, pushes me away, pulls me in close again. I lurch awa and aginst him. Three o ae ithers are kickin a can between them. Anither is runnin ae wall alongside, jumpin ae gate gaps. We bounce across ae swing bridge in single file, ignorin ae sign that says no more than two at any one time, and gettin it goin wi a life o its own so's you canna judge ae up-bounce nor ae down-bounce and your leggies go all funny. Ae creak o ae tension cables is like tall ships and old boots. I danna like ae feel o ae swing bridge, but I know better than til let on. We troop along ae shore line til ae old derelict buildings at ae far end, beyond ae big hoose and ae estate cottages. We throw rocks in ae water, aimin at fish and rusty things at ae bottom.

When we get til ae Ice Hoose, they dare me til take first go at ae Chutes Game. I danna want til, but I danna have ae words til say that. Ae only words I have are their words, half-hearted echoes that I danna get til choose.

It'll be fine, go on.

It'll be fine, go on.

Ae Ice Hoose is where they used til store ae fresh-caught fish in olden times, before refridgeration. It is a dank stone chamber dug and buried intil ae bank, north facin and cold. No windows, one door, and one drop-hatch at ae top-back, and that is where ae chute is, that is where they used til pour ice doon intil ae pit til keep ae fish from rottin.

Ae game is til run up ae bank til ae hatch, climb in head first, whiz doon ae chute, clatter til ae bottom in ae dark, then run back roond again for your next go. It's a race too, til catch ae next one ahead o you, and til not get caught by ae one behind. I've never played before, they've never let me. I've stood watchin, gettin dizzy at ae ither kiddies runnin roond and roond and roond, and feelin secret scared o all that dark and chasin, secret glad they danna want me playin.

But I canna say no. Ae only words I have are their words tellin me I have til.

I have til.

They lift ae hatch for me and when I still hesitate they all stand roond, saying,

Hurry up. Come on. We don't have all day. We want our goes too you know.

So I drop til my knees and start til crawl, in through ae hatch, intil ae black.

It'll be fine, go on.

Halfway in, they kick my knees oot from under me so I go splat in ae grass, and then quick-fast they lower ae hatch. I'm catched, flat on my tummy, my head all alone in ae darkness, my arms oot front graspin at nothin, and my legs flailin behind, feet kickin loose and no use against thin air. I canna see a thing but I can hear ae ither kiddies hootin at ae cleverness o their jest.

Did you just see that?

She SO never seen it comin.

I canna draw a proper breath, and I canna see a thing, so I shut my eyes and squeeze them tight til keep ae darkness oot. I have ae full weight o ae timber-and-steel hatch pressin doon on my back, and beneath me ae frame is cuttin up intil my chest, and it's crushin my breath. And it hurts.

From below, a small voice crows.

Look at ae state o that, she's totally fuckin stuck.

I open my eyes. Ae door til ae Ice Hoose is ajar now, lettin in a slice o sharp-edged light, and in ae middle o it stands ae silhouette o a peedie child, peedier than me, though smarter already and much better liked. It is ae bairnie with ae sweet-sweet voice who asked me oot til play. She is jiggyin with ae excitement o bein a part o somethin as darin-bad as this, and til be hurlin oot such big bad words that she shouldna even know yet. And her wee voice should be teeny in a space o this size, but it isna. Because her words are met with an achin echo that isna even mine.

Fuckinstuck fuckinstuck fuckinstuck.

Her voice is taken by ae Ice Hoose and made bigger, made more, made many. It swirls her words off ae walls like storm waves crashin roond ae geo-cleft cliffs that rise til ae north o our wee village.

Ae lassie shouts again, louder this time.

Fuckin stuck!

And ae echoes oblige.

Fuckinstuck fuckinstuck fuckinstuck.

Ae ither kids hear it ootside. There is a thunder o stampedin feet, then all ae kids are there at ae bottom o ae Ice Hoose, clamour-fillin ae doorway and pushin each ither oot ae way, so's they can all get inside til take their best shot.

Fuckinstuck! Fuckinstuck! Fuckinstuck!

Ae Ice Hoose amplifies, multiplies their voices intil a cacophony o noises, and not a single one is on my side.

Not even mine.

Because ae Ice Hoose isna ae only one who canna help but echo. I danna have ae words til say what I need til say. No matter ae panic nor ae pain, I canna say,

Help me. Stop. No. Please.

Ae words I have are their words, in small involuntary drops. My voice weaves in under ae Ice Hoose echoes, addin a subnote o stricted rasps and sore-sore gasps, and it keeps goin even as ae rest o them fade away, till mine is ae only one left standin.

Ae state o that, ae state o that. Fuckinstuck.

Fuckin hell, are you hearin that? She's sayin it too!

They laugh, this gang o wee nyaffs. But their fun is cut short. From somewhere a ways off doon ae shore, there is a shout, no, a roar.

Oh shit, her mither's comin.

Ae kids scarper, leavin me pinned wi their taunts still drip-drippin off my own sorry tongue like a bathroom tap left on and forgot. I would flood this cavern if left here long enough.

Through ae dunts on ae earth, I sense my mither's footsteps climbin ae bank, and then I hear ae catch in her breath when she sees me. I feel ae grunt o effort it takes for her til lift ae hatch so's I can wriggle mysel oot. She wraps me in her arms and holds me til her tight-as-tight-as-tight, and I bury my face intil her jaikit, so soft and itchy and full o ae smells o safety: her perfume, our hoose, my faither's cigarettes. I sob, my tears and snot and ae sneers o that lot staining her good grey jaikit, and it is a long while till I can get a hold o mysel.

It is only then that I notice ae things that are wrong. Ae beat in my mither's chest is distant, nearly missin. Ae muscles in her face and jaw and neck are strained taut as tension cables fit til snap from too much bounce and burden. And ae worst of all, she's no yet spoken.

I want til say, *Mum?*

I want til say, *Mum say somethin.*

Because my mither aways says somethin. She always kens ae right thing til say, and she says it til me as a gift, clean bonnie words like, *hush bonnie ducklin*, and *shush sonsie dumplin* and, at ae end o whatever she croons til me, she always-always throws me ae safe anchor line o, *It's all fine lassie mine. It's all fine*. So's I can rhyme-chime-align, *It's all fine it's all fine.*

And move on.

But this time she hasna, and she doesna, and all I can say is, *State o that, state o that, fuckinstuck.*

My mither looks away.

She plants a kiss til ae top o my head and she tries for a smile, but all I can see is ae pulse-pulse-pulse o a heartbeat in her neck that shouldna be there, not like that. And I realise, that catch o her breath when she seen ae hatch and my legs, it wasna just breath that caught there. Her heart was hurt, and lurched so bad it lodged in her throat, and now it's stuck there, beatin.

We walk home in silence. In ae kitchen, she checks me over for cuts and bruises, then puts me on ae couch in front o ae fire, with a hot water bottle and my special blankie and a biscuit til make things better. But she doesna speak, doesna say a word, and I'll get no new words til my faither gets home, and that is hours later. And by then I'll have sat too long wi ae cruel words o ae village kids churn-churned on my tongue, so long they're burned on.

Fuckinstuck. State o that.

But worst, I am feart. Because, my mither canna open her mouth in case her heart flies out. And she'll have to at some point. And what happens then?

Jinling Wu
LEARNING GERMAN AGAIN

I've started learning German again –
slowly this time.
Kaffee und Kuchen,
the way snow gathers
without hurry.

The language brings me back –
from Shanghai to Salzburg.

From the taxi window
the mountains glazed with gold at sunset,
a faint blue cloth
stitched with pink light.
Past yellow, pink, blue facades –
a city built of calm, soft light,
the opposite of Shanghai's metallic shine.
Something inside me unclenched.

For three months
I walked along the river,
through forests,
into the city.
Past a white house across the bank
I once photographed through leaves –
a frame of green around pale walls.

At night,
I lay back in my chair
watching leaves improvise
on the windowpane.

Sometimes the night was warmed
by hot wine from Christmas stalls.
The people who kept me company
were also far from home.
We sipped our wine
watching children gather courage to skate on the ice –
some huddling their little penguins,
squealing as they swept past, jumped, or fell.

On New Year's Eve
I watched fireworks with a friend,
then walked home alone in the snow.
The streets were empty,
my breath rising
like a small lantern.

I was neither afraid of
nor numb to the dark.
I walked through the forest
cradling curiosity
to feel the snow and crisp air.

Sometimes I stumbled into strange nights,
believing I had no one –
in what people called the best years, youth.
Then remembered the fireworks,
the burst of pink, coral, amber
lighting up the sky.

Strange
how it all returns
with German again.

HOW TO BECOME SCOTTISH (BY ACCIDENT)

My body may have just turned Scottish.
I used to faint at the thought of winter,
now I complain when heat presses like wet laundry
against my skin.

I slip into the North Atlantic sea in April,
humming at the bite of water,
rise shivering and triumphant,
accepting the admirable gaze from bystanders
with no humility.

When the sun shines, I cannot resist –
shorts, of course.
I walk past bluebells
like a native creature of drizzle.

I knew it for certain in Vienna last year:
on a train journey,
the air swelled to twenty-five degrees,
and I wilted,
a cauliflower in a steamer.
Yet once I endured summers in Shanghai,
sun hammering down,
and I marched on.

It surprises me –
this shift in flesh,
how the subtropical girl
gave way to a body

at home in the chill,
standing quietly
in the long breath
of the north wind.

BIOGRAPHIES

Donald Adamson is from Dumfries. Now living in Finland, he translates poems from Finnish to Scots. He has won first prize in several Sangschaw Competitions (2017, 2022, 2025). In 2025 he was awarded the Brian Whittingham Memorial Prize and shortlisted in two categories of the Wigtown Poetry Competition.

David M. Alper's poetry appears in *Press 53, Harpur Palate, Red Ogre Review*, and elsewhere. He is an educator in New York City.

Emily Arnold-Fernández is an immigrant from California who now lives in Scotland. In a previous life, she founded the global refugee human rights organisation Asylum Access. Her recent poems appear in *Magma*, *Cordite*, *Aeos* and *Black Bough* among others. She tends to live on islands. (Instagram: **@emilyarnoldfernandez**)

Matt Barnard was born in London and now divides his time between London and the Isle of Skye. He has published one collection of poetry and edited the anthology *Poems for the NHS*. He won second prize in the 2024 National Poetry Competition and is currently working on his second poetry collection.

Meg Bateman, born Edinburgh 1959, lives in Skye where she taught at Sabhal Mòr Ostaig. Her poetry main collections are *Aotromachd / Lightness* (1997), *Soirbheas / Fair Wind* (2007) and *Transparencies* (2013). She translated five anthologies of historical Gaelic verse, and with John Purser, wrote Window to the West (uhi.ac.uk) on Culture and Environment in the Scottish Gàidhealtachd: **www.smo.uhi.ac.uk/wp-content/uploads/2021/09/Window-to-the-West.pdf**

Dmitry Blizniuk is a bilingual poet from Kharkiv, Ukraine. His most recent poems have appeared in *POETRY Magazine*, *Rattle*,

The Cincinnati Review, *AGNI*, *Beloit Poetry Journal*, *Five Points*, *The Los Angeles Review*, *The Nation*, *Prairie Schooner*, *Plume*, *The London Magazine* and many others. His poems have been awarded the RHINO 2022 Translation Prize and his folio was selected as a runner-up in the Gregory O'Donoghue Competition 2024 and the 2025 Gabo Prize finalist.

Martin Bowman, an Honorary Fellow of the Association for Scottish Literature, is a native of Montreal where he grew up in a Scots-speaking household. With Bill Findlay he translated into Scots eight plays by Michel Tremblay. *Michel Tremblay: Plays in Scots* was published in two volumes by ASL in 2023.

Julia Cathcart was born in Irvine in 1967 and grew up in Ayrshire. She now lives in Glasgow and is working on her first collection of short stories.

Irene W. Collins is a Nigerian writer of Scottish descent living in Nigeria, crafting stories that blend folklore, memory, and the transformative power of imagination. Her work explores the fluid boundaries between myth and reality. She has been published by Flame Tree Publishing, Reckoning Press, and was a runner-up in the Defenestrationism.net 2026 flash suite contest. She is also a Pushcart Prize nominee.

Rachel Coventry's poems feature in the *Guardian*, *The Rialto*, *The North*, *London Magazine*, *Poetry Ireland Review*, *Southword*, *The Shop*, and *The Moth*. Her monograph *Heidegger and Poetry in the Digital Age* was published by Bloomsbury in 2023. Her third collection, *The West* (Salmon Poetry), will be published later this year.

Jemima Dalgliesh was born and raised in southern Scotland. She studied English literature in Oxford and in London, and thereafter worked in the recruitment industry for several years. She lives in Edinburgh with her partner and child.

Lynn Davidson writes essays, poetry, and fiction. Her memoir, *Do you still have time for chaos?*, was published by Main Point Books, Edinburgh, earlier this year. Her latest poetry collection, *Islander*, was published by Shearsman Books, Bristol, and Te Herenga Waka University Press, Wellington, in 2019.

Eilidh Eglinton writes poetry and short stories in Gaelic and English, with previous work published in *Causeway/Cabhsair* and *PhysiOdyssey*. Originally from the Isle of Lewis, she now lives in Edinburgh with her husband and four children.

Simon Ewing is a writer based in Edinburgh. His work has previously featured in publications including *Gutter*, *Extra Teeth*, *Razur Cuts*, *The New Gothic Review*, *Causeway/Cabhsair* and Forest Publications's anthology *Origin Stories*.

Gabriel Featherstone is a writer, journalist and comedian from Glasgow. His solo show, *Robocop vs. The Terminator vs. Gabriel Featherstone*, co-won the 2026 Luke Rollason Memorial Bursary and was nominated for a 2025 Reykjavik Fringe award. He has written articles for *The Skinny*, *Screen Rant* and *The British Comedy Guide*.

Scott Ferguson is a debut novelist from Kilmarnock. He finished the final draft of his novel in 2024. Since then, he has been writing short stories to grow his profile and secure agent representation. You can read more of his work at **scottferguson.uk**

Nicola Fitzhenry has worked in education and the third sector, and now indulges her passion for reading and writing about women and history. She lives in Glasgow and makes frequent forays to Fife for research on a historical novel about women in the eighteenth century.

Tony Frame is a writer based just outside Edinburgh. His short play, *Jazz Night*, was performed at the Traverse Theatre as part of their Young Writers' Programme. He runs a film, theatre and literature review website and is currently writing his debut novel.

Tony Garner's first novel, *The Hotel Hokusai*, was published by Ringwood in 2024. Other recent work has appeared in anthologies by Tantallon Tìr and Seahorse Publications. He lives in Glasgow and is currently working on short stories and another novel.

Sergey Gerasimov is a writer, poet, and translator who lives in Ukraine. Since day one of the Russian attack on Ukraine, he has lived in Kharkiv, written about six hundred anti-war articles for the *Neue Zürcher Zeitung*, in Switzerland, and DTV published his book, *Feuerpanorama*.

Mirri Glasson-Darling lives in Glasgow, where she moved from Alaska some time ago. She is an avid solo hillwalker/wild camper. She has received a Notable Essay from Best American Essays and been published in *Ploughshares*, the Tantallon Tìr anthology *Call of the Isles*, and other places. She is currently working on a novel.

Mairi Griffin studied Creative Writing at the University of Strathclyde. Her poetry and prose have been featured in *Gutter*, *Wet Grain* and elsewhere, and in 2026 she was shortlisted for the Royal Society of Literature's V.S. Pritchett Short Story Prize. She is currently working on her first novel. Instagram: **@_mjgriffin**

Kate Hendry's poetry has been widely published in magazines including *PN Review*, *Mslexia*, *The Rialto* and *Poetry Wales*. Her first pamphlet, 'The Lost Original', was published by HappenStance Press. Her second, 'MX SIMP' (Mariscat Press), was shortlisted for the 2023 Michael Marks Awards.

Tom O. Keenan is a writer living in the North West Highlands, traditionally published in crime fiction, currently undertaking an MLitt in Creative Writing, where 'Ducks and Donkeys' was written. His work is informed by over thirty years as a social worker. He is currently working on a paranormal thriller.

Áine King is an Irish playwright and poet living in Orkney. Her poems have been published in *Northwords*, *Lucent*, *Aurochs* and *Island Voices*. Her plays have been staged internationally from Texas and Carolina to Cork, Edinburgh, Amsterdam, London and Kiev and include *Burning Bright*, winner of the 2022 David MacLennan Award.

Pippa Little is Scots, living in Northumberland. *Twist* (2017) was Saltire-shortlisted and *Time Begins to Hurt* (Arc) came out in 2022: she's working on her next collection. Recent publications include *The Robert Graves Review* and *Acumen*. A Hawthornden and RLF Fellow, she has taught for the Faber Academy.

Màrtainn Mac an t-Saoir / Martin MacIntyre is an acclaimed author, bard and storyteller, who has worked across these genres for over twenty years; he has written nine works of fiction and three collections of poems.

'S ann à Dùn Dèagh a tha **Donnchadh MacCàba**. Tha a chuid sgrìobhaidh air nochdadh ann an iomadach iris, le *STEALL*, *New Writing Scotland* is *Poblachd nam Bàrd* nam measg, agus air an làrach-lìn andeireag.com. Mar as trice, bidh e a' sgrìobhadh mun àrainneachd, eachdraidh is cruth-tìre ann an ear-thuath na h-Alba.

Wendy MacIntyre was born in Glasgow and now lives in Carleton Place, Ontario. She has a PhD in English Literature from the University of Edinburgh, and has published five novels with Canadian literary presses, as well as poems, essays and short fiction in journals in Canada, the US and the UK.

Iain MacLeod is a bookseller in Glasgow. Born into the thin air between shipyards and shepherds, he has been writing for five years but thinking about it for the prior forty. Work has been published recently in Shearsman, and by Saraband and Renard Press, from five completed collections.

Tha **Robbie MacLeòid** na bhàrd ann an iomadh seagh. Nochd a chiad leabhran de bhàrdachd, *Am Measg Luaithrean, Beò*, ann an 2025. **Robbie MacLeòid** is a queer writer, published in multiple languages and multiple countries. His debut poetry pamphlet, *Am Measg Luaithrean, Beò* (*Living Among the Ashes*), came out in 2025.

Fiona Mossman is a librarian and writer from the Scottish Highlands now based near Edinburgh. She adores short stories and her writing is often inspired by folktales and philosophy. Some of her stories can be found in *Crow & Cross Keys*, *The Utopia of Us* from Luna Press, and elsewhere.

Chris Neilan is an award-winning writer and filmmaker with a PhD in creative writing from Manchester Metropolitan University. He teaches screenwriting and documentary filmmaking at Edinburgh Napier.

Niall O'Gallagher is the author, in Gaelic, of three collections of poetry, of the verse-novella *Litrichean Plàighe* and of *Fuaimean Gràidh / The Sounds of Love: Selected Poems*. He is currently translating poems by Josep Carner (1884–1970) from Catalan into

English and by Florbela Espanca (1894–1930) from Portuguese into Gaelic.

Kailee Parsons is a Seattle-born writer, researcher, and creative producer who has been making her home in Scotland since 2019. She is currently pursuing her MLitt in Creative Writing at the University of Glasgow, where she writes literary, crime and speculative fiction, as well as personal essays.

Martin Raymond's stories have appeared in *New Writing Scotland*, *Causeway/Cabhsair* and *Source*. They have been shortlisted for a number of awards, including the VS Pritchett Prize. His first novel, *Lotte*, was published in 2024. He has an MLitt and PhD in Creative Writing, both from the University of Stirling.

Tracey S. Rosenberg is a poet and spoken word artist. She's the current Loud Poets Inverness slam champion and competed in the Scottish National Slam Championships twice. She's working on a collection about heartbreak and the full-scale invasion of Ukraine, *Unrequited War Trauma*, for which she's received funding from Creative Scotland.

Kerry Ryan has won the Hachette GYOS Prize, the Spilling Ink Short Story Prize, the New Writing South Award and has been shortlisted for the Myriad First Editions Prize, the Writers & Artists Prize, and the HG Wells Prize. Her fiction and poetry have appeared in *The Manchester Review*, *The Kenyon Review*, *3am Magazine* and more. She is the founder of Write like a Grrrl.

Gardener, granny **Finola Scott** writes to try to unravel world events. 'Trembling Earth', her latest pamphlet, considers the climate crisis. Her widely published poems gain competition success. Find her in *The Irish Pages Press*, *Consilience*, *Lighthouse*, and *Gutter*. Read her at FB Finola Scott Poems and **www.scottishpoetrylibrary.org.uk/poet/finola-scott/**

Shane Strachan was the 2022–23 Scots Scriever (National Library of Scotland), during which he began developing *The Roaring of the Sea*. His debut poetry collection *DWAMS* (Tapsalteerie) was nominated for Best Poetry Book at the 2024 Saltire Awards and he was awarded Scots Champion at the 2023 Scots Language Awards.

Lynn Valentine is a poet living in the Black Isle. She has two poetry collections with Cinnamon Press – *Devil's Piece* (2026) and *Life's Stink and Honey* (2022). She has a Scots language pamphlet with Hedgehog Press (2021). She won the McLellan prize (Scots) in 2024. Lynn loves Labradors and bees.

Augustijn van Gaalen is a Dutch writer living in Scotland. His work has appeared in *Stand*, *Gutter*, *Naugatuck River Review*, and elsewhere, and has been listed for various prizes, including the *London Magazine* Short Story Prize, the Clay Reynolds Novella Prize, and the Moniack Mhor Emerging Writer Award.

Katie Webster is from Caithness, where she works as an occupational therapist. She has had stories published in *Extra Teeth* and *New Writing Scotland* 30 and 41. She is working on her first novel.

Jinling Wu is a writer based in Edinburgh, originally from China. Working across literature, theatre and film, she won the 2023 Kavya Prize, has work forthcoming in *Wet Grain*, and is supported by Playwrights' Studio Scotland.